BETWEEN DEMONS AND DEITIES

BETWEEN DEMONS AND DEITIES

BIANCA
WANG-POLENDO

NEW DEGREE PRESS

BETWEEN DEMONS AND DEITIES

ISBN 978-1-63676-731-4 *Paperback*

978-1-63730-036-7 *Kindle Ebook*

978-1-63730-138-8 *Ebook*

CONTENTS

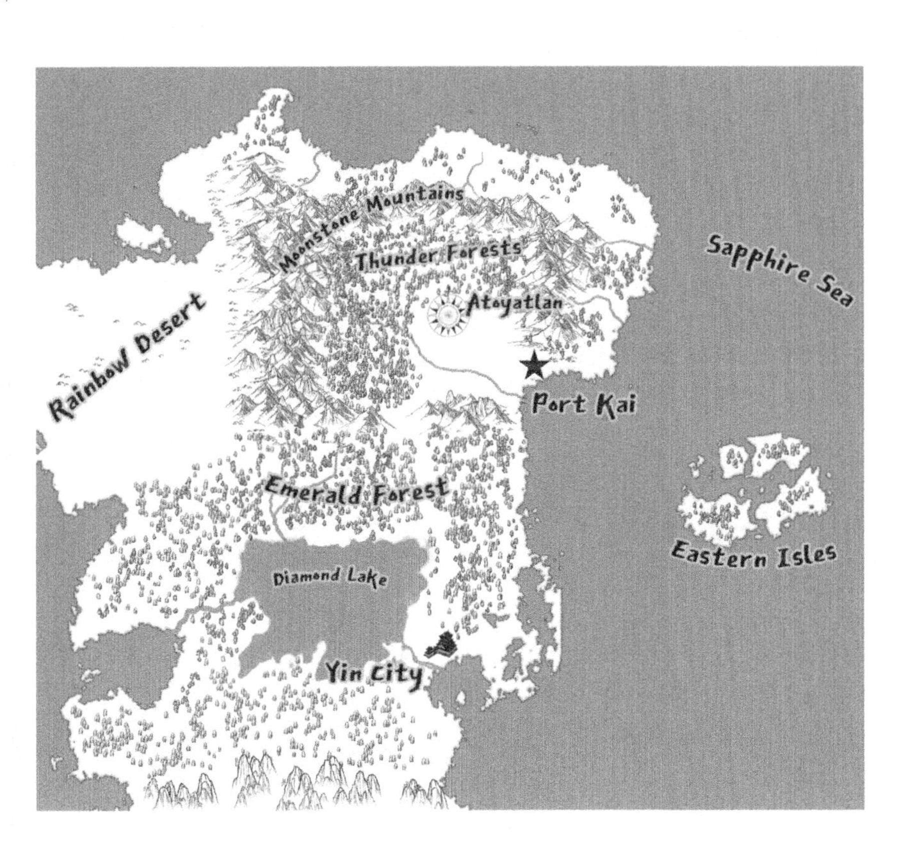
Moonstone Mountains
Thunder Forests
Sapphire Sea
Atoyatlan
Rainbow Desert
Port Kai
Emerald Forest
Eastern Isles
Diamond Lake
Yin City

AUTHOR'S NOTE

Dear Reader,

Thank you for picking up this book and allowing me to share this story with you. It really means a lot to someone who has always dreamed of publishing a book.

I have always enjoyed reading fantasy—from *The Magic Treehouse* series in first grade to spooky ghost stories in fourth grade and basically all of the YA vampire/faerie/demon books that came out when I was in middle school and high school. The world-building, magic, and mythical creatures of fantasy absolutely ensnared me, and I took that interest to write various fantasy stories using good old wide-ruled notebooks and wooden pencils in elementary school and online platforms in middle and high school.

Even though fantasy is, well, fantasy, it really emphasizes that so much more is out there for us to explore and learn. It also provides an opportunity to exercise our imaginations and creativity while coming to understand everyone has a story and every place has its own history. Sometimes, we can find that fantasy is more attainable than we think because the world is large and has a long extensive history.

The opportunity to write this book is special to me because I can put a piece of myself and my experience into my take on a genre I've read and seen many times before. Plenty of books feature half-something characters: half-fae, demi-god, half-angel-half-demon, etc. While these stories are still entertaining and touch on being part of multiple worlds, they don't highlight some of the inner dialogue of what it means to have a diverse cultural heritage. This can so easily parallel what it's like to be multicultural or biracial at an abstract level.

Especially during my teenage years, it would have been nice to read and hear more experiences of other people with mixed identities, knowing others are out there with similar stories as me. Luckily, college and internet meme pages have helped me connect with others in navigating the space.

As a Taiwanese-Mexican-American from Minnesota, I grew up in predominantly white neighborhoods. Though I learned the languages and some of the culture from both sides of my background, my main exposure outside of home was to American pop culture. Ultimately, I was, and still am, a hodgepodge of multiple cultures, some more strongly than others. It wasn't until the end of high school and the beginning of college when I began to meet new people in new settings that I really began to reflect more about myself and my own identity to find a place to belong.

I started out by comparing my experiences with others, and while I found some similarities, I also found enough differences, particularly fluency of languages and lack of some historical and cultural knowledge, that created a sort of distance. I only accepted the differences once I started reading and listening to other multicultural people who had similar dilemmas.

The idea of belonging and identity resonates with me. Some people might think being biracial or multiracial means automatic acceptance to the different parts of their background, but this isn't always true. A group may have shared experiences that you don't have access to. Maybe there is a disconnect between your appearance and your identity, which confuses other people, whether they belong to your identified group or not, and can lead to questions like "Where are you *really* from?" or "What are you?"

Perhaps you aren't fluent in a language that is so closely tied to a certain identity, which can create distance between you and your own family or heritage. At the more overt end, some members of a group, or even members outside the group, may police your identity and directly say you don't belong, which obviously can cause some internal conflict and lead to feeling isolated.

Multicultural backgrounds also come with benefits. It can be quite fun having so much variety within you. Perhaps you have a bilingual or trilingual household, you have even more holidays to celebrate, or you can bond with people of different demographics through some shared experience. Sometimes it's even amusing to ask people to guess what your background is and watch them get it completely wrong; with more familiar people, this can even lead to some productive conversations that center around learning. Each person's experience is a little different, so our definitions should be more encompassing because an average is only one statistic for a data set.

There's no one right way to be a member of a group.

NPR made a great podcast that covers this topic of racial imposter syndrome, basically when people don't feel like they fit in with their people or the people who are presumed to be their people. Often, multicultural/multiethnic people may feel this way—from children and grandchildren of immigrants to people with mixed backgrounds. But even the general phenomenon of imposter syndrome is something just about any person can relate to because our identities are multifaceted and each group seems to have its own rigid concepts. It's important to take a step back and reflect on ourselves.

As a fantasy aficionado, I naturally decided to use fantasy as a tool of my own exploration and was reminded of something I read on a writing blog. *Write what you want to read.* So I reflected on what exactly that meant to me. What is missing that I feel would be valuable reading?

I wanted to read about magic and deities and supernatural creatures. As a biracial person, I wanted to read more about multicultural identities in fantasy settings and see more complex characters whom I can relate to. I also wanted to see more stories of underrepresented groups, histories, and settings. As a person in my early twenties, I wanted to read more about the continual process of self-reflection that extends beyond YA settings. As a citizen of the world, I wanted to read about the hope for a better world that stems from our connections to one another.

Writing this book is my way of giving back to the genre I love by continuing to show more representation of BIPOC and LGBTQ+ people in magic-packed worlds through highlighting some specific experiences they might face in reality, normalizing their existence in media, and making sure they are displayed as important and complex. Fantasy has done a better job with representation in recent years, with more authors of color writing and more inclusion of BIPOC and LGBTQ+ main and supporting characters in non-Eurocentric settings, but this doesn't mean we should stop. Often, there is a specific idea of what fantasy looks like, and we should be normalizing a variety of what fantasy can and does look like.

In *Between Demons and Deities*, you will dive into a world featuring two major empires. The Wei empire is inspired by ancient imperial China while Atonaco is inspired by old Mesoamerican empires, primarily the Mexica (or Aztec) empire. Both the mythology and history in this world are a mixture of reality and fantasy. However, the main focus of this book centers around our three primary protagonists: Esmeralda, an Atonocan-Wei mage with missing memories and mixed abilities; Dacio, a loyal and charming nonbinary healer with secrets up their sleeves; and Raiden, an aloof but extremely loyal Wei fighter.

I hope through my novel, I can both provide an interesting fantastical journey full of magic, demons, and deities while also exploring more fluid definitions of identity with a focus on multiracial identities with an added touch on gender identities as well. No one can fit perfectly into one box, so we shouldn't have to feel forced to squeeze ourselves into one. We should accept ourselves.

So, to all of you, I hope you can appreciate the magic in both the fantasy world in this book and our own.

Thank you again,
Bianca Wang-Polendo

PROLOGUE

Death was waiting around the corner, ready to welcome another soul with a cool embrace.

Raiden stalked his target from the dark winter shadows, quietly blending into the side of the wooden and stone walls. Deep regret rose to the surface, as it did every time he knew death would stain his hands and haunt his memories. However, he was bound to his contract and his loyalty. Death would not be stopped.

He watched as the flighty subject headed toward the teahouse and wondered how the nervous man managed to earn a death order from the prince. Like with all the other targets, he guessed. Perhaps his target disrupted the prince's jubilant mood, or maybe he questioned the glory of one of the empire's military campaigns. Regardless, Raiden never asked for a reason.

The scrawny man constantly looked back and forth before he entered, as if the cold winter darkness made him hypervigilant of his surroundings. Perhaps he knew the prince had sent *him*—the Assassin of the Night. The Hand of Death.

Raiden hated those titles, hated how infamous he was. Not many who knew his true identity still lived, and those who did were skilled at keeping secrets. He wished he could take the mask off and not worry about the looming puppet master pulling his strings. Until that day came, if it ever did, he would continue chipping away at his soul to protect his lovesick fool of a friend.

Crossing the slushy road, Raiden retreated into the shadows and waited for his target to re-emerge. When the scrawny man scuttled out of the door and into the night, the dimly lit lanterns around him flickered and died out. Death was commonplace here, more so than in the smaller neighboring towns. Raiden wondered if this death would be a mercy.

As his target moved toward him, he silently took out his dagger and stepped into the empty path.

"The prince sends his greetings," Raiden apologized, watching the man's eyes look up at him in fearful recognition. Not of *who* he was but *what.*

As quick as viper, he struck. The other man did not stand a chance against a trained assassin's strength or speed, and so he went down with a surprised gurgle as the snow on the ground turned a darker color.

In anyone else's eyes, Raiden was the ultimate killing weapon, with the physical training he had endured and the ability to poison people with just the touch of his hand. But he wasn't the perfect killer. No perfect killer would tremble this much after taking a life for the hundredth time. No perfect killer would feel the deep despair of guilt and anger for acting as the afterlife's emissary. No stone-hearted killer who had the power to poison with a touch would ever wear gloves to cover his skin. Although he was still awake, dreadful nightmares started their whispering torments in his head.

The prince would want verification of the murder, so before he moved the body to the alley to await daylight, he searched the corpse for a personal item, settling on a small amulet. Then he left, trying to keep his internal sickness at bay until he got home. At least he wouldn't have to face the prince tonight, lest he wanted to incur his rage for disturbing his sleep—or worse, one of his celebrations.

Raiden weaved through the streets and retreated into the forest outside the outer walls of the city toward his house. The familiar sounds of bats fluttering and stray gusts of wind rustling dead branches suddenly stopped, making the forest eerily quiet. Too quiet. He stilled, skin prickling in anticipation, and he immediately reached for his dagger. Something was wrong.

"Don't bother with the weapon," a smooth voice spoke from behind him. He pivoted around, eyes widening at the sight of the creature that had spoken.

From far away, the figure would have looked like a normal person with simple robes and tied-up hair, but the creature's glowing, inhuman eyes would give away its otherworldliness. Most telling of all was the oppressive, sticky power that radiated from the creature—one that reminded him of the Dreadful, lost spirits turned mindless demons yearning for the taste of humanity.

Raiden gripped his dagger harder, looking for potential weaknesses. "I might surprise you."

The creature laughed, revealing sharp fangs. "If you insist, but I do not come as an enemy. For now."

"What do you want?" Raiden asked, keeping his balance in control, ready to react.

"Why, that was the question I was going to ask you. I could feel your yearning and self-hatred from so far away," it said, its words hanging in the air between them. "Let's make a deal."

His heart raced. *A deal?* The last time he made a deal, he became a killer for the prince of the Wei empire. Making a deal with an unknown creature was bound to give him an even worse fate, and unlike last time, his hands weren't forced.

"No," he said.

"Even in exchange for your freedom? For your one and only friend to finally leave the prince's company? For you to stop killing to keep them safe?" the creature asked, its voice echoing deeply.

Raiden stiffened. How did this creature know who he was under the mask and what he wanted? What *was* it? Its presence felt more like a demon than a deity, but its appearance didn't seem like strictly one or the other—not that he had ever met a deity.

"What are you?" he asked.

"I am an Evolved, the closest to a deity you will most likely encounter," it said, smiling with its teeth bared. "What you mortals call a demon."

Chills ran down his spine.

A demon. From what he knew, most demons were contained in the spirit realm to feed on the most corrupt and tainted spirits, but those that escaped were so hungry they devoured anyone unfortunate enough to be in their vicinity. Others were formed through the deterioration of lost spirits that escaped into the mortal realm. Not once had he heard of an Evolved, or one that was willing to make bargains. When did starving predators ever ask their prey for permission?

Raiden narrowed his eyes, asking, "You're not going to... eat my soul, are you?" An inkling of horror spawned at the back of his mind. Was he *considering* a deal? How far was he willing to go for his freedom? His friend's?

"Fortunate for you, no. As I said, I'm not here today as an enemy but as an intermediary. I have but one request to ask of you. Lend your power for the rest of the night," the Evolved crooned.

He cocked his head and shifted uncomfortably. The only thing his ability was good for was killing. "How many are you planning to use it on? Why do you need *my* power?" he asked, still uncertain if he wanted to follow through. What kinds of abilities did this Evolved have for it to be able to borrow others' powers?

"One life taken secretly for each life saved secretly. And what are two more in the grand scheme of the world?"

Two more. Two more victims in exchange for his and his friend's freedom. As awful as it sounded, his misery could stop. His hands were already stained. There weren't enough opportunities in the world to ever make up for what he had done. Half of him rejected the offer, but the other half was too tempted for comfort.

"How do I know you won't backstab us as soon we're free?" Raiden asked. Before he agreed to anything, he needed to impose some conditions. Knowing the nature of bargains and knowing the risk of dealing with unknown supernatural creatures, he needed to be particularly careful about how he worded his requests.

"That is simply a risk you will have to stomach," it said.

His stomach churned. This was a bad idea, but perhaps he could make it less bad by negotiating specific terms.

With its teeth bared into a twisted smile, the demon asked, "Now, Raiden, are you ready to discuss?"

CHAPTER 1

"If I don't get my eyebrows burned off this time, I'll consider this mission a success," Dacio called out from behind her.

Esmeralda rolled her eyes and ducked under the large low-hanging leaves. "That was *one* time, and you never let me forget it," she said, even though she did appreciate having those memories. Thunder rumbled closer in the background, making her look up at the canopy of leaves. "I do hope we can find this spirit soon." Although the sun was in the sky, rain worked differently within the forest.

The Forest of Lightning and Thunder, or Thunder Forest, was a place of reverence but also a place of caution. Venture too deeply and one might find themselves lost. For now, Esme and Dacio were only hovering at the edges of the vast jungle that lined the side of the Atonacan empire. The sticky humid air clung to her body and clothes, but that was nothing new to Atoyatlan or Atonaco as a whole.

"I think I see it," Dacio whispered, their voice suddenly next to her ear. It took all of her willpower to keep herself from jumping in surprise and letting the ball of spirit fire in her palm fly out. She looked in the direction they were pointing to spot a moving transparent figure in the distance.

The transparent figure with long floating hair wandered aimlessly through the trees and vines. From the aura of the place, the timeline matched what the high priest had claimed. This spirit recently crossed into the mortal realm and was still safe from morphing into an evil spirit, or worse—a Dreadful, a devourer of souls. Both malevolent spirits and demons caused major misfortunes in the community, so it was in everyone's best interest to simply guide the phantoms back to the spirit realm before they deteriorated into either.

Esme raised her palm and molded the spirit fire in her hand into the shape of a marigold, ready to guide the wanderer toward her. Dacio had infused their magic into hers to create the spirit fire, and while she captured the phantom's attention, they were preparing to ease it back to the realm of the dead. The atmosphere around her smoothed into peace and tranquility—Dacio's magic at work.

When the spirit grew even closer, she could see the recognition in their eyes from having finally found the way. She and Dacio moved fluidly to capture it and send it back to where it belonged. The whole ordeal only lasted seconds with little flair. Before she knew it, just the two of them were left in the jungle.

She turned to face her closest friend, who was a year younger than her. "There. Eyebrows still intact," she stated, to which they flashed a wry smile.

Her gaze swept over their face—from the bottom of their round nose up past their dark eyes to their short black hair. A stray ray of sun piercing through the thick canopy reflected off the jade earrings and necklace they wore, drawing her gaze on the illuminated pendant hovering over their thin, faded turquoise blue shawl.

"Shall we head back to the temple now?" she suggested. They had taken care of the lost spirit, but who knew what else was lurking in the forests. One of the priests had scried the emergence of a Dreadful just a week ago, and she wasn't sure if that issue had been resolved yet.

"I actually might head home first. I found some pretty stones that can be made into a bracelet," they said leisurely and playfully, walking backward in the direction of the city. Their hands were hidden behind their back, perhaps where said stones were.

The anticipation for the surprise overwhelmed her curiosity for what stones they had found. "I'll just wait until you're finished with it then. Let's see how your jewelry-making skills compare with mine," she replied once they exited the forests. An iguana darted into the thick vegetation beside them.

Dacio gave her a grin, its warmth rivaling the sun. "It'll pale in comparison but I can't be good at *everything*."

Esme looked up at the sky, fighting the urge to roll her eyes before shooing them off. "Go. I'll inform the priests and priestesses and will meet you at home."

"I'll see you soon," they said, giving her a last wave before they split directions.

The temple was in the center of the city whereas their home was beyond the floating gardens on the southern edge of Atoyatlan, closer to their current location but in the opposite direction of her trajectory. As she walked along the river, she continued thinking about the spirit and wondered about its life and death. Generally, spirits only escaped into the mortal realm if they found a split in the barrier somehow or if they carried great resentment or injustice from their life. In the second case, the negative energy was an omen.

The sounds of children playing and training outside told her she was passing by one of the military schools. Around the next corner would be the ball field, and then the corner beyond that would be the center. Atoyatlan's liveliness and brilliant colors kept her company as she finally reached her destination.

The Great Temple of Atoyatlan stood in front of her as the brightly painted house of the deities and the place where Dacio was trained as a healer. The entire area was devoted to religious and magical activities—from the large courtyard to the Great Temple. Beside the tall sloping-sided structure were the local academy of magic, the ceremonial grounds, shrines to patron deities, and the stone quarters for the priests. Since she had finished at the academy, it was also the place where she would help the community with her magic when she wasn't crafting jewelry at the craft shop.

Before she could ascend the many stairs of the stone temple to inform one of the priests about sending the spirit to its rightful place, she was stopped by one of the mez children who practiced spirit magic at the academy. Although she didn't know their name, she recognized their face and knew they related to and idolized Dacio. In any other circumstance, she would have greeted them with a wide smile, but their face was scrunched up in concern.

"You live with Dacio, right?" they asked nervously, dark eyes blinking quickly. The sun illuminated beads of sweat underneath their black bangs and the sides of their neck exposed by their high, short ponytail.

"Yes, is there something you need?" she replied.

The next words out of the mez child's mouth made her heart stop. "A group of imperial Wei soldiers came looking for Dacio at the temple and headed toward their house."

Wei soldiers? Why would Wei soldiers be looking for them? Although the people of each empire held little grudge against citizens of the other, the Wei empire kept trying to expand its territory across the natural mountain boundaries and into Atonaco. There would be no reason for imperial soldiers to be after Dacio. They were only a healer at the temple, a pupil of the high priest of Atoyatlan.

"How long ago was this?" she asked urgently.

"Maybe an hour?"

That was more than enough time to get from the temple to their house, and Dacio had probably arrived already.

"Thank you for telling me. I will go figure this out," Esme rushed out, pivoting on her heels and immediately sprinting away from the temple pyramid and in the direction of the house she and Dacio shared.

Imperial soldiers. Cold sweat lined the back of her neck.

By the time she got back to the house, the door was wide open and nobody was there. Her heart raced even more as she slowly stepped in and saw the interior in disarray. Her hand flew up to her mouth. Although they did not have many items, it seemed as if everything had been turned over, as if someone had been frantically searching for something.

"Dacio?" she called out.

Silence.

Shocked, she stumbled back out and saw some of the neighbors giving her concerned looks. One of the old women with silver-threaded, braided black hair walked around her weaving materials and garden to approach Esme.

"You just missed them. I saw those Wei soldiers carry them off half an hour ago," granny whispered, looking back and forth as she divulged what happened. "I couldn't help but overhear that they're all going to Yin City for some absurd accusation. Our dear Dacio would never hurt a person."

This was worse than Esme could imagine. Taken away? Already, she could feel the guilt sinking into her skin. If they hadn't split off, would she have been able to prevent this from happening? Would she be tagging along?

"What were they accused of?" Esme asked hesitantly.

"Attempting to kill the Wei emperor."

Her lips parted and her entire body started trembling. Impossible. Did the guards grab the wrong person? Maybe if she could catch up to them, she could clear up the situation. Dacio would never harm a soul. By the stars, they were a healer at the temple and even offered to be the local community healer. Furthermore, the Wei emperor lived in Yin City, the Wei capital, which was at least a few days' journey south, and they had never been gone for more than a day since she had woken up from her coma. She could only imagine the sheer panic and fear Dacio must have felt when they were taken.

"I'll get them back, granny. Don't worry," Esme affirmed, clenching her jaw. She didn't know how long this whole ordeal would take, so she decided to pack a small bag first as she ran back into the house.

With the chaos left behind, she had to carefully step around the fallen items, suppressing the urge to reorganize everything. She gathered some supplies in her hand and looked for her woven bag, only to find it hiding under some papers. Dacio kept quite a large stack of papers for someone who had impeccable visual and auditory memory. Usually, the doodles they shared with her were atrocious and essentially unidentifiable, more resembling their general state of order and contrasting their neat and pretty handwriting.

That was why the drawing over her bag made her stop. Her hand hovered over the careful chaos of the colors that looked like a woman looking out a window. She hadn't seen this one before. A rush of emotions overwhelmed her: love, yearning, *pain.*

This woman was important to them somehow. Esme's heart ached, but she couldn't pinpoint why. Maybe it was because of how little she knew of Dacio's background sometimes, aside from the short summary they always repeated. Even with her own missing memories, Esme doubted this woman was still in their life if she were real, or else she would have met her by now. Was the subject of the doodle the reason why Dacio had bouts of sadness all the time?

Perhaps she might have pondered more had a loud crash not startled her from her thoughts.

Esme flinched. The noise sounded like it had come from the small, detached healing room. Did Dacio come back? She snatched her bag from underneath the drawings and shoved the items into the pouch before quickly darting out of the house and creeping past the round stone bathhouse toward the smaller building. What if it was an invader? Before entering, she quickly reminded herself of her own powers. Esme might not have been trained at a military school, but she was a trained mage and was perfectly able to defend herself if necessary.

"Hello?" she asked cautiously, peering through the open door. The beaming sunlight revealed a broken glass bottle on the floor inside, explaining the crashing noise. A dark figure inside quickly drew her attention as she drew theirs.

"You," the figure whispered in a faint accent before sharply turning to the side and letting the side of their hood block their face. "Where's Dacio?"

Why was everyone suddenly looking for Dacio today? First the Wei soldiers and now this stranger who stumbled into the healing room. However, as soon she noticed the person holding their side and deep red droplets staining the floor beneath them, her eyes widened with realization. "You're hurt!"

The presumable patient sharply faced her at her exclamation, allowing a better view of his face. From what she could see, he had sharp features and a slightly crooked, slim nose. There were two glinting scars on his face, one down his left cheek and the other leading from his right eyebrow. She wondered how those came to be.

"Dacio's the professional healer, but I can help you too," Esme said, not wanting to turn away someone bleeding at her front door. If she resolved this quickly enough, *maybe* she could still catch up to Dacio. "Please sit down." She gestured at the short wooden stool.

He hesitated but grudgingly went along. She quickly fetched a bowl of water from the side and collected a rag for cleanup before walking over. It was good that she had already tied her thick, wavy black hair back into a high ponytail to keep most of the unruly strands out of her face.

His outfit was odd for the north; it seemed too warm and dark for the hot, Atonacan sun. It also made it difficult for Esme to identify where the wounds were, aside from his abdomen where his palms were placed.

"Where are you injured?" she asked, speaking at the dark hood still partially obscuring his face.

"Just my abdomen," he said curtly, averting his gaze. His entire body was tense. From what she could see, his shoulders were tight and his gloved hands remained clenched.

"My healing magic works best the closer I can get to the wound," she urged. The sooner she could fix this, the sooner she could resolve her original dilemma.

He received the hint and shrugged off some of his outer layers, wincing at the motion. Esme could finally see his black hair, which was pulled back into a long, clean ponytail, with short bangs sweeping to the side of his face. Her eyes swept down and skidded to a stop upon seeing the bloody claw marks across his abdomen. Had he run into a jungle cat? The myriad of old scars scattered across his pale chest hinted at a different story.

"What happened?" she whispered.

The man stayed silent, turning his face to the side.

"Fine, keep your secrets. I'll just assume you lost a battle to a cat." She grumbled and got to work. There was no time to waste. She pulled over another stool and leaned closer to observe the deep gashes. It was a wonder he wasn't displaying more signs of pain and discomfort.

Esme raised her hand and concentrated on her thoughts and powers, remembering what she had learned about healing, *life*, and magic, but most importantly, inner peace and her sense of self. She drew energy from the spirit in her surroundings, from herself, and from the plants nearby, channeling that calming, soothing energy into her palms. When her hands started glowing a soft and faint shade of gold, she moved them toward her patient's abdomen.

He flinched slightly at the motion, but managed to stay still when Esme hovered her hand over the wound. She thought of flowers and trees and nature as she weaved a small tendril of magic through the wounds to stitch them together. However, her healing magic wasn't as good as Dacio's or even as good as her own fire magic, so a faint scar would be left behind from the injury. This newest scar would just have to join the jungle of other scars on his body.

Blood remained on his chest, so she grabbed the cloth and dipped it into the water, which she warmed up with her fingers before carefully wiping the blood off his chest. At closer glance, she couldn't see any more injuries. He was still tense but was now looking at her with his dark, narrow eyes.

What in the nine hells happened? Who was he? How did he know Dacio?

"What's your name?" she asked.

He pulled back, snatched his clothes, and rose to his feet, towering over her. "None of your business," he said, putting on his outfit again.

Esme gaped, letting out a startled and choked laugh. The *audacity.* "A little politeness never hurt anyone, especially when it's directed toward someone who helped patch up your wounds," she said, refraining from unleashing anything on the patient she just healed. Internally, she considered toasting his eyebrows with fire.

When he started walking toward the door, Esme felt herself heat up with frustration. Apparently asking for his name was too difficult a question for him to answer. Or perhaps it wasn't the right approach. He had come here looking for something in addition to healing.

"I don't know what your problem is, but I assure you that you won't find Dacio without me." She raised her voice at his back, causing him to pause. Of course Dacio's name would get a response from him since that was the second thing he had said after the accusatory "*You.*"

"Where is Dacio?" the man asked again, turning around. "What do you mean by not being able to find them without you?"

"Care to tell me how you know Dacio and why you're looking for them first?" she fired back. Her eyebrows arched and her gaze stayed steady, daring him to turn away for the third time.

He looked up toward the ceiling and let out a heavy sigh. "Dacio and I are old friends."

Esme looked at him, and some of her doubt must have shown on her face because he added, "Dacio never takes off their necklace. They have a giant appetite, from both the taxing nature of their spirit magic and their love for eating and cooking. Their family originated from here in the north, although they grew up in the Wei empire. Now, tell me where they are."

Her eyes widened at the quick fire of statements. None of the facts were immediately obvious to a stranger. The third fact she actually didn't fully know the answer to. Although it was clear that Dacio was Atonacan, they had never mentioned anything about living in the Wei empire to her before. With the first two statements being true, she figured the third one could be true for all she knew. Dacio was tight lipped about their past in general.

Staying quiet for a few more seconds, she studied the stranger. Somehow, his aura seemed familiar, as if she knew him from a different life—her own, possibly, from the period of time when she was missing memories. She decided to take a chance.

"They've been taken to Yin City as a suspect for attempting to kill the Wei emperor," she said quietly. Inside, her fury ignited. She still couldn't believe Dacio was accused of this outlandish crime.

The man laughed harshly before swearing and reaching up to pinch the bridge of his nose. "It's a setup. Dacio would never kill anyone," he said. Before she could agree, he added, "But if there was one person in the world they *would* consider killing, it would be the Wei emperor."

What? Esme blinked in confusion from the stark con tradiction.

"Are you serious? Are you sure you know them?" she asked.

"Do *you* know Dacio?" he reflected, his question hitting her square in the chest. "I've known them longer than you have. I've seen both the light and darkness in them. I'm not saying they're a bad person, just that they're capable of bad things, as are we all."

Esme pressed her lips together. "It's true that I don't know every facet Dacio has, but I know in my heart they wouldn't do this, and I'm going to clear this asinine accusation," she declared. "Now, since you aren't going to tell me anything useful and you seem content with my work, I really do need to rush out of here."

"Are you going after them?" he asked, suddenly more curious in maintaining the conversation.

"Of course," she said, picking up her bag.

"To Yin City?" he asked, following her.

"Yes. That's where they're being taken, so that's where I'm going." Esme gestured toward the door and faced the cloaked stranger again. "I won't stop you this time."

"It's Raiden," the man said.

She tilted her head slightly. "What?"

"My name is Raiden," he replied. "I'll come with you to Yin City."

Her eyebrows raised. Did he just invite himself along? "I need to leave now and you're still recovering from your injuries," she protested.

His face relaxed, and she imagined that had he been any other person, he would have been smiling. "It's a good thing I'd be traveling with a mage who knows how to heal," he said. "I'm ready now *and* I know the shortest path to Yin City."

Just from their brief interaction, she could already tell how stubborn he was. "Fine," she said. "But you are not going to bring any of that 'Dacio could have tried to kill the emperor' nonsense with you, and you will treat me with the same respect that I show you."

Raiden let out a soft snort. "I'll be sure to keep that in mind, Esme," he said, finally leaving the healing room. She sincerely hoped she wasn't making a mistake allowing him to come along.

Only after she closed the door, Esme realized Raiden had called her name without her ever formally introducing herself.

CHAPTER 2

Esme had a myriad of questions bubbling inside of her, but every time she looked over at Raiden to see if he seemed to be in a mood for a conversation, those questions remained trapped. It must have been at least a good four hours since they had left Atoyatlan, yet few words had been exchanged. If she closed her eyes, she would have thought her only companions were the constant rumbling of thunder over the forest in the distance and the uneven terrain underneath her feet.

"Spit it out," he said, without turning his head.

She hesitated one last time before nervously asking her question. "Did we... did we know each other before my coma?"

Raiden coughed. "Coma?" he asked before admitting, "We may have been acquainted long ago through a mutual friend."

Esme absorbed the small dose of information. So they *had* known each other somehow. That explained how he had known her name and also why he felt familiar to her even though she didn't remember him.

Two years ago, Esme had woken up from a coma missing memories from the previous seven years of her life starting from when she was thirteen onward. She didn't remember why she had entered her coma, only that Dacio had been there when she woke up. Since then, she could only remember her studious days at the Atonacan Academy of Magic, her father, who had been a high-ranking warrior, and her mother, who had been a Wei mage teaching at the academy. Now, she only had Dacio and some childhood memories as her father had died in battle and her mother was missing.

Even though she was rebuilding her life at the temple, a part of her would always seem unreachable, even to herself.

"Was the mutual friend Dacio?" she asked, to which Raiden nodded. He had been looking for them after all. "Did we know each other well?"

This time, he shook his head and stiffly replied, "No."

Eyes narrowing, she was unconvinced. She turned toward the pearlescent mountain range ahead of them. Yet another pathway closed to her. She wondered if any attempt to pry information out of him would prevail over his stubborn, mysterious air.

A deafening crash of thunder startled her, drawing her attention to the source of the familiar music throughout Atonaco. As a child, she had heard many legends about the Thunder Forests, where more often than not it was raining. Traveling through certain parts of the jungle was difficult, which led to alleged stories of large horned creatures, feathered snakes, and fruits of immortality lurking deep in the green tresses. Although those stories were unconfirmed, the forests did provide many resources for daily life and some trade to other nations, particularly the Wei empire.

She looked back at Raiden, whose features and accent seemed Wei, and remembered he had said Dacio grew up in the Wei empire.

"How did you and Dacio meet?" she asked.

"On the streets of Yin City," he answered quietly after a few steps. "We were both trying to steal the same loaf of bread."

His gaze appeared unfocused, as if he were remembering the scene. Surprisingly, he expounded his answer with more details. "Dacio was more nimble and experienced than I was, so they won. One might think we were rivals because of that, but they were one of the few who showed me kindness."

Esme nodded, trying to piece together the mosaic he was assembling with his words. They had both been stealing bread, perhaps out of desperation from hunger? She imagined the situation—Raiden's hands reaching out for the piece of bread only for Dacio's nimble fingers to snatch it away. If the story was true, that would explain how Dacio was adept at avoiding any pickpockets using their sleight of hand tricks. Wondering if Raiden had the same talents, she looked back at his black gloves.

"Are the gloves not too warm?" she asked. Esme could understand if he were wearing gloves in the south, but outside of the port, Atonaco seldom grew cold, and any other person would have uncomfortably sweaty hands.

Raiden tensed and seemingly tightened the cloak around him. "No," he said unconvincingly. From the way he stiffened, perhaps the gloves were yet another touchy subject for him. Maybe he was self-conscious about them?

"Is it really that cold in the Wei empire?" Esme asked, taking mercy on him by shifting the topic. She had never been there, that she knew of, although her mother was from one of the three kingdoms that eventually united under the Wei imperial banner. Instead, she had lived in Atonaco, which had some of the best schools for magic on the continent and because her father was from Izel Valley in the southwest, near the Moonstone Mountains. "I'm a summer person through and through."

"Yes, it's cold, but a pyromage like you would have the methods to keep comfortable," he said. "Perhaps we should stop for warmer clothes anyways."

As he strode ahead, Esme slowed her step. He knew that she was a pyromage? She quickly thought back to when she healed him and remembered that she had heated the water in the bowl with her fingers. Perhaps he sensed her fire magic in the air then.

Regardless, she looked down at herself, realizing his suggestion made sense. Her loose cactus-fiber skirt, ornamented red and white blouse, sandals, and pulled-up hair weren't suitable for colder weather. All of the skin below her knee was exposed to the elements. Even though she could use her fire magic to warm herself, she knew the cold would drain her energy faster, just like how Dacio's minor ice magic usually dwindled quickly under the hot sun.

"A new outfit sounds like a good idea," she said. On one hand, she was excited about new clothing, but on the other, she was disappointed it would probably cover up her jewelry, particularly the gold serpent-shaped armlet and jade bracelets gifted to her long ago from her parents.

"Port Kai has a market. We can stop for food and rest as well. We've been walking for a while and we're almost there," Raiden said.

Esme looked up sharply. "Port? Are we already that close to the sea?" she asked and squinted at the Moonstone Mountains, only to realize they were much closer than expected. She could even see the marbled white-blue patterns that streaked the mountain range.

"Yes," he replied curtly.

Any port to the Sapphire Sea would mean that the border between Atonaco and the Wei empire was close. Named after the deity of water, Port Kai was the one point of entry between the two sides of the Moonstone Mountains, the southern half of the crescent-shaped range splitting the two nations. After the deities destroyed the nine moons and cast them down as mountains, mortals naturally used the range to demark borders.

"If we go fast enough, do you think we can catch up to Dacio and the guards?" she asked. Hope started rising like a lantern inside her although Raiden quickly dashed it against the stones with his answer.

"No doubt the imperial soldiers have a fast naval ship, and given that we haven't seen them in front of us the entire time, they've probably reached the port already."

She frowned, thinking about what she knew of the Wei empire's naval might with its supposed fleet of ships boasting red, fan-shaped sails and speed that made them all but fly over the waters. They also had the ability to better withstand the power of typhoons that would otherwise shipwreck other boats. Altogether, this meant they wouldn't be able to catch up by sea.

"Don't worry. Remember I know a shortcut, and it will compensate for our current lag," he said, before pointing off to the left. "There. You can see the edge of the city from here."

Near the gap between the two ends of the mountain range were lines of buildings surrounding a few large stone-stepped temples. Esme couldn't quite remember if she had visited Port Kai before or if she was creating false memories, but the port city seemed like a larger version of Atoyatlan. However, as they walked closer, she noticed the one major difference—the system of canals. She could see people floating by on their boats, passing by a larger square with merchants and vendors selling their crafts and food.

The tantalizing smell of food managed to distract her from her mission of getting a new outfit. Her stomach truly had a mind of its own, typically after she expended too much energy. Healing Raiden earlier and walking from Atoyatlan had not been *that* exhausting, but food was food, and she couldn't say no to that.

One of the vendors on the outer layer of the city sold squash and bean-filled tamalli, something that was easier to take along. Esme bought a few and offered one to Raiden.

A flash of guilt crossed his face, but he quickly wiped it off, carefully taking the wrapped delicacy and chomping down on it. They quickly finished up and moved onto the nearby shops before they closed. Night rose from the Sapphire Sea toward the sky.

As picky as she was with her jewelry, she was even more meticulous with her clothing, so much so that after many declines, Raiden gave her a sharp stare and said, "At this point, the shopkeeper and I will be sleeping on our feet tonight."

Esme glowered at him, but the sky seemed to agree with his statement. Darkness had fallen smoothly over them, and the torches on the street were illuminating people's faces as they trickled past.

"Well, some of us like to wear something other than doom and gloom." She sniffed and bargained for a white and light pink robe and a midnight blue cloak worth more cocoa beans than ideal. When she got back to Atoyatlan, she would have to be more frugal with her expenditures. With the reminder of money, she realized she would need to exchange currency for traveling in the Wei empire, so she added that note to her mental list.

She thanked the shopkeeper before heading off with Raiden to find somewhere to sleep for the night. As a gesture of appreciation for Raiden waiting, she let him choose the location. Naturally, he drifted away from the central system of canals and toward the quieter edges of town to find lodging.

Raiden insisted on taking care of the stay, so she let him take the lead. As he acquired two separate rooms, Esme remembered that she wanted to exchange currency, so she waited for him to finish up before approaching the innkeeper.

Before she could even speak, the innkeeper looked at her and greeted her in Wei.

Esme blinked, ill-prepared to use Wei already. As a part of every Atonacan child's mandatory education, some knowledge of Wei was required. She had also heard both languages from her parents. However, she only retained her language teachings from childhood and hadn't touched up on her speaking skills since she'd woken from her coma. How was she supposed to respond? Atonacan or Wei? Panicking, she chose Wei.

"Can I exchange coins here?" she asked, internally flustered and doubting herself.

The older man smiled in response and nodded graciously. "Of course. I can take Wei coins. How many do you need to exchange?"

Managing to understand, Esme replied, "I actually *need* Wei coins."

"Of course," he said. Taking a few copper axe coins from her pouch, she walked over and handed them to him.

The innkeeper was Atonacan and so was she, but did he only choose Wei because she was with Raiden or because she looked Wei? What language had Raiden even used with him?

"How long have you been visiting Atonaco?" the man asked, exchanging the copper coins for silver ones.

Bitter chords struck Esme in the chest, but she kept the polite smile on her face. Being labeled as a visitor in her own homelands always burned her on the inside, even if the comment was neutral and even if she did indeed have some connection to the Wei empire. She felt like she was never enough as herself.

"I'm actually from Atoyatlan," she said, trying to ignore that dull, aching throb of her heart.

"Oh! I didn't realize. I suppose your hair is very northern and I do see some Atonacan features." The innkeeper laughed. "I think your eyes confused me. They are so startlingly pretty."

Esme gave him a pained smile and kept quiet as he handed her the coins and bid her good evening.

Quietly, she turned around, avoiding looking at Raiden on the way to their rooms. Neither of them said anything in their path, nor did they say anything aside from a half-hearted goodnight before they went to their respective rooms. She set her bag down and hung her new outfit on the chair before praying, lying down on the bed and curling up on her side.

She closed her eyes. Soon, everything would be sorted out, and she and Dacio would be back in Atoyatlan. However, her inner doubts thought otherwise, conjuring up a million ways the mission could go wrong. Restless sleep called her name as she fell into its familiar embrace.

CHAPTER 3

Even hours after waking up at dawn, Esme was still wiping the sleep away from her eyes. The only path south was the narrow strip of heavily guarded land between the sea and mountains. Any other path would require crossing through the difficult terrain of the Moonstone Mountains itself. Aside from the small mountainside village they just passed through, she saw nothing but beautiful nature to keep her eyes busy. That didn't change even as they entered the Emerald Forest in the northeastern part of the Wei empire.

Esme couldn't help but look around. The thin, hollow trees were not particularly tall, but they were dense enough to block out most of the midday sun. However, she could already feel the difference between the Emerald and Thunder forests through the lack of moisture in the air and the cool temperatures that descended from the mountains. Although she didn't spend much time in the Atonacan jungles, she still noticed the distinct absence of life and variety.

The forest was too quiet, but perhaps that was because it was the end of winter here.

"Where exactly are we heading?" Esme asked, leaning to the side to better project her voice up ahead to her guide. "You said you knew the shortest path to Yin City?"

From what she knew, only a major forest and large lake separated the Wei capital city and the mountains. So far, Raiden hadn't taken any special shortcuts that would cut down the distance as they only seemed to be traveling on the main trade route.

"There's a hidden portal somewhere in this forest, supposedly a remnant of one of the deities' journey to the continent ages ago. The other side of this portal leads us right outside the walls of the city. It probably saves us a few days of travel, more than enough time to catch up to the fastest naval ship the Wei empire could offer," Raiden said, slowing down his pace so they were side by side.

Her eyes widened. "Portals?"

The corner of his lips curled slightly upward. "Yes, portals. Is that really so surprising to someone who practices magic?"

She shook her head. "Well, not exactly. I just haven't seen or heard about any of them before. Tell me more about them," she said, wondering why no one at the Great Temple had ever spoken of them.

Raiden's neutral frown returned. "Unfortunately, I never paid much attention to learning about the deities, even less so for magic, so I don't know," he said, sounding regretful. "Regardless, only certain people are able to use it. Most people cannot, so that's enough to disguise any portal as a legend."

"Will I be able to use it?" she asked.

He hesitated before answering, "Yes. You have magic in your veins."

Was magic the requirement then? If so, that could explain why most people couldn't use them, as those with magic lineage were uncommon but not rare. Did that mean Raiden was also a mage? Maybe that was a reason why he and Dacio were friends. "You have magic as well?" she asked.

"Nothing so... interesting as that, but I've used portals before," he said, his expression darkening and clearly denoting another sore subject.

After that, he became silent, and Esme had to go back to looking at the forest and thinking about everything. Portals? Were any portals in Atonaco? Were they only found in pairs or were they part of a network? Based on what Raiden had said, it seemed as if they came in pairs, so perhaps none of the portals in Atonaco would have worked for their journey to the Wei capital if they existed.

As for the origins of the portals, she wondered how the deities created them, and which one in particular. Five major deities were recognized by both major empires and were the pure form of their respective element: Jing, the spirit deity; Tayanna, the fire deity; Zoraya, the metal deity; Kai, the water deity; and Alejo, the wind deity. Meanwhile, minor deities ranged from place to place, as did patron deities.

A gentle breeze whispered by, making her shiver. Already she missed the heat of the Atonacan sun on her back.

Of all the deities, Esme felt the most affinity toward Tayanna because of her fire magic. In fact, all magic came from the deities, so she always figured her powers came from Tayanna blessing one of her ancestors. Esme also held an admiration for Zoraya, primarily because of her own preferences for metals like gold and emeralds—her namesake in a language neither Wei nor Atonacan. It was too bad she couldn't control metal although she was still happy with her fire and minor healing affinity.

Raiden let out a soft sigh, bringing her thoughts back to him. Who exactly was he? Mysterious and collected, he still acted a bit prickly toward her, and she had not seen him interact with enough people to decipher whether he had some hidden resentment toward her specifically or if he was as guarded and blunt with everyone. If this was his normal attitude, it only went to show how charming Dacio could be to befriend him.

Hopefully Dacio could use their charm to stay safe until she and Raiden arrived. She was sure she would be extremely upset if she had been falsely accused of a crime and then taken from her home.

Suddenly, Raiden threw his gloved hand up, jostling Esme back to reality. She immediately slowed down and honed her senses on their surroundings. It was quiet except for their breathing.

"What's wrong?" she whispered. Another subtle breeze trickled by, rustling the leaves above them and dragging her attention up toward the hidden sky. Low and dissonant chittering started humming in the background. The hair at the back of her neck raised and she got chills throughout her body. A glint of silver flashed in the corner of her eye, but before she could even process the motion, she saw Raiden holding a dagger in his hand.

"Hells. It's the Dreadful," he hissed softly, scowling. "We need to move quickly."

The Dreadful. The vicious demons formed after a spirit wandered the mortal realm for too long and lost their way. Of *course* they had to stumble upon danger in the middle of this eerie forest. Her chest felt tight, and her breath grew shallow like she couldn't breathe too loudly lest she draw attention. Aside from the rhythmic pounding of blood in her ears, she could also hear the dissonant noises grow louder until they surrounded her like a cloak. Alarmed, she tried to look around, desperate to find the source.

An intense malevolent aura flooded her, almost sending her stumbling backward. She did not want to see what caused such a presence.

"Can you fight?" Raiden asked.

"Not really," she admitted. At least, not hand-to-hand fighting. The obsidian knife she carried in her pouch was mostly for cutting objects or for desperate situations where her magic was not sufficient. Whatever the demons' powers were, hopefully magic would be enough because her physical fighting abilities were lackluster. She'd never really needed to use her knife for self-defense before since Atoyatlan was peaceful, and punishments were severe enough to deter most crimes.

"We better get to the portal before they catch up." Raiden took another look behind them, and his eyes widened. "Wait—"

Before Esme could even turn back to see what he was looking at, she was hit from behind and sent flying. She threw her arms out and her wrists took the blunt of the forceful impact from hitting the ground. Air rushed out of her and her sight blurred for a moment before finally clearing up. Immediately, she regretted regaining her sight because what she saw made her shriek.

Towering over her was a creature that had six thick limbs with countless eyeballs running down them. Protruding out from a round body was its elongated head, which only contained a gaping mouth with rows of teeth and a surrounding plate of bone. All of the eyeballs she could see were trained on her, and its mouth snapped open and closed as if preparing to eat her.

Too close, too close, too close!

She scrambled for her own dagger and slashed up as it lunged down toward her.

"Esme!"

She barely heard Raiden shout her name from afar since her blood pounded furiously in her ears. The majority of her focus was spent trying to get away from the demon, which had shrieked as her weapon made contact with it. Having created a window of opportunity, Esme scrambled back and up to her feet, darting a few steps to avoid the six limbs.

Now the demon was far enough away for her to be able to concentrate on drawing the heat from her surroundings and summoning fire in her hands. Warmth first flooded her body, traveling up her arm before starting to heat up the air around her.

The Dreadful shrieked again and tensed, ready to lunge. Esme instinctively threw her fireballs at it, trying to create more distance and perhaps damage it. As hoped, the demon jumped back to avoid the fireballs. However, the flames landed at the base of a hollow tree and started flickering at the edges.

"Raiden! How do you deal with these things?" she shouted. She didn't bother quieting her voice this time. If her previous scream and the demon's shrieking hadn't attracted anything else, this shout wouldn't cause any more damage. Without waiting for a response, she reached in the direction of where the fireballs landed and sharply drew her arms up, turning the nascent fire into a tall, thin column of flames that started to consume the trees.

The sudden illumination in the forest revealed a second creature behind the first. The second demon was a tall, desiccated creature that looked like a nightmarish cross between an elk and a goat with sharp claws. Its head was bare to the bone as its great antlers sprouted toward the sky.

Raiden swore. "Cover me," he barked, leaping off and dashing toward the two creatures.

When Esme noticed he only had a dagger in hand, she wanted to pull him back and run. The reach of his arm plus the dagger would be no match against the reach of two towering demons with long, gangly appendages.

"Fine, but you still have to tell me how to kill these things," Esme said as she rechanneled her focus on controlling the available flames. Summoning fire was almost as easy as breathing to her; controlling fire was another issue.

"Anything that would definitely kill a mortal will extinguish these demons," he said. The Dreadful screeched and approached him, as if it could understand what he had said.

Raiden struck. He lunged toward the six-legged demon, keeping low to the ground and slashing at its legs. Esme barely saw him move, and she certainly did not see where he had grabbed his sword from, but he was now holding a curved, wide-tipped blade longer than his arm instead of the smaller dagger.

Where did that sword even come *from?* The burning question would just have to wait until afterward.

She lifted her hands and threw them downward, projecting streams of fire at the Dreadful from above while carefully avoiding striking Raiden with her magic. The combination of their attacks forced the first creature, which was now down to five limbs from Raiden's attack, back into the second one. Meanwhile, Esme kept the second one at a distance by forcing it to dodge her ranged attacks.

Lifting his elbow and lunging forward, Raiden continued his pursuit of the Dreadful and cut the first one down with brutal and experienced efficiency. One leg detached, then another, and another until finally he drove his sword into the demon's head. The creature exploded into a cloud of gray dust, disappearing to deities knew where.

The explosion took her by surprise, which gave the second demon an opportunity to charge through the ash cloud and knock Raiden back. Esme yelped when she saw one of its giant antlers stab him.

He grunted, and stepped back from the force. Even with an antler piercing his body, he still managed to use his weapon to cleave off the bone from the demon's head. The Dreadful jerked back, widening the gap between them, and Raiden stepped forward to slash at it again. It parried back, swinging its remaining antler into him and sending him flying into the ground, the sword tumbling to the side.

When he looked over at his weapon, he started to take off his gloves.

What is that fool doing?

However, with him now out of the demon's immediate range, Esme stepped forward and took over again. Time to show the Dreadful the consequences of playing with fire.

She jerked her arms up, letting the nearby flames from the burning hollow trees shoot up like winged serpents of fire. The heat only fueled the energy around her, but it sent Raiden scrambling back. His motions must have been painful because he groaned even after he stopped. Esme was about to run over to check up on him, but he waved her off and moved to staunch the blood flow from the puncture wounds.

Trusting his judgment, she returned to her mission and moved her hands to fold the fire walls to surround the elk-headed demon. The tips of the flames began to curl inward, boxing it in from above like a slowly constricting room. Through the gaps of the flickering fires, she could see it step back. *Promising*, she thought.

If whatever could absolutely kill a human could kill a demon, surely trapping it in a prison of fire would do the trick—or at least inflict some major damage.

Stepping forward, she turned her palms inward toward each other and began to close the walls of fire together. The edges of her face and the back of her neck grew damp, and breathing became difficult, but she kept her focus and energy. The fire grew hotter and whiter, like a star, sending the demon mad in its attempt to find an escape. She brought her palms together, collapsing the box of fire onto the Dreadful before light exploded from the collapse.

Esme threw her arms up to block the blast of wind and blinding light, which quickly faded. When she opened her eyes again, the demon was gone, a pile of ash all that remained where it once stood. Embers sprinkled the ground around it, eating away at the remaining vegetation. Raiden was now behind her, his arms raised from having blocked the light. Still wary, she looked around to see if she had missed anything.

Nothing moved. She waited, listening and listening.

A bird chirped from the tops of the hollow trees. Tension eased from her shoulders. That insidious sense of unease drained from the atmosphere, and Esme had a feeling they were free from demonic troubles. *For now.*

CHAPTER 4

Raiden huffed, drawing her attention back to him. His hair was disheveled and dirt smudged the glimmer of pain on his face. "Why didn't you just start with that trick?" He groaned from the ground, leaning forward and still covering his wounds with his hands.

Esme didn't know whether to laugh or glare at that comment. "You're the one who charged right in before telling me anything useful, and mind you, your comments were vaguer than oracle bones," she retorted. Regardless, she walked over and offered him a hand.

He glanced at her outreached hand and promptly ignored it, choosing to pick himself off the ground with only a wince. She narrowed her eyes, feeling slighted.

"Let's just get to the portal, and then we can fix other… problems," Raiden said, picking up his glove and tucking it into the belt wrapped around his waist. His exposed fingers were stained garnet red with blood.

She pressed her lips together. "How far away is this portal? Your injuries should be addressed," she said, looking at where he was clutching before cocking her head to the side. "Where's your sword?"

Raiden used his free hand to gesture at the sheathe strapped to his side. She could only see the handle of the dagger, and it was clear that he could see the doubt on her face because he said, "A metallomage enchanted this dagger to be able to transform into a sword."

Taking the dagger back out, he murmured something, and they both watched it glow and extend its length until it became the slightly curved sword she saw earlier. After giving the sword a wave, Raiden murmured something again, making the sword shrink back into the dagger.

It was always astounding to see other magic. According to her studies and the priestesses at the temple, all mages were limited to one major affinity, which was inherited and fell under the domains of one of the main deities: fire, water, wind, metal, and spirit. In addition, mages could also inherit and develop a minor skill, a highly specific subcategory under another realm. Dacio's minor magic was ice, a subcategory of water, whereas Esme's was in spirit—healing. Neither of them could manipulate metal, but metal was the only magic that could be sustained away from the mage, as shown through Raiden's blade.

However, these past two days had made her appreciate her healing abilities, especially as she eyed his covered wound. With mages being few in number, he truly was fortunate to travel not only with a mage but with one who could heal. Not all those who had magical ancestors became mages or developed powers.

"If that portal's far from here, I insist on addressing your wound now. You don't want to aggravate it even more," she said.

"I don't think we should stay here longer than necessary. We don't know where they came from and more might be lurking around," he said, scowling. Based on his answer, she guessed the portal was further than comfortable. "I'll be fine. I've been in worse situations."

Esme narrowed her eyes, skeptical at first, but then she remembered his sorry state when she first met him.

He sighed and offered, "Maybe you can heal a little now and the rest later?"

"Fine." She nodded and stepped closer. Based on her initial examination, she could start working on the wounds on his torso now and then perhaps the wounds on his arms later if the tears in his clothing were any indication. Not only did he have puncture wounds but also claw mark damage.

She froze. They looked like the same type of claw marks she had healed yesterday. Slowly, she returned to healing him while considering the implications of his injuries and abilities. Was demon hunting his occupation? The scars only reminded her of why she only stuck to dealing with lost spirits in Atoyatlan. Dealing with demons was hazardous—and frightening. She couldn't imagine encountering the bone-faced creatures day to day.

"You weren't completely surprised by the Dreadful," she stated, glancing up.

"I'm paid to take care of them, but I've been getting sloppy." He glared at his own wounds.

Esme looked back down and focused on manipulating the spirit around her and channeling it to artificially heal the wounds for now. Luckily, his wounds weren't as bad or deep as they could have been since he wore a hard scaled leather vest over a silk shirt.

"Sounds dangerous," she said.

"I'm good at killing things," he said, his tone flat and cold, yet certain. The way he seemed to fully believe that ominously worded statement made her feel a little uneasy. As quickly as the darkness entered his tone, it left. "Okay, that's good enough. We should hurry before we run into any more surprises."

She pulled her hand back. They really should hurry. When she truly healed Raiden, the combination of fighting the demons with her fire magic and expending more magic to heal wounds would be enough to exhaust her, and she did not want to be caught exhausted in a demon-ridden forest.

Raiden prowled ahead without hesitation. Every few minutes, she looked over to see how he was doing. His back was unnaturally straight and his jaw was clenched, but she didn't see him wince or flinch from any of his motions. He simply continued to guide them in the direction of the portal, away from the main trade path.

Eventually, they started following a stream. Even before she saw it, she could hear the faint roar of a waterfall. There, spawning from the top of the rising rock formation, flowed the considerable waterfall that fed into the stream. However, neither sight nor sound could explain the tingling sensation prickling at her skin. Magic.

"Here," Raiden said, verifying her suspicion. She looked around for the portal, although she wasn't quite sure what a portal even looked like. "It's in the cave behind the waterfall," he added, upon noticing her confusion.

They followed the small stone banks of the stream that led to the side of the waterfall. Cool mist slowly sprinkled onto her face and accelerated the closer they got to the base. A crown of mist covered Raiden's hair, and she imagined that her dark hair was spotted with silver-glinting droplets. Esme had to squint to see the gap between the falling water and the rocks. *There.* She could see the cave now, once hidden by the waterfall. If Raiden hadn't told her about the existence of the portal, she might have walked past and wondered about the magical energy of the place.

Neither of them needed to cross underneath the water, but the mist was enough to dampen their skins as they walked in. Raiden quickly rinsed his bloody hand under the fall and immediately donned his gloves afterward. The energy Esme felt earlier suddenly amplified to a level she had never experienced before. Her eyes widened, trying to take in her surroundings as best as she could with limited light. This overwhelming energy was not of this realm. No mage could create something this powerful and lasting.

Sharp rocks rose from the stony bed into a field of pikes. She could see writing on the far end of the musty, misty cave. One sentence was scrawled over and over in the stone but in multiple languages: *Blood Divine Enter Here, Else Risk Eternal Fear.*

After Esme read the warning out loud, she pondered over its ominous meaning. "Blood divine?" she asked.

"Magic," Raiden said from behind before striding past her, around the spikes, and toward the wall. "Not sure what the eternal fear part of this warning means, but it might just be an empty threat. I know we can use the portal."

She eyed the wall cautiously and approached. "If you insist."

Raiden's face relaxed, and he gestured to the wall. "After you."

Esme looked at him again, reassessing her trust in him. She had just met him the day prior and now she was walking into a cave and going through a suspicious portal with a foreboding message next to it. But he could have let the Dreadful eat her, so she had faith that she could continue to trust him.

Magic stemmed from the wall. Her hand seemed to raise without her permission because suddenly she found it had passed through the image of stone. *An illusion?* Certainly not magic a human could cast. Taking a deep breath, she walked forward, her foot passing through first followed by the rest of her body.

When she stepped through fully, she couldn't tell whether she was dreaming or whether she was still stuck in the portal. Esme squeezed her eyes shut, rubbed them a few times, and opened them back up again.

Everything was in shades of gray: the buildings in the distance, the sky, the grass, the tall trees next to her, and the boulder behind her. All of it. Gray.

Wherever she was, this was not what she had expected to see upon crossing through the portal. She continued to look around, her eyebrows furrowed together, before she realized Raiden wasn't by her side. Her heart sped, and she quickly whirled around to see if he had stalked off without her knowing, but he was nowhere to be seen.

"It's okay," Esme told herself. She closed her eyes again, trying to steady her breathing and heart rate to no avail. Maybe some of the effects from using the portal took some time to wear off. Maybe there was some staggering in time for beings to pass through the portal. Raiden was just fine and she was overreacting.

As soon as she opened her eyes once more, she yelped from the skeletal face that appeared right in front of her. She leapt back, throwing one arm up and using the other to wrap around her chest as a shield. Her eyes devoured the changes to her environment. Suddenly, many transparent, clothed skeletal figures gathered around her, all in grayscale. All of them stood here now when just a few seconds ago, they weren't.

The skeleton who stood in front of her captured her attention with their wide gaping gaze and simple robes.

"You're so colorful," they fawned in a high chime, looking over her.

Esme's mouth just gaped open. "Er, thanks," she stumbled. What was she supposed to say in response to a talking skeleton? She never expected Yin City and its citizens to lack so much... color. Maybe crossing the portal somehow temporarily messed up her vision. Either that, or she was in some very, *very* wrong place—a place of death.

Even though their skeletal face seemed to have an eternal grin, she felt like the being smiled at her. "Is this what we look like right before we move onto our next destination? I do miss having flesh."

Their words knocked the air out of her. She felt like she could faint. Her body became more and more agitated, and she tried her best to calm herself down again. The lack of flesh wasn't just something she was imagining. *Oh stars above, I'm not in the spirit realm. Am I?* Did she happen to make a wrong turn in the portal? Was that even possible? Was she stuck here forever? She hadn't imagined that spirits would look skeletal in the afterlife. Perhaps these were just the forms they wore in this stage.

Most importantly, how was she going to get out?

"At ease, my dear," another voice soothed. Esme looked back up, and for the first time since she stepped through the portal, she saw color.

The figure standing serenely in front of her was beautiful, ethereal even, and was the only one who was opaque. She had long, silky black hair that flowed over her shoulders, partially covering her pearly and opalescent dress. It was hard for Esme to pin down the exact color of the dress because every breath she took shifted her gaze enough to catch different hues of blue, white, and purple.

"You should not be here now, little one," she spoke, drawing Esme's eyes back up to her face. The newcomer's narrow eyes sparkled radiantly in every color possible and her voice was like a lullaby, enchanting and alluring. "Return," she commanded.

Return where? How?

The ethereal being smiled. "Return as you have returned other lost souls," she said and then faded from view.

Esme threw her hand out. "Wait!" She was now alone.

She tried to decipher the hint. *Return as I have returned other lost souls?* Like the spirits she and Dacio guided back out of the mortal realm? Could she guide herself out using a similar method? It couldn't hurt to try. She looked up to the sky, where the sun might be, but saw no shining ball of light hovering in the heavens. Somehow, it was just a lighter shade of gray, enough to distinguish between the sky and the ground. The temperature around her was neutral and offered little kindling for her to extract magic from the surrounding elements.

Regardless, she could create her own.

Locking her fingers together and drawing from her inner magic and the heat of her own blood, she felt the rush of warmth flow through her body before releasing it through the tips of her fingers and igniting a small flickering flame. When nothing happened, she wondered if she needed to surround herself with light. She closed her eyes, raised her arms, and enclosed herself with a barrier of fire. Even with her eyes closed, she could tell the light from the flames was bright.

Hopefully, her plan would be enough as she didn't think she would have energy to make a second attempt.

She dropped her arms and the fire.

Opening her eyes once more, Esme found herself standing in the shadow of the same tall trees as before but in color. Her heart leapt and she had never been so happy to see a green tree in her life. Immediately, she whirled around to check if she could see Raiden.

"Esme?" Raiden called out. She looked up in the direction of his voice and was elated to see his concerned face. "Where were you? I couldn't find you."

Her smile faded slightly as she began to process what had just happened, her shoulders sagging slightly. "I think I was just in one of the afterworld realms?"

Raiden paled. His eyebrows furrowed, eyes glancing over her. "Are you okay?"

She looked down at herself, felt a creeping sense of weariness settle into her bones, and then looked back up. "I feel fine, but I am confused and exhausted," she said. Fighting demons, crossing through a portal, and blazing her way out of what she guessed was the spirit realm all within a day had drained her.

After another examining glance, he said, "We should find a place to rest. We've both had an eventful day, and the naval ship probably won't get here until tomorrow morning."

Esme's eyes widened. "Truly?" Had the portal cut down that much time from their journey that they had beaten one of the fastest naval ships in the world?

"Yes, we avoided going through most of the Emerald Forest and around Diamond Lake, which probably saved us at least a week of travel on foot," he said. "Now, let's find shelter in the city and prepare for when Dacio arrives."

His comment reminded her that she was in Yin City. Her head darted back up, looking into the distance where in the other realm, she had seen buildings. The same exact shapes were present here too, like a mirror image, but in color this time. From the outskirts of the city, she saw frosted, gray tiled roofs of the many dwellings and buildings past the fortified walls bordering the city. Further yet, she could see a complex of tall, tiered buildings on top of a large hill at the far end of the enclosed city—the palace, she guessed. Beyond the city and bordering the cliffs was the gleaming coastline of the Sapphire Sea.

"Stop gawking. Start walking," Raiden said, dragging her attention back to him. She wrinkled her nose at him but followed along. She would have time later to admire the Wei capital city and at a closer distance too.

They made their way to the outer walls of the city, but instead of going toward the guarded main gate, he led her to another section. Hugging closely to the side of the tall stone structure, Raiden kept looking at the segments of stone in the barrier. Soon, he stopped and faced the wall. In front of him was a small painting of a cephalopod with six tentacles. *A secret entrance?*

Esme's guess was confirmed when he pressed his finger into the middle of the hexapod and a small rumbling sound gave way to a pathway. Her eyebrows raised. Raiden really knew his way around Yin City. She wondered why he knew about this alternative, and somewhat suspicious, entrance.

Nevertheless, she walked behind him, just in time for the wall to close up behind them as darkness swallowed them whole.

CHAPTER 5

The welcoming musty tunnels, though secret, looked well-kept, as if people occasionally used them. Based on the way they were headed, Esme figured they were moving within the wall, parallel to their previous path outside. However, instead of passing through to the other side of the wall, they descended a staircase. Her eyebrows furrowed. Where were they going?

Her wrists were still sore from catching herself on the ground, but healing them could wait until after her magic replenished. "Just to let you know, if I don't take a break soon or eat something, I won't have enough energy to address your other wounds today," she informed him, moving her wrists in small circles.

"Noted," Raiden replied, still looking ahead.

After a few turns, they reached what seemed to be a dead end. This time, a different symbol was painted on the wall—plum blossoms. She already preferred the flower painting over the one outside. Raiden walked forth and pressed the symbol. Unlike previously, the wall didn't immediately open up; instead, one of the blocks of stones moved, revealing a flower-shaped indent.

Raiden reached down to his sheathe, drawing Esme's attention to a jade pendent in the same shape. After unclasping it, he placed the small amulet into the hole and twisted it like a key. She heard some clicking noises—locks—before the wall pushed out toward them, forming a door she wasn't able to see before. When the door opened all the way, she could see a cloaked figure standing next to a seat cushion in a nicely lit, well-furnished foyer with bookshelves and intricate wooden furniture.

The interior had enough lanterns for Esme to see the stunned face. Long, straight black hair lined her sharp features and light skin. A simple pin held back the hair from her face.

"Is she in?" Raiden asked the cloaked woman in Wei as he entered.

She nodded at him, passing a quick glance over Esme, and then called out in a smooth low voice, "Reina, you've got visitors."

Esme looked in the same direction just in time to see a tall woman yanking a door open hard enough to send her dark, tightly braided hair flying back to leave streaks of yellow-orange in the air from the jewelry intertwined throughout. Esme's eyes trailed up from her black leather outfit up to the studded silver earrings going along the rim of her ear, which twinkled like stars in a night sky against deep brown skin typical of those who came from the northwestern deserts. The woman's dark eyes narrowed as soon as they landed on Raiden.

"I distinctly remember you saying you would never return to this cursed nightmare of a city, Raiden," she said, leaning against the door frame by the end of her sentence.

"Then you understand the severity of the situation," he replied without hesitation. Their familiarity with each other made Esme guess this person was Reina.

Reina hummed in response before examining both of them. Her neutral expression somehow seemed to ease and tense at the same time with her lips pulling back into a grin as her posture straightened. "And who is this ray of sunshine?" she asked. "I'm Li Reina."

For a brief second, she wondered which name to give: Esmeralda, Esme, or the Wei name her mother had endearingly called her. After second-guessing Wei greeting customs too, she went with introducing herself as Esme. Reina continued grinning at her, but slowly her smile faded and her eyes sharply cut back to Raiden, who went stiff at the questioning look.

"We came here for help," Raiden rushed. "Need intel and a place to stay."

Esme looked back at him. Intel. In a hidden underground room found through a secret passage in the walls of the city. *Not suspicious at all.*

"Are you all spies?" she blurted out. She had to say the last word in Atonacan since she couldn't recall the Wei word for spy.

Everyone's gaze turned to her. While Raiden's eyes widened almost comically, Reina and the cloaked woman's remained neutral.

"What gave it away?" The cloaked woman smirked mysteriously, easily responding in Atonacan.

"I'm a former spy, actually," Reina said in such an offhanded tone that it was as if she were talking about the weather. "But given how well Raiden keeps his secrets, I could see why anyone would think him to be a spy. He is, after all, a man of few words." She gave him a pointed look.

Raiden scowled. Esme had to hide her smile at that comment. After all, her first interaction with him had been very limited in information and she all but had to pry anything out of him. *Few words indeed.*

The former spy kept her smile and walked closer to them. "Magic words, dear," she sang.

If anything, he scowled harder. "Please."

Reina clapped her hands together and glided across the stone floor. "Daiyu, feel free to continue resting. I can take care of welcoming an old friend," she said, turning toward the person who had greeted them. The cloaked woman—Daiyu—nodded and sat down onto her cushion and pulled out a book. Facing Raiden and Esme, Reina said, "Do not fret. I know of a small place for you to rest for the evening."

At the mention of rest, Esme was beginning to *taste* the promise of sleep.

"I will gather information about Dacio in the meantime. I assume that only a situation regarding Dacio would drag you back here, Raiden," Reina added, verifying for Esme everyone's connections. Reina started to guide them back into the tunnels. The stone door shut behind them, depriving the passageway of the foyer's light.

Every few steps, she looked back at Esme. Was something on her face? Suddenly self-conscious, she raised her fingers toward her face and hair, to which Reina laughed gently.

"Nothing wrong with you. I'm just trying to figure you out," Reina said. "Feel free to use any language you want. Successful spies know all the major ones."

"Thank you," Esme responded, dropping her hand. She could understand Wei but needed some adjustment period before she started voicing her thoughts on complex topics like the exchange back in the room. "You said you were a former spy, but I have to admit that this venue"—she gestured to the tunnels, almost hitting Raiden—"still seems very secretive, and you're also a source of intel."

Reina nodded, saying, "That's a fair assessment. Since you are a friend of Raiden's and Dacio's, I will tell you." They both looked over to Raiden, who tensed again but didn't say anything, so Reina continued. "I was once a part of an organization called The Six as a spy. You may have even seen their logo when you entered the wall."

Recalling the painting of the hexapod at the city wall entrance, Esme raised her eyebrows. Based on how Reina was setting up the story and how the two paintings were different, she guessed the two symbols indicated two different organizations.

"I hated every second while I was involved, but they trained me well. I quickly left and decided to use my skills for something better," Reina continued, glossing over details. "Undoubtedly many at The Six wish they weren't involved but stay out of desperation. The palace has drained too much of our resources." Her face grew cold at the mention of the palace. "Now, I spend my days—with the aid of Daiyu and other fellow defectors—helping people, both ordinary and those trapped in The Six, escape and keep themselves informed."

They finally reached the end of the pathway and a stone staircase with a cloth-covered entrance above. Reina reached out and pulled the cloth to the side, leading them into the back of a noodle shop. Immediately, the scent of savory food smacked Esme in the face, making her whimper. She was simultaneously starving and exhausted.

"The owners, Mr. and Mrs. Chen, will help you with food and shelter for the night. They are two of the first people I helped and are always willing to host people in their spare room," Reina said, nodding toward the shop. "I will leave you here and will send Daiyu back with information later. Just let the owners know I brought you here and keep out of trouble."

The former spy blended back into the shadows and slinked out of sight, leaving Esme to trust they were now in a safe location. However, she wasn't sure why they were hiding in the first place and why they couldn't have just strolled through the front gates of the city. The shady nature of the whole ordeal made her guess that Raiden was trying to stay hidden.

Esme easily spotted one of the owners standing outside the kitchen, and as the more affable one, approached him and mentioned Reina's name. The friendly owner gladly welcomed them, inviting them to a corner table where Esme sank down to rest her feet. She all but devoured the bowl of warm, soul-replenishing soup and noodles shortly offered to them before following Mr. Chen upstairs to the residential part of the building. After taking her shoes off and putting on indoor slippers, she thanked the owner and let him return to his duties.

Raiden entered the room first, but sharply froze, causing her to crash into his back. She peered around him and realized why he stopped. There was only one bed.

"You can take it," he said, turning away. "You've drained yourself."

In the midst of scanning the rest of the room, Esme failed to catch her words before they left her mouth. "There's probably enough space for both of us."

Both of them froze again. *Oh, stars above,* she panicked internally, *I've made him uncomfortable. Why in the nine hells did I say that?*

Surprisingly, when he turned to face her, he wore a mirthful smile. "You're too kind, Esme," he said, his smile fading away. "I don't want to accidentally hurt you in the middle of the night so I would probably sleep better in my own space. I can use that extra bed roll. Just take the one in the canopy."

He was firm enough that she didn't push further. "Fine, then let me at least finish healing the rest of your wounds. It would make me sleep better if I knew I didn't make an injured person sleep on the floor," she said.

Raiden sighed and begrudgingly walked past the short wooden table, rolling up his torn sleeves and looking out of the small round window that faced the street. She dropped her full bag onto the table, followed him over, and raised her hands, drawing the last of her magic to close some of the scratches on his arms before beginning to feel dizzy. Something wet started to leak from her nose. Her sniff must have caught his attention because he yanked his arm back.

"Stop," he said in an alarmed tone. "Your nose is bleeding."

Esme reached up to wipe her nose, pausing when she saw blood on her knuckles. Hesitantly, she touched her nose again to wipe away more blood. Luckily, the flow seemed on the lighter side, enough for her to quickly pull out some cloth from her bag and wipe it from her face.

When she looked back up, she saw him scowling. "It was selfish of me to let you heal me when I knew you already used so much of your magic. Just go rest. Don't argue with me on that. Sleeping on the ground is nothing new to me."

Had she been less drained, she might have argued, but the bed was calling her name. Raiden was right. She had used too much magic today and needed to let her body rest to replenish it. Frowning, she walked over to the canopy and lay down, barely bothering to remove her slippers before closing her eyes and letting the darkness overtake her. Thinking about demons and realm hopping could wait another day.

CHAPTER 6

Uneven panting noises woke Esme from her sleep. Her eyes, which had been stubbornly glued shut, slowly peeked open to peer into the darkness. Although she wanted to go back to sleep, she realized the sounds were coming from the part of the room where Raiden was sleeping. Wondering what was going on, she took her hand from underneath the covers and produced a small flicker of fire from her fingers to better illuminate the room.

Curled up on the floor under the window, Raiden was asleep, but his eyebrows were furrowed and he was making sharp, agitated motions. Only when he whispered out the word "no" did she realize he was having a nightmare.

Immediately, she slid out of the bed canopy and down the low platform to go to his side. Now that she was closer, she could see the strain on his dimly illuminated, sweat-lined face. Should she wake him from his nightmare? Dacio also frequently had nightmares and had always appreciated it when she disrupted their bad dreams.

"Stop," he mumbled again, jerking his head to the side.

"Raiden," Esme called softly.

When he didn't wake, she reached down to gently touch his shoulder and give him a little shake. As soon as her hand met his shoulder, he jolted and grabbed her back. The next second was a blur. One moment she was crouched near Raiden and the next, she was on the ground with a hand wrapped around her neck.

Instinctively, she threw her hands up and called upon her magic, trying to pry his hands away with her now-flaming hands. The heat must have shocked him enough to make him realize what he was doing because Raiden's eyes widened and he wrenched himself off her to scramble away. She took the time and access to air to try and breathe again, but a fit of coughs came out instead.

She pushed herself back into a sitting position, coughing and glancing up to meet his horrified expression.

"No," he choked. "*Hells.* What have I done?"

Even though he had just grabbed her, Esme understood he had just been jolted out of a nightmare. People reacted differently to being woken from their sleep, and his reaction was just one of the possibilities she should have prepared for even if she hadn't expected such an atypical and sudden move. Nevertheless, it didn't seem intentional. Better yet, she had managed to get him off her quickly and neither of them seemed too injured, so she didn't quite understand why he was acting so extremely.

"It's okay," she spoke, having finally regained her breath. "You were having a nightmare."

"I'm still in a nightmare," he rasped, his face twisting with anguish. The harsh shadowed lines across his skin were defined from the light of her palm and the nascent dawn. "Oh, Esme, I'm so sorry," he apologized profusely.

"Raiden, I'm okay. I know you didn't mean it," she insisted.

However, her words only seemed to exacerbate his feelings because he started breathing shallowly and quickly, which concerned her. *Stars above, I really startled him.* She never expected him to have such a strong reaction to anything, especially with how stoic he had acted in the last two days.

"I've killed you." He buried his face into his hands. "Forgive me," he repeated over and over.

She was even more confused now. *What in the nine hells was going on?* "Killed me? Raiden, I'm *fine.*"

"My bare hands touched your skin. You won't live for much longer," he said, still not making any sense. His face crumpled into an agonized half-snarl. "Everything I touch dies. Oh hells, *Dacio...*"

Esme closed her eyes. That was a lot to unpack, but the first step was to calm him down, which shouldn't be too hard as it only required her to stay alive. When she reopened her eyes, she cast her gaze down at his bare hands and was surprised by what she saw—or didn't see. They weren't as expected and had no abnormalities, no scars. His hands seemed normal, except for the fact that Raiden insisted he had a killer touch.

"How long does it take?" she asked. As long as she cleared the time limit, she could show him enough evidence to address his fears.

Raiden gave her a miserable look. "You'll feel it in your chest first, like you can't breathe, and then the pain and blood comes," he said, looking at her as if waiting for the symptoms to manifest. Her eyes widened at the morbid description, but no symptoms arrived.

"This always happens when you touch someone with your bare hands?" she asked. "The day we met and even yesterday, I healed you and nothing happened."

"Only my hands are cursed," he said, glaring off to the side. "I should've kept my gloves on while I slept. This is my fault."

The cloud of self-blame around Raiden seemed to suffocate him and almost latched on to her. She decided to take further action, approaching him slowly and watching his eyes widen as he scrambled away.

Esme held up her hands and paused. "Look, you've already grabbed me, so we have two options. One, I'll die as you insist I will, so touching your hand again won't negate anything. Or, maybe everything will be fine and we can prove that together," she said patiently. She supposed it was possible she could exacerbate the situation but she didn't mention that.

"*Or* you're tempting fate," he said, but he stopped moving away. Enough time had passed where she could start seeing a glimmer of hope peering from behind his eyes. She recognized the curiosity—the same expression held by any wide-eyed child.

Slowly stepping forward, she stopped in front of him.

"Shall we tempt fate together?" she asked.

He blinked a few times and then nodded. Esme reached forward for his trembling hands, and as she captured his cool fingers with hers, he exhaled sharply.

They waited in the slowly fading dark as dawn arrived and announced its presence through the small round window. Jaw clenched tightly, he stared intensely at her, as if monitoring for the first sign of blood and pain. Still fine, Esme looked back into his worried dark eyes and the scars on his face, hoping her calm state would reassure him.

"Anything?" he asked.

She shook her head. "If anything, I'm sleepy."

Still, nothing happened except for the room brightening.

"I don't understand." Raiden's voice shook in disbelief. "Why? How?"

Esme gave him a small smile. "Maybe you're not as cursed as you think?" she suggested, releasing his hands. "You're immune to your own powers, right? Maybe I am too."

Grief and doubt still managed to crawl onto his face. "You shouldn't be… yet here you are," he whispered. "I… I need to see if…" he trailed off. Raiden scrambled toward the table that held a small bowl of water apples. When he grabbed the rose-colored fruit with his bare hands, Esme wondered if his death touch applied to all life—if it was even true.

They both waited patiently, looking at the fruit. After a few seconds, she saw it. From where his fingertips touched the fruit, a black shadow consumed it, shriveling everything until the whole piece was covered. Her eyes widened as she saw the water apple crumple into itself, sagging along the way. Raiden dropped it and they silently watched the rotted fruit fall apart and turn into dust.

Her mouth fell open. "Was that supposed to happen to me?" she whispered, feeling faint. His death touch was real.

"Fruits and plants are more fragile, so they disintegrate, unlike humans," he said hollowly, giving her chills. His earlier anxiety seemed to have morphed into disappointment.

Meanwhile, she was numb from surprise. A literal touch of death, and somehow she had survived not one, but two touches. *Unlike humans? Did that mean he…*

Esme laughed nervously. "Would've been nice to know about the death touch earlier," she said. At least this explained many of their interactions, primarily his hesitancy to be in close proximity to her. Maybe his nightmares, in addition to his ability, was why he had requested two rooms in Port Kai.

"It's not something I like revealing. I'm either used as a tool or viewed as a plague to avoid. As long as I keep my gloves on, there's no need to disclose my *ability*," he muttered.

On one hand, she could understand that. On the other, it would've been nice to have had a warning.

"I have many questions," she said.

Raiden looked up at the ceiling, seemingly already tired from the oncoming barrage of questions. "Go ahead," he sighed, closing his eyes.

"How long have you had this ability?"

"It's a curse, and I've had it for as long as I can remember."

Esme paused. "It's supposed to affect every living thing? How do you eat fruits? Pet animals?"

"Yes, all living beings. That's what the gloves are for," he said, opening his eyes and looking around the room before his gaze settled on his gloves by his pillow roll.

"Do you have any other magical abilities?" she asked. He had evaded her question back in the forest, but perhaps his answer would change now that she knew about his curse.

He shook his head. "I don't use or have magic. My hands are the only exception and unfortunately, I don't know how that happened."

Esme looked down. Now that she thought about it, his death touch was an odd ability to have. She had never heard of magic that granted the power to kill or poison someone with the barest brush of skin, and it didn't seem like he had any control over it given that he wore gloves. Which domain would a death touch fall under? Probably spirit, since Jing, deity of spirit, was also the deity of life and death. She wondered if her healing magic, which fell under the spirit umbrella, could have shielded her from the fatal consequences. Did she heal faster than the poison? Or was there another explanation?

"Do you have any idea why I wasn't affected?" she asked.

Raiden stayed silent, staring into her eyes.

"Am I truly the only one who has ever survived your touch? Has anyone been healed immediately and survived, perhaps?"

He closed his eyes once more. "Let me tell you a story," he started and opened his eyes. "When I was around the age of five, I washed up on the shores of Yin City and lived on the streets as an orphan, hungry, scared, and alone. But I had this... *ability,* something I discovered when I was attacked by cruel thieves. When The Six found me, they didn't even bother training me in all six divisions before assigning me. Why waste a child with a death touch in forgery, theft, or espionage when one of the divisions was assassination?"

The implications dawned on her, inflicting a turmoil of reactions and emotions: sadness for his desperation, anger at the injustice, shock for the reveal of his past occupation. Behind all of these emotions lingered a stab of fear. Assassin. His job has been to *kill* people. Their sneaking into the city and his connection to Reina made sense now.

Raiden smiled bitterly. "Yes, I killed people. Killed them on behalf of The Six's clients. I was taught, molded into the perfect killer. I know and have used at least a dozen ways to kill someone with just my hands, even without using my curse. In my lifetime, I've given many targets a slow, painful death sentence with just a touch of my finger," he said. His stare was unflinching, trained solely on her. "And yet here you are, standing before me now. Alive."

She stood there speechless. What could she say in response to any of that?

He cast his gaze away, toward the window, and sighed deeply. "I hate this city," he stated. His face was calm but she could sense his shame and guilt. "I hate what I did to it. What it did to me. Even when I tried to escape, it managed to claw me back."

"Is it really that horrible?" Esme asked, her eyebrows furrowed tightly. So far, everyone she had come across seemed helpful, so surely, some spots of light broke through the dark clouds.

"No," he admitted. "I don't think it was always like this, from my understanding."

"Always like what?"

Raiden looked back at her. "Let's take a walk."

Her eyes widened. "What about waiting for Reina or Daiyu?" she stuttered, taken aback by the suggestion. Not that she didn't want to explore the city, but she hadn't expected him to offer a tour since he was clearly in hiding.

"She can easily find us. Her network, though smaller, puts The Six to shame," he said. Raiden finally grabbed his gloves, slipping them on like a mask. "Follow me."

CHAPTER 7

Raiden clung to the shadows beside the wood and stone buildings, as naturally as Esme suspected an assassin would. She kept pace, trying to blend into the darkness as well. As they navigated through the twists and turns of the cobblestone streets, she pretended she too was trained to be one with the shadows, even though everything about her yearned for the sun and light—from her abilities to being raised in the north. Growing up, she often heard the claim that Atonacans were people of the sun and the Wei were people of the moon.

Nevertheless, she followed Raiden's lead. Perhaps she could treat her movement like magic, imagining the cooler shadows underneath the trees on a hot summer day. Even thinking about shadows made her feel cooler, though perhaps some of that sensation could have been attributed to the sharp wind bristling through the city and the sudden overcast hanging over them. It was good that she had stopped back in Port Kai to buy warm robes. She couldn't imagine how cold the middle of winter would be.

She must have done a good job at blending in because at one point, Raiden looked back in her direction and did a double take, his eyebrows furrowed and his eyes darting back and forth. "Esme?"

"Yes?" she said, pausing and turning her head to see what he was looking at. However, nothing was out of the ordinary; only red banners and lanterns hanging from curved-tip roofs drew any attention. Since it was so early, barely anyone was out. When she turned back to face him, he wore a puzzled look.

"Were you there the entire time?" he asked quietly, to which she nodded. His eyes narrowed before relaxing with a hint of mirth. "You could be a professional if you wanted," he mused.

Esme blinked. "Professional what? Assassin?"

"Professional spy," he clarified quickly, eyes widening as he threw his palms up.

Still, she wasn't sure if that was meant to be a compliment. After all, Reina had been dissatisfied as a professional spy and preferred not to be labeled that way.

"Forget I said anything," he said and stiffly resumed guiding them past the market district.

So far, the city seemed normal. Unlike the wood and clay houses in Atonaco, the houses here were made of stones and had gray tiled roofs. Wide streets sprawled between the lines of tightly packed buildings, all of which appeared well-kept. Many potted plants and flowers decorated the balconies on the higher levels where people hung their clothes out to dry—a hint of green within the business district. Raiden led her past a nice square courtyard with a beautiful flowering tree in the center.

Nothing here reconciled with the picture he had painted with his tone.

However, soon they started walking down dilapidated streets. Glass from broken liquor vases littered the ground and the buildings were both more cramped and less pristine than the ones in the market district. The walls of stores had cracks and holes. Somehow, despite the shorter buildings, it seemed darker here, as if even the slightest hint of light was devoured immediately.

Her skin began to prickle from the hints of despair she felt in the air. Reina's comments from the previous day started to make more sense. She could see how Raiden might view this place as a cursed nightmare, even disregarding his problematic former occupation.

"This is the Yin City I grew up in," he said, gesturing to the area. "Some of my earliest memories are from these streets, though fewer cracks were in the walls." His eyes became unfocused, as if he was seeing visions of his past.

They continued walking and Esme saw barefoot children running in the street. She cringed, worried about the broken glass on the ground and their exposure to the cold, but the children seemed to avoid and flitter around the glass like butterflies. Her concern was quickly addressed when the children's parents called for them to come back and bundle up.

"You asked me if Yin City was horrible. A sense of hopelessness remains here of never escaping your fate. People in some areas die young and many fight each other just to survive," he said. "But it's not their fault. They're doing the best they can with what's been stolen from them. Since the unification of the three old kingdoms, people have been stolen and made into soldiers, and other resources and livelihoods have been taken from civilians for the crown to exploit."

His face darkened with anger and shame. "And I was complicit," he continued, swallowing before confessing, "I became a nightmare for these people on behalf of the prince. So much of a nightmare that I was called the Hand of Death."

Esme held her breath. Not only had he been an assassin but an infamous one at that. "I thought you worked for The Six."

Raiden closed his eyes, clenching his jaw and his gloved hands into fists. "I was so good at my job the prince took notice and extorted me to do his bidding for him."

She reached out and gently put her hand on his forearm, making his eyes jolt open. His large eyes widened even further as if he wasn't even expecting the silent offer of comfort. If she sensed any hesitation from him, she would remove her hand, but he only seemed surprised.

"From what I understand, it didn't seem like a choice," she said. "You were just trying to survive."

He gave her a wry, sarcastic smile. "I survived at the expense of others. I cannot take that back. I can regret and own my actions all I want, but the damage I caused on behalf of the crown should make anyone sick. When I die, I will not be cast into the stars. At best, I'll probably be reborn as an animal after a short stint in one of the nine hells. There aren't enough good deeds in the world to balance all of the destructive actions I've committed."

Esme retracted her arm. His eyes were jaded, and he seemed so sure of his fate in the afterlife that she doubted anything she said would make him budge from his convictions. Despite the fact that he was helping her and her general intuition was to trust him, she still didn't know him well enough to give an effective argument to counter his guilt.

"Are you Raiden?" a high-pitched voice asked in Wei, shattering the trance they were both in. They looked down to see a small pale child wearing ill-fitting clothes and looking up to him with a toothy smile.

Raiden nearly stumbled back, but Esme had to hold back a small laugh. If she didn't know any better, it looked like the child had startled him. If people had known small children could scare the infamous assassin, maybe his story might have ended up differently. Perhaps he had been too focused on adult-sized threats that he disregarded any potential child-sized ones.

"What?" he sputtered.

The girl beamed brighter, contrasting the dark atmosphere of this section of the city. "The Lady of Shadows told me to find a tall grumpy man and said I should bring you over to see her because she had something to tell you," she rambled.

Esme and Raiden eyed each other. Lady of Shadows? Sounded like Reina. She hadn't expected the messenger to be a child, though.

Raiden crouched down until his face was at the same level as the girl's. "Is this safe for you to do?"

"When the Lady is here, her shadows keep watch and make sure the bad things stay away," she replied, nodding vehemently. "Follow me!"

The two adults looked at each other with no further argument as the child led them through the narrow streets and into a small park with a stone-rimmed pond in the middle. On the bridge over the pond was Reina, who was perched comfortably on the side. When she saw them, she hopped off and strolled over to meet them in the middle, greeted by the child tackling her legs.

Reina quietly laughed and fondly smiled down. "What a warm welcome."

"Why are you using children to deliver messages?" Raiden asked.

The smile dropped off Reina's face as she looked back up at him. "I don't, but this one was bored and wanted to help out. I know as well as you do what it means for a child to enter the realm of shadows at such a young age, but this area is under my protection now. I'm surprised you didn't notice my second in command following you three at a distance and watching over her," she said, tilting her head to the right.

Esme followed that direction with her eyes and saw Daiyu casually leaning against a tree with her arms crossed, a small smirk peering from under the hood of her dark cloak. She certainly hadn't noticed anyone else following them and started to wish she could move that easily undetected.

Something Reina said made Esme pause—entering the realm of shadows at a young age. How old had both of them been when they had joined The Six? She couldn't imagine being put in that kind of position and maintaining any youthful innocence with what they'd had to do. Her own childhood had been simple up to her last memories: her loving family, her studies at the academy, her community with celebrations and dances and music. None of them looked much older than her twenty-two years of age although if she had to guess, Daiyu and Reina were probably in their mid-twenties and Raiden a year or two younger than them.

Regardless of when they had joined, it seemed as if they had left The Six with many painful stories and hardened skills.

"Go back to your parents," Reina ordered the child, who pouted but complied.

Raiden kept his gaze on the girl and only relaxed his shoulders when Daiyu started accompanying the child back.

Once the girl left, Esme asked, "Do you have any information about Dacio?" She chewed on her bottom lip, preparing herself for the worst while hoping for the best.

"Yes. The naval ship landed in the port this morning. They're on the way back to the city now and should arrive at the palace within the hour," Reina started. "Although Dacio was accused of a failed assassination attempt on the emperor, my sources told me the palace isn't any more secure than before. No extra guards. Nothing."

Esme's eyes narrowed at the report. *How odd.* Why wouldn't there be more guards? Even though Dacio's involvement in the accusation was complete nonsense, perhaps the assassination attempt itself was real.

"I could understand that, given the emperor's powers, so what *does* concern me is the Spirit Festival. Only commoners and some Atonacan dignitaries were invited to the palace, but none of the nobles or high-ranking government officials," Reina continued, reaching up to rub her chin.

"Why is that troubling?" she asked.

Two days a year, on the equinox, the barrier between the spirit and mortal realm grew thin enough for spirits to briefly wander out. As a child, she had celebrated the holiday in both Wei and Atonacan manner, where in either case, food, festivities, and ceremonies would be thrown in honor of the dead before the spirits returned to their realm. In the last two years, she and Dacio helped guide any stragglers back to the spirit realm.

Regardless, she didn't see how the Spirit Festival related.

"With the empire still undergoing expansion, there should be no reason why he doesn't use this festival to continue creating more alliances and consolidating power among the elites," Reina explained. The frown on her face quickly turned bashful, as if embarrassed from going on a tangent. "The point is, I don't trust this situation at all. I would suggest you two go to the palace now before Dacio arrives and stay hidden."

"Why can't we just clear Dacio's name?" Esme asked, frowning.

Raiden scoffed. "The emperor lacks a sense of justice. We are better off extracting Dacio and leaving the city. Let's just go and get this over with."

"Be careful," Reina warned, looking at Esme. "When you're done, stop by the tunnels."

Before she had a chance to reply, Raiden pivoted and started walking out of the park, distracting her. When she turned back to give Reina a quick farewell, no one was to be seen.

Lady of Shadows indeed.

Maybe Raiden's earlier comment about being a professional spy *was* a compliment.

CHAPTER 8

It would be nearly impossible for anyone to miss spotting the palace from anywhere within the city walls. Sitting on top of the giant seaside hill, the tall, white-stoned building loomed over the city. Unlike the gray tiled roofs that painted the rest of the city, the tiered palace complex had blue tiles so dark they almost looked violet. It was like a small city within a city, expansive as it could be while limited to the surface area of the hill and as guarded and walled as the borders of Yin City.

Again, instead of going through the front gates like normal people, Raiden led Esme through a hidden side passage near the bottom of the tri-tiered complex surrounded by trees. Before they entered, he paused.

"Do you want to wait out here?" he asked.

Even though she occasionally ascended the many stone steps of the Great Temple in Atoyatlan, Esme was almost offended he would make her climb up such a tall hill just to ask her that question. "Absolutely not. I didn't walk all this way from Atoyatlan just to entertain myself with fire flowers at the last second. I'm going in, with or without you."

He reached up to pinch the bridge of his nose and sighed. "Follow me closely. Don't let anyone see you. If they do, I'll take care of them."

Impatient, Esme waved at him to go. Raiden looked at her face, perhaps re-evaluating his decisions, and then turned back to continue their infiltration into the palace.

Once they made it up to the end of the narrow, inclined passageway in the walls of the palace, he paused at the intersection, looking around.

"Where are we going?" Esme whispered. "What's our plan?" She wished she had asked earlier.

"Haven't decided yet," he whispered back.

"*What?*" she hissed.

"Depends on where Dacio is taken," he replied quietly, remaining vigilant of their surroundings. Esme had no clue where they were. "Extracting them from the civil buildings is different than extracting them from the dungeons."

He quietly darted out of the passageway and beckoned for her to follow. She quickly tiptoed after him, afraid to make noises across the dark stone floors. The wider hallways were empty except for some decorative pots and the endless doors lining both sides. They were approaching an intersection when Raiden stopped and held up his hand, blocking her from going anywhere. Before she could ask what was going on, she heard footsteps coming their way from one of the hallways. From the sound of soft metal clinking, she guessed these were guards and not officials.

Raiden stiffened, pivoted around, and immediately started pushing her back in the direction from which they came. She felt like a leaf in the wind, directed only by unknown currents, and was surprised when he shoved her through an open door into an empty room.

"Hide," he hissed.

"You in the cloak, stop right there!" a guard shouted from down the hall. Raiden froze, but the look he gave her silently communicated his order to stay quiet and in the room. It seemed as if only he had been spotted.

"Don't worry about me," he told her quietly, spearing her with one last look and quickly closing the door, giving her a chance to find a place to hide.

"Halt!" the guards shouted outside followed by the heavy pitter patter of feet hitting the ground, chasing Raiden.

Esme turned her attention toward her current location, a large, open salon with sleek wooden chairs surrounding short tables and priceless statues on them. A large brass ceiling light hung from above, the flame inside the metal sphere cage strong enough to shine patterns along the floors and walls. Her head whipped around, desperate to find something to hide behind or under, but the only semblance of a hiding place was behind the room divider. *Oh stars above, deities save me,* she thought, her face twisting in panic.

Suddenly, the door creaked. She flinched before darting behind the divider and hoping whoever was at the door wouldn't come in. Unfortunately, heavy footsteps entered the room. Fear gripped her heart like a snake constricting its prey.

"Check the perimeter," a guard called out, a different voice than the one she heard in the hallway.

The footsteps grew closer.

Blend into the shadows, she repeated to herself while trying to slow her heartbeat and avoid thinking about how she was currently trespassing on royal grounds of a foreign nation. What would she do if she was found? Both Raiden and Reina had told her to not be seen. Maybe she could sneak to another hiding spot.

Clink. Clink. Clink. Esme closed her eyes, concentrating on the sound of the guards' metal armor alone. When they checked under the short table, she eyed the tall wooden pedestal with a small bronze statue of a lion on top and shadows behind it. It was a midpoint between the divider and the door and out of the guards' immediate visual range.

It was time to emulate what she thought a spy or an assassin would be like. *Be silent and stick to the shadows.* Maybe she could make it there in six strides. *Be like a shadow, Esme! Move fluidly, like magic,* she chanted to herself.

However, when she took a step, her body moved unnaturally. Her physical essence seemed to painlessly scatter and blend through the shadows of the room until she suddenly appeared by the statue. Esme had to catch herself on the bottom of the pedestal once she materialized again. Her entire face froze in shock as her mind caught up with the rest of her body and the situation, her eyebrows furrowed and her lips parted.

What in the nine hells just happened?

Just a second ago, she had been halfway across the room, and somehow with only one step, she was crouched next to the statue. Along the way, it didn't just feel like she had sneaked through the shadows; it was almost as if she had *become* a shadow, blending into it and gliding through any trace of darkness in the room. Like warping through space.

Her mind quickly wandered to just a few hours ago when she and Raiden had been in town and he had been unable to find her for a few seconds. Had he truly lost track of her? Or had she unknowingly and literally blended into the shadows then as well?

The guards walked toward the divider, forcing her to shift her position to be out of sight.

Was this the result of the portal? Ever since she stepped through that portal and traipsed into the spirit realm, she had demonstrated some strange abilities, ones that she never had before and did not fall under the realm of fire or healing. Whatever this was, she didn't even know it was possible for even trained mages to know more than two elemental categories.

"Perimeter clear," one of the guards announced. Esme ducked down as they turned back. She could figure out the origins of these abilities later. Meanwhile, perhaps she could experiment with what she would call shadow magic and see if she could find Raiden or Dacio.

The door creaked open and another guard called from the hallway.

"The mage from Atonaco has arrived," he said. Esme's eyes widened and her heart stuttered. Dacio? "We are to relieve the others."

"And the intruder?"

"Dealt with."

Esme absorbed the implications, closing her eyes. Raiden seemed to be in a precarious situation, but he had told her to not worry about him, which made sense because he was a former assassin with a death touch. She was more concerned about Dacio. Although they were a powerful mage in their own right, particularly with regards to spirit and ice, they were a pacifist. Also, she didn't know how they were treated on the way over.

Trail the guards, it is, she decided.

As soon as the guards left the room, she darted for the door, making sure she could see which direction they were headed. She made sure to look both ways and wait for the guards to reach the end of the hallway before sneaking out of the room and quietly chasing after them.

After another turn, she wanted to replicate the strange shadowy phenomenon again. Esme eyed the hallway, scanning for darker areas. Luckily, no windows lined this hallway, so shadows aplenty loitered on the sides. She took a deep breath before leaping forward and centering her thoughts around smooth velvety darkness, treating this like she would any other magic. Once again, she felt her body free itself from its physical confines and travel the darkness until she reached the end of the hallway and was jolted back into her body. Her heart pounded from exhilaration. This new magic was fascinating—and terrifying.

She looked around the corner and back at the guards, who were approaching a towering set of black metal doors covered by intricate whirls of gold. Unlike the wooden doors to the other rooms, these were unique and elaborate enough to possibly guard a special room. The presence of additional guards placed in front of the metal doors further added suspicion to what the room could be.

Her palms started to feel clammy. *Can I really sneak past* four *guards?*

But then, perhaps she didn't need to try out her shadow magic again right now. After all, she still had her fire magic at her disposal. Just a distraction might be enough of a cover, and with two guards now entering the room, she only needed to evade the other two.

Esme twirled her hand so her palms faced up and drew up a small spark of fire barely the size of her thumb. She looked down the opposite side of the hall to see if she could find anything to catch on fire. The only objects on the floor were potted plants and… a nice wooden table holding an expensive-looking vase. *There.* Now, to get the tiny fireball over to that table.

She looked up at the high ceilings of the hallway and sent the small ball of fire up toward it so it was out of sight for the helmeted guards. After it was high enough, she sent it flying down the hall and down onto the table with two flicks of her wrist. Once the growing flame caught the guards' attention, she would sneak past.

"Smells like something is burning," one of the guards said, sniffing the air. "I wonder what they burned in the kitchens this time. Someone's probably getting exiled for this."

The other one also sniffed the air, saying, "It does smell like something is—wait, the table!"

They darted toward the table, trying to extinguish the fire before it burned anything else. Once the guards were distracted and had their backs turned in Esme's direction, she ran for the door, trying to keep her feet light. The door was still open from when the previous guards walked in, so she quickly slid into the room before the other two returned.

Upon entering the room, she immediately found the nearest shadow and blended in, thinking of being one with the darkness. Adrenaline spiked through her body as she quickly found a place to hide in the corner of the grand room. A large decorative pot stood nearby to hide behind, so she darted in that direction and crouched down.

Luckily, she managed to get in just in time to avoid one of the concerned guards rushing out to see what the commotion was. The other stood at the bottom of the dais where an empty throne sat. She gave a mental thanks to the deities for having evaded capture.

Finally securely hidden, she let herself breathe and take in her surroundings. The room was massive and gaudily decorated, even to her. Gold and navy-blue colors assaulted her eyes everywhere she looked, and though she loved the colors and the designs, she thought it excessive. Gold banners larger than her person hung from the walls. At the end of the room, where the one guard still stood, squatted a throne with gold trims and dark blue fabric.

This must be the throne room, which meant the guards were waiting for both Dacio *and* the emperor. Chills ran down her spine.

Barely a second after the realization, more guards walked through the open doors. Behind the front line walked a man dressed in fine black and red robes that flowed elegantly around him with every step he took. She only got a glimpse of the disdain on his face before becoming distracted by the crown on his head, with jade beads hanging from silk threads swaying from his motion. The shiny gold of his hairpin further emphasized who this was.

The Wei Emperor—Jin Jianli.

Who was much younger than Esme expected—around her age by the looks of it. He was maybe even younger, if she squinted hard enough.

He marched confidently to the throne, and the guards kneeled as he sat down. A group of advisors with black hats approached and bowed. With a flick of his wrist, they all stood up once more.

"Bring them in," the emperor ordered in formal Wei, his low voice resonating throughout the vast room.

Even before she saw Dacio, she felt them, felt their steady aura that was so familiar to her, both cool and warm at the same time. She would recognize them anywhere by feeling alone, but laying eyes on them and seeing they were physically unharmed relieved a tension in her shoulders she didn't even realize she'd carried.

Despite the relief she felt from seeing them again, she had to restrain herself from leaping into the throne room from the shadows. The challenge became even more difficult when the guards marched in through the doors, towing along a familiar cloaked figure—Raiden. Esme's gaze darted back toward Dacio, whose dark eyes were widened upon seeing Raiden's face.

"We found him sneaking around in the palace," one of the guards announced. Esme wondered if Raiden let himself get caught so he could be taken here or find out more information.

The emperor's face quickly morphed from surprised curiosity to smug disdain. "Ah, how lucky I am to be reunited with both my best assassin," he mused at Raiden, who was glaring at him with unadorned hatred, before turning to face Dacio with an arched eyebrow, "and my best spy."

CHAPTER 9

The words slammed into her. *Spy? The emperor's* best *spy? Stars above, am I dreaming? Did I hear that correctly?*

She was glad she was already leaning against the large pot or else she would have tipped over and revealed herself in front of the emperor, his guards, and his advisors.

"You know, Dacio, I must admit you were a hard one to find. I should have known you would have a false name as a spy, but you really took creating a new identity to the next level. Why, look at your hair! Half is gone now," the emperor mused from his throne. "What was it like to hide in plain sight in our neighbor to the north?"

"What do you want, Jianli?" Dacio asked back in perfectly fluent Wei.

If Esme hadn't known them better, she wouldn't have caught the subtle twitch in Dacio's eyebrows and the slight tension in their shoulders. To anyone else, they might have seemed disinterested and calm, aside from the clear lack of respect from directly addressing the emperor by name. It seemed Dacio knew the Wei emperor personally.

The revelations of discovered secrets sank her heart. She was going to have an extensive talk with them once this was over.

Emperor Jin kept his smile, but his eyes grew colder. "That's Your Majesty to you," he said. "Son of heaven and earth, if you are truly regretful."

Dacio smiled back although it didn't reach their eyes. Esme was startled to see such a cold smile on their face when they normally had beautiful, warm smiles. Occasionally sad ones, too, but never cold. She was suddenly reminded of what Raiden had said the day they met—something about knowing what Dacio was capable of. Was this a hint of what he had been referring to?

"Of course, *Your Majesty*. Please forgive my slip," they said in a higher register, dropping their head into a deep bow. "I admit I am quite distraught to have been accused of trying to assassinate the leader of a foreign nation."

"Assassination? Is that what the ambassador and guards told you?" the emperor asked, eyes widening. "Why, we must get this cleared up immediately. You are neither asinine enough to take me on, nor do you have a murderous bone in your body. Perhaps local Atonacan officials prohibited the squadron from entering for a simple theft case, so they needed to stretch the truth."

So, a lie, Esme thought. The accusation still didn't make sense, but at least Dacio wasn't being accused of attempted assassination anymore.

"Rest assured, I shall punish them for that accusation accordingly," the emperor said, his gaze sweeping toward his advisors before returning to Dacio. "However, I could not help but notice you referring to the Wei empire as a foreign nation. Is this not your nation as well? You grew up here."

He rose to his feet and all but floated down the stairs of the dais with his hands casually crossed behind his back as he approached Dacio until he hovered just beyond their reach. Esme felt her shoulders tense up as tendrils of cool, sturdy metal magic weaved through the air from the dais. Emperor Jin Jianli must be a metallomage—and a strong one at that, from his presence. The magical aura quickly faded like a stealthy jungle cat, an unseen threat.

"What do you want?" Dacio asked again. This time, they didn't bother hiding their contempt.

The emperor stopped in his tracks. The jade beads on his crown swayed back and forth, partially blocking his eyes. "I want what you stole from me."

Esme's eyebrows shot up, but Dacio remained calm, asking, "What could I have possibly stolen that an emperor couldn't replace?"

"Don't play coy, Dacio. Need I refresh your impeccable memory of a fateful night when your lover died and—"

"The sword."

Dacio's face was so hard and rigid it could have been sculpted from stone. Meanwhile, Esme was trying to piece together all of the scraps of information she was hearing, her heart throbbing from the tragic undertones of the message. Was the death of their lover why Dacio never mentioned any of this history?

Her thoughts about love and death quickly pivoted to the main subject of the current story—a stolen sword. The recent events seemed rather extreme for the theft of a simple weapon. Lying in general normally had severe punishment in Atonaco, but lying to the nobles to gain entry and seize a citizen without agreement could inflame tensions between the two nations, even if it was supposedly over a theft.

"Why do you need that specific sword when you have an army's worth of weapons at your disposal?" Raiden asked, startling Esme. She almost forgot other people were in the room because she was too focused on Dacio and the emperor.

Emperor Jin also looked surprised, as if forgetting everyone else's presence as well. "Questions, Raiden? That is new," he said, evading the inquiry. "Nevertheless, I do not owe either of you a reason, only a command. Bring it back to me."

The implied *or* saturated the air.

"If I retrieve it, will you finally leave me and Raiden alone?" Dacio asked. Their eyes narrowed in caution.

The lines on the emperor's face smoothed out. "Of course," he said. "You have until the Spirit Festival to bring it back. I have waited long enough, and it would be the perfect day to celebrate the lost sword's return."

The Spirit Festival again. Was a week enough time? Esme looked back at Dacio to see what they thought of the timeline, but their expression didn't reveal anything. They didn't protest it either. She shifted on her tiptoes, starting to feel her legs losing sensation from staying in the same position for too long.

Emperor Jin walked toward Raiden. "You are, however, a rather slippery person, Dacio, so I do need to keep you in line," he said without looking at them. The short hair along the upper edge of Esme's neck raised as a warning.

"Have you heard of the Starbright Berry?" he asked, starting to circle around the former assassin.

She froze. *The poisonous fruit that could slowly kill someone if not prepared correctly?* The effects of the poison were so slow and insidious that by the time the person felt any symptoms of dizziness and nausea, they would need to get medical attention within the hour to survive. The worst part was that it might take a week before any symptoms showed up, so it was notoriously difficult to diagnose the cause of symptoms.

"It is highly potent and sticks to a schedule. However, it has an antidote—both through magic and through herbs," the emperor continued, taking an object out of his large sleeves. Instead of a bright red berry, it was a shiny silver pin. "The best aspect about metal magic is that although it requires significantly more energy and time to create something, its castor's influence remains long after the object is made."

"I'm afraid I don't understand," Dacio interrupted, their jaw clenched. Esme wasn't quite sure why the emperor brought up the two topics, but she had a feeling it wouldn't lead to anything good.

He whirled around. "You know, in the past three years, I've done some more research on you, Dacio. You are not as effective at hiding your weaknesses as you think, particularly when you know what spies do. Your money trail led me to your father, and although I was going to bring him here to act as *assurance*, Raiden is a welcome surprise for me to use my magic on instead."

Dacio inhaled sharply, breaking their mostly even composure as they threw a concerned glance Raiden's way.

Oh stars, Esme thought, understanding the connection. The emperor had made his very own Starbright Berry with metal and magic, something he could control and couldn't just be healed away.

The only warning she had before the Wei emperor struck was the sudden flash of magic prickling the air. She didn't even see what happened, only that Raiden gasped and fell to his knees. The silver pin was no longer in the emperor's hand, leading her to horrifyingly conclude that it was now in Raiden.

"Raiden!" Dacio called out sharply, stepping in his direction. Esme clenched her hand, her nails biting into her palms. She had to force herself to stay hidden.

"Not another step," the emperor ordered, making them freeze. "Good. Now let me demonstrate what will happen should you disobey."

"You can release him now," he told the guards before flicking his wrist and eliciting a pained groan from Raiden. "Every day, this pin will creep closer to his heart. If you bring back the sword by the festival, I will extract it and my former assassin here will only have suffered a minor inconvenience along the way. Should you fail... well, you understand." He looked down at Raiden, who jumped up to his feet and immediately came crashing down with a groan—the emperor's magic at work. Although she always knew magic was a double-edged sword, the display of power only reminded her of magic's potentially wretched applications.

Dacio bared their teeth at him, and their hands started to frost over from their ice magic. Although they stayed silent, their message was clear to everyone in the room.

The emperor leaned down to whisper something in Raiden's ear. Whatever he said made Raiden's face twist with disgust and his own grow smug. Swishing the sleeves of his robe, the emperor turned toward the door and started walking away. "Better get started, Dacio," he sang as he strolled out of the throne room with his entourage of guards trailing behind him. To his advisors, he ordered, "Fetch the grand chancellor."

The deep thud of the door jolted Esme out of her anxious waiting state, so she sagged against the pot to finally exhale. She peered around the edge once more to double check that it was only her, Raiden, and Dacio left in the grand hall. Her feet remained glued to her location and she could feel her legs trembling slightly. Never did she want to be in the emperor's presence again. She couldn't imagine *working* for him as Raiden and Dacio had done although from his use of pressure points, it might not have been willingly.

"Rai," Dacio called out, rushing over to him and hovering their hand over his shoulder. "I'm sorry."

He held up a palm and said, "Just give me a second."

The interaction freed her from the confines of fear, allowing her to stand up and her head to poke above the top of the decorative pot. Her motion drew both of their attentions. Dacio's large eyes widened as they realized she was there.

"Esme?" they whispered.

They blinked a few times and then reached up to rub at their eyes, as if in disbelief. She took a step toward them, and then another, before finally running over and throwing herself at them. Dacio yelped in surprise but caught her reflexively. She hugged them tightly and pressed her cheek against their neck, clutching them to tether herself to reality. How easily they could have been hurt and she wouldn't have known if she hadn't come.

Dacio hugged her back before sharply pulling away, their eyebrows pinched together. "You shouldn't be here."

As if she would ever leave them in their time of need.

While they nervously scanned the rest of the room, Esme took the opportunity to check in with Raiden, who had managed to rise to his feet and was currently rubbing a spot on his chest. Was that where the pin had entered his body?

"How do you feel, Raiden? Do you need one of us to heal you?" she asked him. Although she couldn't tell if blood stained his black gloves, she couldn't see anything dripping onto the floor, so he was at least in a better state than when they had first met.

He shook his head, frowning. "Not here. We should get out."

"You two... met each other?" Dacio asked quietly. Esme looked back at them and nodded, watching their face morph from confusion to fear. "Wait, how long were you hiding?"

"Long enough to hear the Wei Emperor call you his favorite spy," she answered, raising an eyebrow at them.

"Oh," they cringed, "so the entire time."

"Yes, you have a *lot* to explain," she said sternly. So much to explain, in fact, she could imagine this conversation taking hours.

Raiden cleared his throat. "Perhaps we should leave first."

Dacio nodded. "Right, priorities. There's never a shortage of eyes and ears on palace grounds and you shouldn't be seen, Esme. Since you don't know the palace well, Rai and I can visibly walk out first and then sneak back in to lead you out, or I can lure the attention while you and Rai take a more secret path."

"There's still a risk of getting caught. It's a long way from the throne room to anywhere outside," Raiden said. It *had* taken them climbing many stairs before they even reached the highest-level tier of the palace.

Esme considered the two options. The guards had found Raiden on the way in, but they should now know he and Dacio were on their way out with the emperor's mission. *She* was the unknown visitor. "Raiden and I can take the more secretive route. I have an extra skill up my sleeves that we didn't know coming in."

The other two both raised one of their eyebrows in sync.

One corner of her lips tilted upward. "Perhaps a demonstration would be better."

Taking a step back into the shadow of the closest pillar, she looked around to find where to warp to. After deciding, she closed her eyes and recentered her energy and thoughts, drawing in more energy from her environment. *Deep, smooth darkness.* Magic rolled over her like the cover of the night, cool and steady. Like pulling a curtain to the side, she slid into the shadows, once again feeling her form dissipate into smaller pieces before warping to the side of the main doors.

When she opened her eyes, Dacio's lips parted open in shock and Raiden's eyebrows rose halfway up his forehead.

"What in the heavens?" Dacio whispered at the same time Raiden exclaimed, "Hells!"

Although the last hour had been full of dread, horror, and confusion, Esme couldn't stop the small smirk she wore earlier from slipping back onto her face. Their bewilderment was simply too amusing, and she needed something else to think about other than secrets and lies.

"Talk later, remember," Esme reminded. "Let's go sneak out of a palace."

CHAPTER 10

By the time they all reached the noodle shop, the mood was sullen once more. After all, Dacio was being blackmailed, she was reeling from the discovery of secrets, and Raiden had the magical metal version of a Starbright Berry inside him. Although they had managed to leave the palace smoothly and undetected, she was ready to fidget out of her skin from the silent air around them all. As much as she was used to the unknown, given her missing memories, she had never been too comfortable with missing out on information that was readily available.

Suddenly, Esme was struck by how condensed all of the recent events were. Had it really been just two days ago that Dacio was taken? She had traveled so far and discovered portals, demons, Yin City, and new powers, just listing off the top of her head. That was excluding the massive pile of secrets that everyone was keeping. She hoped she would get some time soon to just sit and process everything.

As soon as they returned to the private room above the restaurant, Raiden turned to Esme and asked, "Do you mind notifying Reina that we're back?"

Dacio nodded and added, "I can check on Raiden in the meantime."

"Do I just go into the tunnels?" she asked, unable to stop the disappointment from creeping in. Although she knew that Raiden was probably the first priority here since he had gotten hurt, she was eager to get information.

He shook his head. "Just let the owners know."

"I'll be right back," she said, giving the two one last look before closing the door behind her gently.

Esme wondered how Reina's network even worked. Had they unknowingly passed by one of her informants? How exactly did one get in contact with her? What was it like being the keeper of so much information?

The noodle shop owners were preoccupied with diners, so she had to wait. Trying to stay out of sight, she stood in the area between the staircase and storage. Customers entered and left in rotation, each one enjoying their meal. Her stomach grew envious of the spicy noodles they were eating. The dish reminded her of her childhood, of the Wei food she ate with her family, paired with typical Atonacan dishes—the best of both worlds. Food was an invisible string of connection that tied her to strangers and acquaintances alike.

After a few minutes, Mrs. Chen finally came over to listen to her request.

"I'll let Reina know you're back," the sweet owner said with a smile.

Esme ducked her head and thanked her, turning around to head back upstairs.

Just before she reached the room, Dacio and Raiden's hushed voices made her stop in her tracks. The temptation to eavesdrop reared inside her, so she tiptoed toward the door, hoping neither former assassin nor former spy would hear her over the sounds of the restaurant below, and started listening.

"You know how dangerous it is for her here," Dacio murmured. Esme pressed her ear against the cool door to hear the conversation better.

"She was coming with or without me. Since it seems as if you haven't told her anything, it's not as if she knew the stakes," Raiden replied.

Casting her gaze down at the wooden floorboards, she wondered if they were talking about her. If so, why would it be dangerous for her here? Dangerous in general? Or for her specifically? Questions flooded her mind.

"It's not like I don't want to tell her, I truly do. You of all people know what she means to me," they said. This time, Esme narrowed her eyes. What was happening here? More secrets? She grew warm from frustration and she resisted tapping her feet to release energy—and sound.

"Interesting conversation?" a melodic voice quietly asked from behind her.

She yelped in surprise, whirling around to see Reina leaning against the wall with her arms crossed and a half-smile on her face. When had she gotten there? Although Esme was the one with shadow magic, she was sure everyone around her moved like shadows as well.

"Esme?" Dacio's voice called out in concern followed quickly by the door opening. Their eyes widened but quickly relaxed when they saw her and Reina.

Reina pushed herself away from the wall. "Glad to see everyone made it out in one piece. Perhaps we should take the conversation into the tunnels, where stragglers won't stumble upon any sensitive information."

Esme felt the tips of her ears burn.

"Good point," Raiden said, walking into view and swinging on his cloak. "Although I'm only in one piece for now," he added dryly. His morbid humor did not amuse her.

Dacio's shoulders slumped. "Unfortunately, my spirit magic is ineffective against Jianli's here, unless I want to physically extract the pin from Raiden's body. I was only able to heal the entry point and everything up to where it's at now," they said, giving him a guilty look. "The best course of action is probably to fulfill our side of the *deal* and get Jianli to remove his metal. For the most part, he does follow through with his bargains."

"Shh," Reina hushed, looking back and forth in the upper hallway. Only the four of them were upstairs, and the ambient dining atmosphere was still going strong downstairs, but she repeated, "Again, why don't we head to the tunnels?"

"Let me quickly fetch all my things," Esme interjected, breezing past the other two into the room and collecting her bag. On the way out, she avoided making eye contact with anyone else, even as Dacio handed her shoes over to switch from the indoor slippers. The secrets kept nagging at her.

The lingering smell of pork bone broth weaved into her half-tied hair, staying with her as they all descended back into the shadows. When they seemed far enough in, Esme started.

"The sword. Spill," she ordered Dacio, trying to recall the conversation from the palace. "Why did you steal it? Was it related to your—your lover?"

Dacio flinched, avoiding her gaze. "Jianli had plundered it from one of his battles—a souvenir. Something precious, rare. I overheard him saying to one of his advisors that it was the key to expanding his power. I could have easily disregarded that statement had I not felt the strong spirit magic resonating from the sword. So I took that exact sword when I wasn't in the right state of mind. Even though he had everything, he still stole from others. I just wanted to take something away from him."

"Stole from you?" Esme asked, still thinking about their former lover.

"Stole from *her*," they said, lips curling up sadly. Their shoulders were tense and the other two were awkwardly quiet.

Her eyes widened. Were they implying the emperor had something to do with their lover's death? Based on what the emperor had said, it seemed like Dacio had swiped the sword on the same tragic day, and they had just said they were angry because Emperor Jin had stolen from others. Stealing a life?

When Dacio looked over at Reina, Esme's mind stopped functioning. *Wait, is Reina... no, didn't the emperor say Dacio's lover died? Why are they looking at her? What if their lover isn't dead? They are a powerful healer...* Her eyes darted back and forth between the two.

"Oh dear, I can see those thoughts being led astray," Reina said, her normally narrow eyes widening. "Rest assured, I'm happily involved with Daiyu."

For some reason, the statement made her feel better although she didn't know why.

"Past aside, where is this sword now?" Reina asked, stopping at an intersection with better lighting. When Raiden seemed to notice his body was partially blocking the light, he stepped closer to the walls.

"It's somewhere on the Eastern Isles. At least, that's where I left it. I threw it into a cove of one of the smaller, less-populated islands," Dacio said.

Esme's eyes widened. "That's so far away! Will a week really be enough time for us to get there and back?" The trip from Port Kai to the port of Yin City was a two-day journey on the fastest naval ship in the world, but that was along the coastline, and not across the Sapphire Sea toward the Eastern Isles.

"It's a good thing portals exist," Raiden said.

Dacio nodded. "When I left here three years ago, I wanted to put as much distance between me and the capital in as short a timeframe as possible. Reina told me of the existence of a portal in the Moonstone Mountains that led to the Eastern Isles, as well as the one between Yin City and the Emerald Forest, which I assume you took on your journey over given I was on one of the fastest naval ships the Wei empire has to offer."

More and more revelations seemed to both clarify and confuse at the same time. The timeline of many events began to bother her. Three years ago, Dacio left Yin City. Prior to that, they had apparently been a spy, probably for quite some time if the emperor called them his best spy. Afterward, they had spent some time in the Eastern Isles before making it over to Atonaco. Two years ago, Esme had woken up in Atoyatlan with Dacio by her side, and they had apparently been friends for a few years before her coma. As the emperor's assassin, Raiden also had lived in Yin City, but had apparently met her prior to her coma.

"Wait," Esme interjected, still thinking about the floating details. Something major was missing here. "This isn't my first time here in Yin City, is it?" She only had memories from the north and Dacio had only ever mentioned that *she* had lived in Atonaco, but how would she have crossed paths with them if it seemed as if they had stayed in the Wei capital city? Furthermore, the brief snippet of the conversation she had eavesdropped earlier indicated that Yin City was dangerous to an unnamed *her.*

While Reina closed her eyes, the other two stiffened. Raiden's gaze quickly darted over to Dacio before returning back down to the stone floor. As transparent as she was, she was astounded by how obvious the two were. *Some spy and assassin they were.*

"You all know something!" Esme accused when their silence verified her suspicion. "Why didn't you ever mention I had been here before? Why are you still keeping these secrets—all of you?" Technically, it wasn't fair to lump Reina in with the other two given their limited interactions, but she'd been with Raiden for two long days and had spent the last two years of her life with Dacio. Half of her past was still largely a mystery and both of them were keeping clues away from her. Any thoughts about the stolen sword were dead and gone, soaring their way into the heavens.

Raiden looked like he was trying to fuse with the wall while avoiding her gaze. Dacio floundered, reaching up to scratch the back of their neck, and unlike the other two who were dressed in all black, they still had their faded turquoise shawl on, preventing them from blending into the wall.

Esme narrowed her eyes at both of them. Finally, one caved.

Dacio leaned forward and took her hands in theirs. She froze from their touch. "I'll tell you once we leave the city. I promise. Let me find the right words," they said with pinched eyebrows.

Why couldn't they just tell me now? Whatever it was, it seemed like the three of them knew, even if partially. She felt hurt—no, betrayed even. They were keeping *her* memories a secret. Her own life. She had floundered in the dark unknown, blindfolded when the lantern had been beside her the entire time. Her entire face felt tight, and when she realized she was clenching her jaw, she forcibly relaxed the muscles and frowned at all of them.

Dacio cringed again, either from having read the visible frustration on her face or from her slipping her hand out of theirs.

"Perfect discussion for the trip you will all be embarking on," Reina murmured, her dark eyes open again.

"You're not coming?" Esme asked, trying her best to keep her tone even. Reina was the only one who wasn't stepping on eggshells in her mind, and she wished she could learn more about the Lady of Shadows.

"Unfortunately, someone needs to keep an eye on Jianli. I don't trust this situation at all, and this sword, along with the recent occurrences in the palace, throws off many warning signs." She frowned. "From what I've gathered, you seem to be on a deadline."

A small rustle brought Esme's attention back to Raiden, who tugged at the clasp of his cloak and then glided past them, grumbling, "It's too stuffy in here."

Esme found herself agreeing with that statement. The tunnels were starting to suffocate her, and the sooner she learned about the past, the better. Fresh air would also help relieve the pressure building at her temples.

"Yes, let's leave," she said, her words clipped.

"Good luck," Reina said gently. Esme didn't want to leave her on a bad note, so she nodded back. Dacio murmured something but she didn't catch it.

The Lady of Shadows retreated to her base while everyone else made their way out of the tunnels and beyond the city walls. Silence hung over their heads like a dark cloud all the way to the portal. The further from the city they were, the less tension was in both Raiden and Dacio's shoulders. It was as if Yin City had stifled them and distance from the city, particularly the palace, freed them. However, suspenseful secrets lingered in the air among them.

Although it wasn't fair to judge Yin City for what had happened since the morning, Esme was beginning to understand why Raiden had referred to it as a cursed nightmare of a city. The sheer number of secrets only indicated something big had happened—and something wretched.

CHAPTER 11

This time, Esme kept her eyes open as she stepped through the portal. Gray streaks flashed by, making her stomach drop in fear of being trapped in the spirit realm again, but they quickly blurred into hints of blue and green when she stepped out of the portal and into the poorly lit cave in the Emerald Forest. Her heart only relaxed when Raiden and Dacio arrived.

One portal down, one more to go. She was glad for no detours this time, so hopefully whatever happened last time wouldn't recur. Although using the portal felt as normal as walking through a doorway, her first experience tainted her thoughts with anxiety. Luckily, the peaceful dark of the cave and the scent of fresh water slowly alleviated her jitters.

"The next portal is somewhere in the Moonstone Mountains. Right? Is it difficult to get there?" she asked, following Raiden as he walked around the rock spikes toward the mouth of the cave.

"It'll require a short hike, but otherwise shouldn't be too difficult to reach if nothing has changed since last time,"

Dacio answered from behind. "We can get to the Eastern Isles by nightfall if we go directly to the portal."

They all stepped out and back into the crisp, fresh air of nature. Sometime within the last day, it had lightly snowed in the forest, with white dust covering the ground and the tops of the thin hollow trees. The chill in the air made her glad again for her warm Wei robes and cloak, and she took advantage of the fact that her normal body temperature ran warmer than most people due to her affinity to fire. Mentally, she thanked the deities and her ancestors for having fire magic running through her veins.

Raiden stalked off to the left, cloak and long black hair swaying from the sudden acceleration. Esme looked back at Dacio, catching the countless emotions flickering across their face. The one that stood out most was sadness, which quickly melted into something more neutral. However, she guessed from the nervous tension in their shoulders that they were probably still thinking of the conversation from Yin City.

"So," she stretched out, subtly trying to remind Dacio of their promise. Her nails bit into the bottom of her palms, the suspense of waiting giving her a phantom itch.

Dacio exhaled and finally complied. "You guessed correctly; that was not your first time in Yin City."

Instead of feeling validated like she thought she would once her guess was confirmed, Esme felt lost. Her heart throbbed painfully, and she had to force her hand to keep steady at her side rather than clutching at her chest. She would never get used to not remembering her past. That part of her was unavailable and was only present when someone else told her about her own history. Whenever she paused and thought about her dilemma, one question always came up: who *was* she?

Esme reached up to rub her temples. She knew she had been born and raised near the Moonstone Mountains on the Atonacan side. In the first twelve years or so of her life, she had not visited the Wei empire, so it must have happened afterward.

"Why was I in Yin City? Do you know how long I was there?" she asked.

"You moved to your mother's family home in the Wei empire when you were almost thirteen years old—shortly after your father died. A year or two after, your mom grew ill and came to Yin City to get medical treatment, bringing you along," they replied.

It seemed as if she had completely forgotten about her entire experience in the Wei empire. She tried picturing her mother from fragments of memories, recalling her long black hair tied into a bun and a moon-kissed complexion, unlike Esme. Her mother had been so ill that they both needed to move? Where was she now? Was she still alive?

Before she could get drawn deeper into that death spiral of thoughts, Dacio spoke again and brought her to the present, quietly asking, "Esme, did you hear me?"

"Why didn't you tell me this before?" she whispered. The truth was like a viper's sting, but it was made worse by Dacio's involvement. They kept this from her. What else was hidden?

The silence before their answer was deafening. She could hear the crunch of snow under everyone's boots, Raiden's being the softest since he was stiffly walking in front of them.

"The reasons were many," Dacio eventually admitted, gulping before elaborating further. "I was afraid and unsure. When you woke up forgetting who I was, I was hoping your memories would come back eventually, thinking you hadn't completely healed yet—which you weren't because you suffered from awfully debilitating migraines in the beginning. Recovering memories is out of my magical scope."

Esme squeezed her eyes shut. "Not telling me immediately makes sense in that context, but it's been two years. I've healed. Why haven't you told me anything since then? Don't my memories, the ones I theoretically have access to, belong to me? Are they not a part of me?" she asked, her lips and words starting to quiver slightly.

Her life felt like a mask on a hollow body.

"They are," Dacio admitted. Esme opened her eyes to meet their pained and remorseful expression. They opened and closed their mouth a few times, as if trying to find the strength and words to continue speaking. "Shortly after you woke up for the first time, I went back to Yin City to notify your mother."

Yin City. Did her mother still live there? *Oh stars above, had I unknowingly passed by my own mother while I was just there?*

"We didn't know whether you would ever come out of your coma, but when she found out, she said it would be best if you never returned to Yin City again, and that meant not letting you know about your life there," Dacio said. Although they tried to say it as gently and carefully as possible, she felt as if she could be knocked off her feet by even the barest of breezes. "You would be safer away from Yin City."

Esme was ready to explode, but she had to contain it for the moment, lest she wanted to accidentally hurt Dacio, Raiden, or herself with any outburst, particularly one that included uncontrolled fire magic.

"Safer from what?" she asked sharply. What could possibly make her own mother want her away from Yin City and make Dacio so afraid of sharing her history with her? She'd seen that brief panic that flashed in Dacio's eyes when they saw her in the Wei imperial palace. Had there been something more behind that?

Her eyes narrowed into a withering glare, which Dacio floundered under. Her stomach clenched tightly, awaiting the inevitable freefall. However, the answer came from an unexpected source.

"Neither of them wanted you to be killed again," Raiden interrupted their conversation.

Esme's mouth dropped and she froze, her breath stolen by his words.

What? Killed? Again?

Dacio jerked their head to glare at Raiden. "She didn't *die*," they hissed.

She let out a whimper. *By the stars.* It took all of her willpower to not fall to her knees.

Raiden ignored them, walking back toward her and giving her that serious and solemn look he wore naturally. "Three years ago, Esme, you died. And while Dacio had, and still has, a hard time accepting that, they know the truth," he said.

Each word was a brutal blow to her, making her chest feel tighter and tighter like a cage slowly enclosing around her. *No, it couldn't be. Could it?*

Dacio turned toward her again, giving her a pleading, placating look. "You were in a coma, but that doesn't mean that you died," they said before throwing Raiden another hard look.

Suddenly, she *knew*. Something in her recognized it, having found the words to describe what it knew but couldn't say or piece together. Her body started shaking, curling in, and she squeezed her eyes closed. What else could have completely wiped out her memories like that? Most coma-related memory issues involved difficulty in recalling one's most recent memories or the inability to form new memories—not half of one's life memories just gone. But waking from death? That was fair game.

Furthermore, what else could have scared both her mother and Dacio into trying to keep her away from the Wei empire but fear for her life? Perhaps her visit to the spirit realm when she walked through that portal the first time wasn't so much an accidental detour but a subconscious return to somewhere she had gone before.

She had died.

Then, something about the way Raiden phrased his comment struck her. He didn't just say that she died; he said she had been *killed*.

"Wait a second—" Esme started before getting interrupted.

"Hells," Raiden snarled sharply and quietly.

"Stars above, what now?" Dacio hissed.

Esme pulled herself out of her own crumbling thoughts to see what the other two were clamoring about. There, far beyond the rows of hollow trees and blocking the path further up, stood two large gangly creatures, pale as bone and eerie as a nightmare. Somehow, the demons neither heard nor saw any of them yet.

"The Dreadful," she whispered, finally noticing the ominous chittering sounds coming from in front of them.

Had her thoughts been so oppressive that she had completely missed the ominous change in the aura of the forest? What about this forest attracted so many demons?

Raiden exhaled quietly, tossing the bottom edge of his cloak back so he could more easily access his blade from his sheath. "There seems to be more demonic activity as of late.

We might as well take care of them while we're here since there are three of us and two of them. Not to mention that you two have magic," he said, face focused yet jaded.

She frowned. Her magic would likely refuse to cooperate given the cold atmosphere and the recent revelations about her own history. No way could she fully concentrate and harness the energy from her surroundings. She could barely even stop her hand from trembling from the awful, spirit-draining truth, and they hadn't even finished discussing her past.

"How exactly do we deal with them? Guide them back into the spirit realm?" Dacio asked.

"Close. We have to destroy their living bodies like any other living creature. Where they go after that, I don't know. I think they're sent back to where they belong," Raiden answered.

Suddenly, the air around her cooled even more, sapping away the heat from her body and depleting external sources of her magic. Heat seldom bothered her, but lingering cold always crept deep into her and drained her faster than anything else. A flash of blinding light caught the side of her eye, and she followed that light down until a gleaming shard of ice came into view. Holding the razor-sharp shard with frost on their hands was Dacio.

Her mind and eyes almost felt like they were disconnected. Reconciling the image of Dacio making and holding a weapon of ice with her memories of them healing people and using their ice magic for small, cheerful snowy displays was like trying to picture the sun next to the moon in the sky—incompatible with her perspective of reality yet theoretically possible.

When would the world stop spinning and inverting upon itself? She wished it could slow down and give her a chance to breathe. The pressure within started to overwhelm her, bleeding out into the open.

Malevolent spirits and demons alike were drawn toward emotions and life—both of which were something they had lost. Perhaps her turmoil had suddenly brought the Dreadful's attention onto them, drawing their gazes and hisses.

Raiden's blade glowed and lengthened into a sword. He gave it a swing and dropped low into a steady stance in front of both of them, ready for the demons' charge while Dacio lifted their hands and shattered their own shard of ice into a myriad of smaller hovering pieces. Although his impatience showed in the tightness of his lips, Raiden didn't have to wait long before the Dreadful barreled into him.

The two demons didn't look as nightmarish as the last two, but they were nothing to laugh at. The faster one, with a body of a half-decayed bull, held its head down so its horns met the edge of Raiden's blade. The raucous clash made Esme flinch and step back whereas Raiden took the blunt force in stride.

Next to her, Dacio flicked their wrist and sent the army of floating ice shards at the slower eagle-winged demon like a deadly shower of knives. It swerved some of the blades of ice and used its wings to block the rest. A few shards managed to puncture through the wings, skewering though and knocking it down. After crashing back to the ground, it lifted its head and unrolled its long protruding tongue so it could hiss at them, but Dacio didn't hesitate to throw out their frost-covered hands and shoot ice at its feet to trap it on land.

Suddenly, a large, dark object flew over Dacio's head and toward Esme. Her eyes widened and she threw her hands up to try to call upon her magic, not that fire would necessarily stop a moving object. A cruel repeat of history blasted her off her feet. Wildly in mid-air, she reached out for any tendril of magic, anything she could reach with no direction or focus, and so she clung to the nearest welcoming shadow.

Her body dissipated into the shadow to transport away. Just as quickly as she blended into the darkness, she manifested once more, stumbling back on her feet. Esme almost tripped back but managed to catch herself against one of the thin, emerald trees. Chest tight with worry, she looked over and saw Raiden groaning on the ground where she would have landed had she not warped elsewhere. He must have been the large, dark object flying at her.

The demon he had been fighting was missing its horns now. Enraged, it charged at Raiden, who quickly rolled over and jumped back onto his feet, reaching down to grab nothing. His head sharply swiveled back and forth to find something.

Where is his sword? Esme panicked.

A shiny silver glint near her feet answered her unspoken question. He was too far away from the weapon but not far enough from the demon, and no way was she going to properly use a sword to defend them both with no training or precision. She didn't think it would be wise for him to use his death touch against the Dreadful either.

The air near her was cooler from the shadows but warmer than where Dacio was, so she had enough to build on. She reined in the energy currents within her and let them flow up her arm to her hand, where heat burst out of her. A small fireball flew at the ox-headed demon, distracting it for a moment. The distraction gave her just enough time to grab the sword near her feet and test out whether she could bring objects along as she traversed through the shadows.

The heavy sword lightened in her grip and miraculously managed to reappear in her hand when she warped over to Raiden's side. Although his eyes widened in surprise, he didn't let that distract him from reaching out for the sword. He turned around and swung it just as the oncoming demon jumped at them. The blade struck true and separated the Dreadful's head from its body, both of which immediately turned into dust that rained on them. Esme coughed and shook the dust off in disgust. At least it was dry.

Her attention went back to find the remaining creature, which was still trapped by ice covering its body. Before either of them could step forward and help out, Dacio thrust their hands up, and along with the motion, four large icicles shot up through the winged demon. It gave one last squawk and then fell apart.

Raiden huffed loudly beside her, his sword back in its smaller form. Esme looked at the other two, and when she saw that they both seemed unharmed, she exhaled in relief. Dacio must have felt the same because they languidly strolled over to them.

"Well, that was exciting. Wasn't it?" Dacio smiled.

"Fuck off," Raiden grumbled, slipping his gloves back on.

Shaking her head, Esme reached up to pinch the bridge of her nose. *What a mess.*

CHAPTER 12

With every remaining step she took in the Emerald Forest, Esme prayed to the deities that no more demons would show up. Every sudden noise placed her on high alert. Perhaps that was why when Dacio spoke, she nearly jumped out of her skin.

"We never discussed those new abilities of yours," they said, reminding her of the changes in her life. "You certainly didn't have these abilities before—either pre- or post-coma—and I've never heard of anyone being able to travel through the shadows like that with magic. If I had to guess the domain of this power, I would say spirit, but even I don't have that in my skill set."

She gently chewed her bottom lip. "I only discovered it in the palace, but something strange happened to me when I stepped through the portal to Yin City the first time. I'm certain I crossed into the spirit realm, and I think that might have done something to me."

Dacio froze. She and Raiden stopped as well.

"*Heavens,*" Dacio whispered, their posture completely rigid as they gave her a glance over. "Are you sure?"

"The walking skeletons kind of gave it away." She laughed nervously, rubbing the back of her hands under the large sleeves of her robe.

Although Dacio looked ill at the idea and seemed stunned into silence, they resumed walking through the forest with uncertainty lining their eyebrows.

She was still thinking about how close she had been to being trapped there. Upon crossing over to the other realm, spirits were supposed to be judged for their actions and were sentenced to one of three fates: be consumed by a Dreadful and sent into one of the nine hells, be born again as a new creature or person, or ascend to one of the thirteen heavens and become an eternal star.

Where do I fit into this then? After all, she had apparently died at some point, and she was still here, so she hadn't been consumed by demons nor had she ascended to the heavens. Did her case count as rebirth? At least she knew her past self was neither too good nor too evil but somewhere in the middle.

Esme seemed to live her entire life in the middle—half her time in the temple, half in the craft shop. Half in the past, half in the present. Good, but not good enough. She almost felt like the Moonstone Mountain range they were starting to traverse through, neutrally separating two nations while being part of both.

Although some of these middle grounds were natural, the one of life and death was not. Why had she been killed?

"Raiden?" Esme called out once they officially left the forest and entered the rockier region at the base of the Moonstone mountains.

The former assassin tilted his head and slowed his pace. "Yes?"

She hesitated before asking her question. "You said I was... killed. Do you know what happened or who did it?"

Dacio choked softly beside her, like someone had punched them in the stomach. Raiden didn't seem any more comfortable, shifting uneasily, his back rigid with tension. The only time she had seen him more distressed was when he thought he had killed her with his death touch.

Surprisingly, Dacio gave her the direct answer this time. "Jin Jianli attempted to kill you," they said, making her eyebrows jump up in surprise.

"He *did* kill her," Raiden murmured his protest.

Back to this argument again. She sighed, only letting it momentarily distract her from the increasing absurdity of the past. The Wei emperor had killed her? Why? How? Even if it didn't make logical sense to her, both Raiden and Dacio's behavior at the palace, of making sure she wasn't spotted, made even more sense under this context. Furthermore, running away from Yin City seemed like the most prudent option if the literal leader was threatening her life.

"Why would the emperor bother to kill me?" Esme asked. How had she gone from being a gifted young scholar at the Atonacan Academy of Magic and the daughter of a renowned Atonacan warrior to being the target of the Wei emperor? Fire ignited within her. She was tired of being confused and lost.

"You were a threat to him," Dacio said. Esme turned back to face them, watching them squirm uncomfortably before they mumbled, "You two were actually cousins."

"*What?*" Esme shrieked. Some birds in the dry brushes scattered from the noise. The other two winced. "By the stars, that mediocre marblehead is my *cousin?*"

Raiden snorted at the insult, but when she looked over at him, he schooled his face.

"He's your cousin on your mother's side of the family. From what you told me before, your mother was estranged from the rest of her family when she married your father so you didn't meet much of her side of the family until you moved to the Wei empire. However, she belonged to one of the ruling families of the three old kingdoms that merged into the Wei empire. Jin Jianli is the son of your uncle, the former king and current province leader," Dacio stated.

Every time she thought reality couldn't break any more, another revelation shattered it. The one who had casually threatened both Dacio and Raiden within the same hour? That person was her cousin? She closed her eyes and took a deep breath to recenter herself. "That doesn't explain why he's the emperor now nor why he would want to kill me."

"Does Jianli need a reason to be cruel?" Raiden muttered.

"The short answer is politics," Dacio answered. "The former Wei emperor started off as one of the three kings south of the Moonstone Mountains before he decided to form an empire. Although he directly conquered the weaker kingdom in the northwest by force, the kingdom in the northeast, where your family was from, was more powerful and so there was an agreement to have a political marriage between the former emperor's child and a child from the northeast."

Thinking about the timeline of events, Esme felt sick. The Wei empire was only about a quarter century old. A political marriage of the former emperor's child and a child from the northeast would put her in the age category, although she never heard about any of this growing up in Atonaco.

"Jin Jianli was betrothed to the sole daughter of the former emperor, and there weren't any problems until a few years after you and your mother arrived at the capital for her medical treatment. While Jianli was out to expand his future territory, a group of angry conquered people snuck into the Wei palace and kidnapped the princess," Dacio continued, sounding a little winded from explaining and hiking at the same time.

Her eyes widened and she almost tripped over a stray rock in the mountain path, but Raiden silently caught her elbow with a gloved hand. *Stars above*, the situation already sounded messy and she wasn't even involved—yet. However, she could already see how she might be involved, given her ties to nobility.

"After a few years missing and no information, the princess was officially declared dead. That put Jianli's path to the imperial throne at stake, and the former emperor and empress were suddenly heirless and on shaky grounds with the former northeast kingdom. Throughout this entire time, you had been at the palace because your mother was friends with the former empress, who sponsored your studies and provided royal healers for your mother. By the time the princess was declared dead, you had been at the capital for long enough to be a favorite of the former empress," they said.

Esme tried to connect the dots but still didn't see how she would pose as a threat to Jianli. "Before you continue, how did you know about all of this?" she asked.

They blinked at her. "My job required me to be politically knowledgeable."

Oh yes, Esme remembered. Dacio had been a spy.

"Anyway, the climate at the imperial palace was toxic after that and everyone changed for the worst," Dacio said with a pained expression. "The emperor withdrew into himself and started ignoring the political chaos within his halls. Court officials and nobles alike wondered about who would lead the empire. Rumors started including your name, as you were the favorite of the empress and more magically powerful than Jianli once you started mastering lightning itself."

Lightning? Her mouth dropped. That was possible?

"Were those rumors even true? Also, how did he k— attempt to kill me? Isn't trying to kill your supposed competition to the throne, especially a relative, frowned upon and probably disqualifying?" Esme asked. She was focusing so intensely on trying to wrap her head around the complicated politics and the idea that she had died that she only barely noticed the change from pebbled path to smooth shimmering rock.

"He poisoned you somehow. I wasn't there when it happened, but I found you… after," they answered, their guilt shining through their eyes. How bad of a state had she been in when they had found her for them to recall that memory with such pain? Dacio kept insisting that she hadn't died but based on their expression and the fact that she had been in a coma told her that she had not been in a pretty state.

When she looked forward again, she noticed Raiden's shoulders tighten and wondered if he had been there too in her final moments.

"The emperor also mysteriously met his final fate on the same night, which was more pressing, and no one ever found you or your body. Jianli blamed both the emperor's death and your disappearance on the same group of rebels who had previously kidnapped the former princess, but I know for certain he was behind it. Too many convenient coincidences for it to be otherwise, and I along with other spies had done our jobs too well that Jianli was protected from potential repercussions," Dacio gritted out, seemingly spilling the secrets they had held onto and crushed within them for so long.

Her eyes burned at the injustice, but her heart felt so, so cold.

A few years ago, she had been poisoned—killed—by her own cousin for the throne and her cousin was now emperor. Her life had changed dramatically, had been stolen from her, yet Jianli seemed unperturbed by the whole incident and had only gained more influence.

Murdered for a throne.

Her head felt murky, like she could wander in its foggy recesses for days. Dacio hadn't been understating how overwhelming the truth was, even though it was important for her know.

With a gentle touch on her shoulder, Dacio pulled her out from getting lost in her head. Turning to the side, she gazed into their dark, flickering eyes.

"I'm sorry," they said, "for the half-truths and omissions. For the pain you're in. For not stopping everything in the first place."

A wry smile forcibly clawed its way onto her face. "You carry too much responsibility and guilt for things you cannot control. I think it's safe to say that Jianli is responsible for the last two things you mentioned," she said before her smile slowly fell apart. "However, all of these secrets hurt. I can understand why you kept them, and maybe you being a former spy also plays into that, but you have to promise to tell me the full truth from now on."

They closed their eyes and nodded. "I will."

Not long after, they all finally reached their midpoint destination. Along the milky white and blue cliffs of the Moonstone Mountains was another noticeable marking with the same inscriptions as the ones in the cave followed by the familiar potently magical aura. At least portals seemed consistent, and it would be easy to identify a stray one in nature by feeling alone, even when the mountains themselves already had a low, consistent level of magic—a reminder to all of the remnants of the deities' power and Jing's specifically.

Raiden approached the hidden pathway first, stopping only to give them both a silent glance. Sadness lay in his eyes, so familiar it reminded her of the trials of sadness Dacio had every once in a while back in Atoyatlan.

Before she could read too much into it, he turned around and walked through the portal first. Esme went next with Dacio close behind her.

A cool sea breeze greeted her on the other side. Raiden was on the other side, shaking water off his boots and grumbling something about hating water before jumping into the nearby sand. He must have stepped in the shallow puddle of sea water that she narrowly missed.

Esme was too stunned by the sight to share his sentiment. They were beside a small cliff, surrounded below by the clear blue waters of the cove. Within a blink of an eye, they had jumped from the cooler mountains and into the tropical waters of the Eastern Isles, bypassing any potentially dangerous naval travel. The blue-purple waters of the Sapphire Sea under the setting sun mesmerized her, as did the pink sand. Tall formations of rocks scattered in the water of the bay, standing firm like steady guardians and casting their shadows onto the sand. She had always wanted to explore more of the world and perhaps once this was all done, she could do more traveling.

"Wow, it's so beautiful," she gasped, breath startled out of her. *Now, if only I could swim*, she thought as she eyed the crystal-clear waters.

"It is beautiful," Dacio agreed, biting their bottom lip. "We lived here for almost a year while you were in your coma."

Air left her lungs for a different reason. "Oh."

Another place she didn't remember, but because of her coma rather than the erasure of her lived history.

"Rai and I took you here after that night. We wanted to be as far from Yin City as possible. Nobody knew us here, so we were safe from Jianli realizing his plan partially failed," Dacio said. "Also, the abundance of water and the islands' affinity for spirit magic, with Jing as the patron deity, made it easier for me to keep you in a steady state."

Oh. Esme had never thought too much about the conditions of her coma since she had eventually come out of it, but it should have been easier to see all of the hidden connections. As a spirit mage, a healer, Dacio must have used their abilities to try to keep her—her body?—alive.

She threw a worried look at them, her eyebrows furrowed tightly. "How often did you use your magic?" she asked.

"Every day for a year," they answered.

"Please tell me you took breaks," she pleaded. That much usage of magic without breaks would be draining, damaging even. That was why healers at the temple had rotations.

They cringed and scratched the back of their head. "I mean, I wasn't using magic all the time, but I had to make sure you didn't go anywhere you couldn't return from."

Esme turned to Raiden to verify. "Did they?"

He cast his eyes away. "I only helped bring you here. I didn't stay."

She closed her eyes. As much as she wanted to berate Dacio for endangering themself, she still felt grateful that they tried so hard to heal her—or bring her back to life? Everything was still confusing and it was starting to chip at her head. Even for someone who had learned magic and religion, some mysteries of the world were perhaps not made for mortal minds.

"At least we're both still here, thank the deities," she said.

Dacio gave her a tender smile. "Shall we head into the village?"

Esme nodded, and they led the group away from the glistening waters and further onto the island.

CHAPTER 13

Deep oranges and reds streaked across the sky as the sun descended to the horizons with darkening blues trailing behind. On the opposite side of the sky was the only moon left by the deities. Glimmers of stars were visible to the naked eye, spanning the center gradient.

Even with the evening soon to settle in, Esme realized that both her and Raiden's outfits were ill-equipped for the island climate. While Raiden unclasped his cloak, sweat lining the side of his face, Dacio was still in their thinner Atonacan clothes. With their ice magic, they might not have even noticed the cooler temperatures back in the Wei empire and were back to being appropriately dressed for the circumstance. Technically, she was still comfortable, but she could tell that any typical person would've felt otherwise.

"It's been a while since we were here last, Rai," Dacio murmured, still leading the way. The rocky cliffs faded into forestry.

"Mhm," he hummed. "Better circumstances this time."

"And this time you're staying with us. Right?" they replied. When he nodded in agreement, they asked, "Why didn't you stay last time? I could have used your support."

Raiden's lips thinned out and he cast his gaze down. Just as she was about to remark about how everyone was conscious—alive?—this time, he uncharacteristically stumbled in his step, reaching up to clutch at his chest.

"Rai?" Dacio glanced back in concern and rushed over. "Is it the metal pin?"

Pain crawled over his face as he nodded. With everything that had happened in the Emerald Forest—from demons to revelations—Esme had forgotten it had been just this morning that Emperor Jin had implemented the timed metal poison into Raiden. Her own stomach tightened in worry.

Luckily, Dacio the professional healer, was ready. She felt a calming energy radiating from them as they reached up to place one of their darker hands on his paler forehead and the other over his heart. A soft white glow surrounded their fingertips, seeming to do its job given Raiden's pinched expression relaxing.

"Better?" they asked, pulling their hands back. Their eyebrows were furrowed together in focus.

"Thank you," Raiden sighed. "I think it stopped moving before you used your magic though. Jianli isn't lying, at least for now, about the incremental movements."

Esme glared at the ground. Even though she couldn't remember any of her personal memories of Jin Jianli, she despised him for the effects he had on everyone. Raiden didn't deserve to be used as hostage, especially after he had been an assassin. Dacio didn't deserve to be made into a puppet beholden to the emperor's whims either.

"Well, we're almost there, so you'll be able to rest soon," they told him.

As relieving as that might have been for Raiden, Esme was looking forward to resting as well. They had all been walking the entire day and her feet were sore. Back in Atonaco, the uneven terrain between cities wasn't made for easy transportation so she was used to walking, but an entire day of walking was still draining.

The minute they stepped into the village, Dacio was greeted with warm welcomes and deep hugs from stunned people who managed to recognize their fire-lit face. From the way everyone seemed to know them, Dacio had indeed taken breaks from trying to heal her to develop relationships with the villagers. Raiden was clearly more hesitant with the amount of exuberant attention occurring in the lively group and drifted further out into the edges. Esme was tempted to join him but was quickly pulled in.

One villager's round eyes widened when she finally saw Esme, exclaiming, "She's awake? What a blessing from the deities! This calls for celebration!"

Esme's own eyes widened with uncertain anxiety and a hesitant smile froze on her face. She had not been prepared to be the center of attention, but Dacio flashed her a crooked smile and gently pulled her in, giving her support through their mere presence.

"This is Nami, the matriarch of the village. She took care of me, us really, while we were here, and she specializes in water magic," Dacio said.

Esme gave her a more thorough examination. With her gray hair tied back into a simple braid, Nami wore a fiercely friendly smile that shined clearly on her round brown face. The matriarch's smile and entire presence could probably make anyone feel like they were embraced by warmth personified, which seemed to be verified through Dacio's fond expression.

"Nice to meet you," Esme said, bowing her head slightly to show her respect and gratitude. From what she remembered, customs on the Eastern Isles were more similar to that of the south.

Nami stepped forward and embraced her just as warmly as she had embraced Dacio. The old woman was even smaller than she was, despite her large presence and energy. "I am happy for you, child," she said before releasing her. "Life is so precious and you managed to hold on through even the most terrible of tempests. Be sure to cherish it and the time with people you love too."

Her words tugged at Esme's heart. "Thank you for your kind words."

The matriarch turned back to the other villagers gathered around the fire on the beachside. "Will someone come fetch some fruit for our guests?" she asked.

A small child jumped up to his feet and excitedly volunteered himself, running off further inland before anyone could argue. Nami laughed at the boy's eagerness and turned back to face Dacio and Esme, pausing when her gaze passed the two of them.

"You look weary from travel. Please, come and sit around the fire," Nami ordered. "We were just about to sing some songs."

They walked over and sat in the sand around the fire pit. Esme felt particularly drawn to the fire in front of her, hearing the crackling of wood and the sound of its movement. The bright crimson burned strongly.

Without prompt, someone began to sing a song in a language Esme didn't know—something not quite Wei and definitely not Atonacan. More voices joined in, followed by some drums. She simply sat there beside Dacio and enjoyed the harmony and rest, watching joyful faces dance around each other and loose clothing sway to the beat. The moon swung higher in the sky like a lantern in the dark, a beacon of reunion.

After the second song, Nami leaned over and asked, "What do you think so far?"

Esme softly smiled at the islanders. "This reminds me a lot of Atoyatlan. The dancing, singing. The festivals. It's an honor to listen in."

"Hmm yes, we mortals are connected in so many different ways. Music is a universal language, even if we have different beats and styles. We share the same joy and devotion," Nami remarked. In the distance, the child from earlier was running back with a deep plate full of colorful fruit. "We also share the language of food, so I hope you will enjoy our welcome. If I had known you were coming, we would have prepared a great feast for you. Alas, that will have to wait until tomorrow."

Dacio ducked their head. "We are very grateful, as usual."

"I got the fruit!" the child exclaimed in a winded voice as he handed the plate over to Nami.

She smiled up at him as she took the plate and set it on a flat rock. "Thank you," she said, earning her a toothy grin before the boy ran off to join the rest of the dancers in the background.

Esme leaned over with her eyebrows raised in curious anticipation of the available fruits. Slices of starfruit and dragonfruit lined the edges of the plate with shelled lychees surrounding an empty bowl in the middle. Her eyes widened at the treasure. All three fruits were common in Atonaco, but lychee was one of her favorites.

Reaching over for the lychee, Esme accidentally brushed her hand against Dacio's, who was reaching for the dragonfruit. She looked up into their dark eyes and tried to fight the heat rushing to her face.

"You first," she laughed nervously.

They grinned back at her and then widened their eyes with exaggerated surprise. "She of Eternal Hunger is letting me eat first?" they gasped.

Esme feigned an outrageous glare and indignantly snatched a lychee off the plate. "Well, not anymore," she huffed, peeling the shell off, popping the fruit into her mouth, and then throwing both the shell and seed into the empty bowl. It almost seemed like she was home where everything was fine and she and Dacio were simply playing around.

Dacio snorted and then dove for the dragonfruit, eating three slices before offering the plate back to Nami, who smiled fondly at the two of them.

"You are the guests, so I insist that you eat them," she said before gesturing inland, where the rest of the villagers seemed to be heading, morphing the communal dancing and singing into more intimate conversations. "Though perhaps you can invite your last friend over there to share some of the welcoming gifts."

Looking over in the exact direction, Esme saw Raiden still hovering in the edges. She thought he had disappeared to his own company earlier.

"Of course," Dacio replied, turning around to call for Raiden, who straightened up at the call and looked at the three of them near the fire. They picked up a lychee and waved it at him, beckoning him over.

When Raiden got close enough, Dacio tossed the lychee up at him. With his trained reflexes, he caught it easily with one gloved hand and then ate the whole thing, shell and all. Esme's mouth dropped in horror, and she had to blink a few times, wondering if she really had seen him just eat the whole fruit. The crunching noises coming from his direction verified what she saw.

"Did he just..." Esme asked Dacio, who laughed.

"Yes," they answered mirthfully. "Almost puts me to shame. If you thought the way I eat whole tomatoes from the inside out is strange, just wait until you see how Raiden eats other things."

Her nose crinkled. "Deities save me, I'm surrounded by chaotic people."

By now, Raiden was close enough for the light from the fire to illuminate his smirking face. He seemed to be enjoying her shock.

"Raiden?" Nami whispered from beside them. The matriarch's eyes were now glistening in fearful hope as she gazed upon his wary face.

"Yes, that's my name," he said, confused. Unless the two had met last time, Esme didn't think Nami should have known his name since they hadn't exactly introduced him.

"Oh, in all of the heavens," Nami gasped, choking slightly and stumbling up to her feet. "It can't be."

Everyone froze, unsure what was happening. Nami reached for him, her motion causing him to flinch away, but she still tilted her head up to look at him, her gaze sweeping diligently, repeatedly over his face. "You look how your father did when he was your age."

Raiden went completely rigid, his arms hanging stiffly at his side and his eyes widening like he had seen a spirit. *Oh no.* Esme knew where this was heading. It seemed as if she wasn't the only one who would get a dose of startling truth that day.

"My grandson, you've returned," Nami said, trembling.

He jerked back as if he had been stung. "That's not possible," he immediately denied, scrambling back from the tiny woman. His face turned hard. "The deities would not be so forgiving. No, this is a punishment."

Nami's eyes widened and she tried to calm his agitation, to no avail. Raiden all but bolted away, his tied hair whipping around behind him like a tendril of shadow attempting to mask him.

"Raiden!" Nami called out, her arm still stretched out. The wrinkles in her face seemed etched in deeper agony under the shadows of the fire.

True to his title, the Assassin of the Night darted back into the dark to hide under its cover. When Esme looked over to Dacio, she could see the same confusion and concern reflected on their face.

What just happened?

CHAPTER 14

Given their long history, it was for the best that Dacio was the one who darted after Raiden, leaving the other two shocked on the sand. The matriarch slowly sank down to her knees and rubbed her hand over her face. This was a surprise to everyone. No one could've fathomed a situation like this.

"Is he really your grandson?" Esme asked after waiting for a few moments and letting the shock roll off. Gently biting her bottom lip, she examined the old woman to see how she was faring with the revelations.

Nami rubbed her face one last time but her eyes were still unfocused. "He has the same name as my grandson, and I see my son in him. That arch of his eyebrows, his nose, and smile—all of it, like his father, even though his mother's features are strong too. I can't believe he survived the shipwreck," she choked. "He was so young when he left with his parents and none of them ever returned. He must not have known how to get back, if he even knew where to go back. My poor Raiden."

What had he said when he told her about his background? Something about washing up on the beaches of Yin City? *By the stars, he had meant that* literally. She tried to remember what else he had said, but she couldn't remember information as clearly as Dacio although very few could match their ability.

"I don't think he knew. He said he didn't remember much before Yin City," Esme said quietly, interlocking her fingers together. How awful it must have been for Nami to have lost her family like that. The sorrow must have been devastating. "I'm sorry for your loss. May they rest amongst the stars."

She didn't know what else to say, so she offered her presence until the other two came back. With the rest of the villagers back in their homes, only the sound of waves crashing on shore kept them company. Her gaze also unfocused, settling on the smooth sands.

"Nami," Dacio's smooth voice called out. When she looked up, she also saw Raiden grudgingly straggling aside them.

"I'm ready to listen," Raiden said quietly, kneeling down in the sand in front of Nami and sitting on the back of his feet. Any glimmer of amusement from before was now gone.

"What do you wish to know?" Nami asked hesitantly. Her presence seemed smaller, more uncertain now.

Esme looked at Dacio, who had returned to her side, and gave them a questioning glance. Should they both be listening in? A quick jerk of their chin toward Raiden and a raised eyebrow told her it would be up to him whether he wanted privacy or support. With no objections from anyone, she and Dacio stayed in the area.

Raiden floundered for words, but eventually found his voice to ask a question that struck Esme in the chest. "Who am I?"

Esme asked herself the same question all the time. It implied many others and had no simple answers.

Nami gave him a gentle and sorrowful smile. "You are Raiden of the Kunhai village, the son of my son and a Wei merchant's daughter. The playful wind of Kunhai."

One detail caught Esme's attention. He was like her too: child of Wei and of the Eastern Isles—one who was also disconnected and being connected once more.

"So, I have family?" he asked, to his own grandmother's face, as if to verify. His voice held a wavering degree of vulnerability, like he couldn't even believe what he was saying. She could certainly relate when just earlier, she had been wondering about her own mother and the rest of her Wei relatives, particularly the non-murderous ones.

"Of course." Nami smiled. "You have a very large family here and an even larger one if you count all of Kunhai."

"Why did we leave then?" Raiden followed up, as if he couldn't imagine any reason to leave family behind. Esme was reminded of how he said he had essentially grown up alone on the streets.

The old woman slumped. "Your parents were taking you to meet your mother's family in Yin City."

"I have family there too?" he asked, his eyes widening again in fear. Trembling slightly, he looked like he was going to be ill. Esme didn't understand why he seemed afraid until she remembered he had been an assassin, primarily prowling in Yin City, where part of his family lived. She too would have been afraid of those implications if she were him. Hells, her past was also murky to a point where she didn't know what kind of person she had been at the palace and what sorts of things she had done.

"Yes. Did you manage to find them?" Nami asked, fragile hope in her voice. "Were you able to have a good life?"

Raiden dipped his head and covered his face with his gloved hands. His shaking turned into quiet gasps of breath, alarming his grandmother, who shifted over and hovered her hand over his shoulder without actually touching him. That might have been the correct move given his apparent aversion to being in close proximity to people. After a few deepening breaths, he dropped his hands and kept his face tilted down. She withdrew her hand but stayed close.

"An old couple pitied me and took care of me for a few years before they died. Whether or not we were related, I don't know," he murmured.

Esme's leg started losing feeling, so she shifted positions and continued listening with Dacio, silently absorbing the heavy grief saturating the air. The night breeze made her shiver despite the general warm temperature.

"Was I born cursed?" Raiden asked quietly.

Nami's eyes widened. "Cursed?" she exclaimed. "I know you must have experienced a lot of hardship and it may be hard to believe, but you were born on an auspicious day blessed with gentle sea breeze and waters."

"Then why are my hands like this?" he asked, glaring at his open palm and visibly frustrated. "Did I ever kill someone here? Did either of my parents have hands of death? Do you?"

"Hands of death?" Nami echoed, wrinkles deepening from worry. "That's not even a power any mage can hold."

Esme's head jerked up. What else about magic did the matriarch know? Did she happen to know about shadow magic? Melting into the darkness didn't fall cleanly into any of the realms of magic either.

His left eye twitched and he cast his gaze over to the rock, where the plate of fruits remained. Quickly taking off a glove, he reached over and grabbed a lychee, widely avoiding Dacio who was next to the flat stone. In his hand sat the shelled fruit, and this time, Esme knew what to expect. They all observed the way the lychee blackened and then deteriorated into dust, just like the rose apple had back in the Chens' spare room. Nami let out a sharp gasp.

"You certainly did not have these abilities when you were younger. I… I still can't quite believe this is possible," the matriarch whispered, her fingers digging into her flowery skirt. "Do you have any other magic? Water? Wind?"

"No," Raiden replied flatly, yanking his glove back on. "Ever since I washed up on the shores of Yin City, this is the only ability I have, and I *have* tried to see if I could demonstrate magic." He curled his fingers into claws.

With a deep frown, Nami asked, "What happened the first time you demonstrated this ability? Tell me everything you remember."

The question made him pause. "I remember waking up in wet sand with coral jewelry around me. I didn't remember much before that and was trying to figure out what happened when some thieves came to collect everything on shore. Instead of helping me, they tried to take me. I don't know exactly what happened, but I was afraid for my life and the next thing I knew, they lay dead at my feet. It took me a few occurrences with animals to figure what was going on—that my hands were cursed."

"So, fear," Nami whispered. "Again, I haven't heard of this happening before outside of legend…"

Still thinking about her own abilities, and having the opportunity to be in the presence of someone who might know more, Esme interrupted the conversation. "What about shadow magic?"

Although she was torn between feeling apologetic and anxious for inserting herself into the conversation, Dacio hadn't had any answers for her when she had shown them her newly discovered magic.

Nami looked over, her eyes widened as if she had forgotten she had an audience. "Shadow magic... I haven't heard of that either. How odd. Shadow magic and a touch of death?" she murmured. "If I had to guess, I would say both of those could fall under the realm of spirit, but mortal-wielded spirit magic is usually restricted to healing, divination, spirit-walking, and aura-reading."

Then she let out a gasp, looking at both Esme and Raiden. "You two must have been touched by death, the deity Jing herself. Raiden, it's highly likely that the shipwreck might have been fatal for you, and last time you were here, Esme, you were stuck in that horrible state of stillness. Both of you, with strange powers and almost fatal fates. It's like the old legend of the fisherman who drowned at sea but somehow survived and came back with the power to resurrect the dead, which had only been discovered when he revived his wife."

The legend of the fisherman? Esme had never heard of that particular story before. Was it an island legend? Even though the Eastern Isles, the Wei empire, and Atonaco shared the same religion recognizing the five major deities, they each had their own pantheon of minor deities and minor stories. Perhaps this was one of the differences, and with Atonaco being rather landlocked, it made sense she might not have heard many stories regarding the sea.

Regardless, the hypothesis could make sense, as Raiden claimed that she had died, and she certainly did not have shadow magic beforehand. However, she had been out of her coma for two years now and only just discovered her new abilities. Had she had these powers the entire time but never acted upon them? Mages did need to focus on the specific realm in order to manifest any powers, so it had never been a possibility in her mind. Her magic had only manifested itself when she actively thought about shadows.

Raiden frowned. "I thought Jing was the creator of life, or at least the deity who breathes spirit into all living creatures," he said.

"Yes, as the deity of spirit, Jing is involved in matters of life and also of death. You two must have brought back powers from the spirit realm that should not exist here, and with the legend in mind, it may have been given by Jing themself," Nami continued.

"So you're saying because I drowned as a child but somehow actually survived, I happened to pick up the ability to kill people with the touch of my hand," Raiden said astounded. "How do I get rid of it then?"

"I don't know the answer to that, my dear grandson," the matriarch said sadly, covering one hand with the other.

Esme's eyebrows drew together as she compared both her and Raiden's situations. Why could she control her possibly deity-given abilities but Raiden couldn't? Was it because she already knew how to use magic? Perhaps the legend would provide a better clue.

"What happened in the legend of the fisherman? Was he able to control his ability?" Esme asked.

"As my grandmother told me, and her grandmother told her, it is said that the fisherman's power was an indication of Jing's favor, but his abilities and his island's perception of him filled him with great hubris as he converted his island into the Isle of Eternal Springs. No one died—or at least, no one stayed dead for long," she replied.

"What's wrong with wanting people to stay alive?" Dacio asked softly, startling Esme with their sudden entrance. They had been quiet by her side the entire time, and their fire-lit expression looked vulnerable from asking that question.

Quickly, she wondered if they asked that because of how they took care of her after her death, healing her day after day in Kunhai more than two years ago. Even though death was natural and just a step in one's journey, she remembered struggling when her father had fallen in battle. Every time she had seen a hummingbird afterward, she had broken down in tears. The yearning for loved ones to stay was equally natural.

"Because the world needs balance, and his use of magic severely disrupted it. What they didn't know was that every life he saved only reduced his own life, and that he tied their lifeline to his," Nami answered.

"So everyone on the island died with him?" Raiden asked. His grandmother nodded.

Heavens, what a tragic story, Esme thought. She wondered if there were any particularly negative consequences from her shadow magic and Raiden's death touch aside from the personal mental toll.

"Well, given your abilities and the drive for balance, could it mean something good happened elsewhere whenever you used it?" Dacio suggested weakly.

Raiden glared at them. "A lot of good things would have to happen to balance out each kill I made with my hands. Regardless, I wish I didn't have this power. I don't need it. I can kill without it. I want to not have to obsessively wear gloves all the time for necessity. I want to not see life die under my fingertips when that's not my purpose. Either it needs to go, or it needs to be controlled."

Esme quickly threw Nami a glance, watching her reaction for the killing part. She wondered if his grandmother was able to piece together his former role as an assassin.

"Are you sure you can't control your abilities, Rai?" Dacio asked. "I know we've tried to deal with this together before, but neither of us knew what we were doing. We were stumbling in the dark."

"I *have* tried. It never fails," he snapped and then drew back, turning toward Esme. "Well, it only failed once."

Although Esme realized what he was referring to, Dacio didn't, so their entire body stiffened as they seemingly tried to piece the information together.

"What are you talking about?" they asked slowly. When he looked away, they pressed on the topic with a warning in their voice. "Rai..."

His jaw clenched and he started fidgeting slightly before giving her another glance. "Esme happens to be immune."

"What?" Dacio barked immediately, flinching against her. "How?"

A guilty look crossed his face. "There was an incident."

"It's fine, Daci," Esme soothed, interjecting quickly and reaching out to touch their arm. "I startled him from his sleep and we both found out that nothing happens to me if I touch his hand."

"Heavens," Nami murmured quietly as Dacio started fuming. Esme was just glad all of the villagers had left earlier and weren't witnessing what was about to turn ugly.

"That... that... why didn't you mention any of this? She could have died!" they exclaimed, gesticulating vividly and shrugging off her hand.

Raiden rose to his feet. "She's still here. Isn't she?" His voice was strained.

"I suppose! But that could have ended much differently, and that's why you need to learn how to control it, and I do think you are able to do so," Dacio insisted, their voice raised a higher pitch as they stood up.

"I don't. I can't," he replied. His entire body language appeared locked up, and she could almost see the walls he was building around him.

"Well, something different happened with Esme, so there must be some way to—"

"Maybe it was because she had already died before!" he snapped, making Esme shift uncomfortably. "Maybe my death touch or magic or whatever it is only works once because it can't kill a person twice."

Before she could even process the last statement properly, Dacio was ready with their counter, striking back with their words and frustration. "You are *afraid* of yourself," they claimed. "Properly wielding magic requires both external and internal control, and your aura is constantly turbulent. You don't even trust yourself. How would you trust magic?"

Now Raiden was baring his teeth at them, like a cornered animal. "You used your aura-reading on me?"

Esme froze at the harsh tone, her eyes widened.

"I don't need to use my magic to see it. Trust me, you are not and have never been very subtle with your fears, even if I wasn't trained to glean these things," Dacio said, breathing heavily. After another pant, they took a step back and tried to lower the temperature. "Rai, I'm just trying to see if there's a way to address your power. I know how much it torments you."

The atmosphere had deteriorated enough for Raiden to signal he was done with this conversation. Stiffly, he faced Nami, bowed his head slightly, and said, "Thank you for your answers."

Without saying anything else to Esme or Dacio, he turned around and disappeared back into the arms of the darkness.

This time, Dacio didn't follow him.

CHAPTER 15

Raiden still hadn't returned by the morning and Esme was worried, even though Dacio insisted he needed time to reflect on everything he had learned last night. The best thing they could both do for him would be to find the sword and give him some breathing room.

Dacio led her along the pink beaches under the morning sun, its peaceful rays putting her at ease with the tropical sea breeze rustling through her flowing clothes and the crisp scent of salt and flowers in the air. The reflection of the sun on the water nearly blinded her as much as the reflection of the rays of light on her golden snake armlet or Dacio's pendant.

Although they were both going to search for the sword while Nami wrapped up some village dispute, Esme couldn't help but get distracted by her surroundings. The waters around the isles were so clear she could see the rocks and sands of the seafloor and the small creatures swimming around. A patch of orange coral added more color to the brilliant blue-green hues of the water, and she could even see some hexapods lurking near the intersection of the coral and rock. The small creature with six tentacles reminded her of The Six.

"Why did you end up joining The Six?" Esme asked. She still wasn't sure what the job entailed. Sneaking around in the darkness and eavesdropping on people?

Dacio paused mid-step before easily sliding back into their natural languid gait. "Originally, I wanted to be a mage scholar, but I had to stay home to help my family—although this included thieving on the side, to my parents' absolute dismay," they said with an embarrassed smile. "I wanted to join The Six as a thief because I could support my family by using my skills to steal from petty, squabbling nobles, but my memory was a valuable asset for espionage, so that's where I ended up."

She could only imagine how their parents felt about the idea of their child resorting to theft and espionage—probably upset.

"What was it like being a spy?" she asked.

"Well, the information-gathering wasn't bad. If anything, I felt more like a performer than anything, which was sometimes amusing. I also attended many decadent celebrations at the palace and met many people. Ultimately, I *was* sent to learn secrets and observe people for sensitive information in plain sight," they said before letting out a sad sigh. "However, I had to stay away from my family to protect them and my identity, and it was tiring to wear many masks that ill-fit me."

"That must have felt isolating," she murmured before turning her head to look at them and the way the light seemed to bronze their skin. "Were you working when we first met?"

"Yes," they admitted, rubbing the side of their neck. "When you and your mother started living at the palace, I was directed to see how much of a threat you were. This was before the former princess was kidnapped and you were new to court politics, so Jianli didn't initially think of you as too much of a threat. He never completely dropped his guard, but it was relaxed enough where things were somewhat normal."

"What was considered normal?" she asked, trying to imagine her own past life.

What a strange concept, having lived in the imperial palace for some time. From what Dacio had told her yesterday, she had continued her magic studies there too, so perhaps it was similar to what she remembered from childhood with the added backdrop of political intrigue. She could easily imagine Dacio flitting around in the palace as a spy in plain sight with their charming and adaptable personality. They had said their memory was their most valuable asset, yet she would argue that their ability to easily converse with and understand people was perhaps why they would've made a great spy.

"Well, Jianli would go on military campaigns to expand the territory and cement his own renown, so he wasn't always at the palace. The nobles would scheme amongst themselves, even seeking help from The Six sometimes, and try to curry favor from the emperor and empress. I'd keep track of them and report any concerning details to Jianli, but otherwise I spent my time with you, practicing magic, healing some of the patients in the royal clinic, and actually being myself. Not a spy, not a false friend, but myself," Dacio said, fondly looking back at her with their eyes framed by long, black eyelashes—ones enviously longer than her own.

The last part didn't sound so bad. It reminded her of their life in Atoyatlan given their dedication to beneficial applications of spirit magic. However, she could imagine that the overwhelming burden of keeping secrets must have crushed Dacio despite their former occupation and talent to adapting to people and situations.

"Did I know you were a spy back then?" she asked, feeling the breeze on her face and her long hair flowing behind her.

"Yes," they said, tilting their head to the side. "Before, I used to tell you everything, which, now that I think about it, had been a big risk to take as a spy since you could have easily taken advantage of that information..."

Esme's heart throbbed slightly and she could feel the air between them grow awkward. What would her life and Dacio's life have looked like in Atoyatlan had she known the truth? She found herself missing the closeness they must have had in the past.

"Oh, we're here," Dacio said.

She blinked and noticed they had arrived at the edge of a small cove. The beach was short; she imagined that at night, the water would rise up high enough to reach the feet of the rocky cliffs. Seaweed and large rocks sprawled across the pink sand.

"You threw the sword somewhere around here?" she asked. With Dacio's perfect visual memory, she didn't doubt they had found the correct place. The retrieval of the sword was more dependent on whether or not it had been disturbed from its last known location.

They sighed. "Yes, I threw it in the water."

Her head turned toward the sea, and she went on her tiptoes to peer through the crystal-clear waters for any sign of a sword. "How far did you throw it?"

Dacio winced, telling her all she needed to know. She wouldn't end up fetching the sword, as she never learned how to swim in her memories. Briefly, she wondered if she had learned to swim in Yin City given it was near both a large lake and the Sapphire Sea.

"I'm going to check that it's still here while Nami is busy so it's not futile to bring her over and help us out," they said.

Esme nodded. "Okay, do you need me to help with anything?"

"Emotional support if you're so generous." They winked playfully. "But you can watch over my body as I spirit-walk into the water. Defend me from any diving birds."

The last sentence shattered the tense air with familiarity, making her laugh. Even though she and Dacio had many issues to resolve together, she had faith they would always be on her side. "Oh no, the terrible birds. Fear not, I will protect you," she said, grinning and earning a pout.

They both knelt down into a sitting position on the warm, coarse sand. Dacio sat in front, back to her. Since she had seen them spirit-walk before, she guessed they were probably closing their eyes to concentrate and focus their energy. A silver-white light started glowing along their outline—a sign of their magic. After a few seconds, they slumped back into Esme's waiting arms. They were now spirit-walking, even though she couldn't see where their spirit was.

Although Dacio only mentioned protection from birds, she was also there to make sure they had a tether back to their body. From what she was told, spirit-walking was when a mage's living spirit walked through the spirit realm, and in this case, it would allow Dacio to walk through water without needing to breathe. However, it was dangerous for a mage to wander the other realm for too long, else they might get lost.

The situation reminded her of her own stumble into the spirit realm. *Did that count as spirit-walking?* Maybe not, given that she must have stayed in her own body because Raiden couldn't find her. She would have to ask how spirit-walking felt when Dacio returned. The air around her was potently infused with spirit magic, and she wondered if it was solely because Dacio was using their magic or if the island itself really was blessed by its patron deity.

Keeping her eyes on Dacio, she gently—sadly—brushed their hair back from their face and observed their peaceful, relaxed expression. If it weren't for the glow of magic hovering over their entire body, they would have looked like they were sleeping. Suddenly, their eyes opened and they took a deep breath, startling her. They blinked a few times and realized that their head was resting on her lap. The color on their cheeks deepened slightly, and they quickly jolted up, narrowly missing the bottom of her chin on their way up into a sitting position.

"Is the sword still there?" Esme asked, her chest feeling a little more restrictive than normal. Was she too optimistic to hope that the mission would be so simple?

"Thank the deities, yes. It's still there, and surprisingly not rusty. Must be the magic," they answered, to her relief. "But it is resting on the seafloor, farther down than I can swim comfortably, so Nami will still be needed."

"That's good," she said. "By the way, what is it like spirit-walking? What did the spirit realm look like for you?" Would it be similar to her experience, whatever it was?

Dacio hummed thoughtfully. "The spirit realm looks much like this world, like a reflection, but in shades of gray. Are you asking because of what happened when you first crossed through the portal?"

She nodded before questions poured out of her. "Did your body have color when you were over there? Can you feel anything?"

"I imagine spirit-walking is like how a spirit would traverse through the realm—no color, no physical feeling."

Esme frowned. She definitely hadn't spirit walked then because she had some color and had felt heat from her own magic. It must have simply been her entire body stumbling into the spirit realm. Perhaps the barriers between realms were just weaker near portals, unless that had perhaps been a manifestation of another power she had brought back from death.

"Shall we head back?" Dacio asked.

Still thinking about her mysterious abilities, Esme declined. "I want to test my powers out, but I also want to see Nami use her magic, so I'll stay in the cove."

A faint aura of disappointment hovered over Dacio and then disappeared. "I'll be back soon. If you do end up leaving the cove and happen to get lost, at least it's a small island and you can just follow the coastline back to the village."

"Don't worry. I'll stay near here," she said, nodding and waving them off.

They gave her one last look and headed back to the village, leaving her to her own devices.

Esme tilted her face up to the sky, closing her eyes and soaking in the sun, the natural representation of Tayanna, the deity of fire. The sheer heat and light offered her enough to use fire magic, even with the large body of water near her. However, her fire magic wasn't what she wanted to test out. Upon reopening her eyes, she realized there wasn't much shade on the shallow beach to test her shadow magic.

With this much light around, she could test out the limits of her powers. Given her knowledge of magic in general, a little inspiration could go a long way. The only thing left was to simply try.

She focused her energy and thoughts on the cool, welcoming darkness awaiting her, even one as small as the shadow at the edge of the tall rock formation in the middle of the beach or the one she cast at her own feet. Recalling the last few times she shadow-warped, she let the cool magic wash through her and dismantle her physical form. Wind rushed against her as she transported herself to the rock.

"That's promising," Esme said to herself. "Now, what else can I do?" Could she manipulate shadows like she could manipulate fire and heat?

Leaning against the rock, she looked down at the shadow at her feet. Applying her knowledge of magic, she reached her hand down and tried to treat it like manipulating fire. When she moved her hand to the side, she expected and hoped the shadow would follow the motion, but nothing happened. Frowning, she tried again, thinking of bending the light, but again, the shade failed to move.

Esme sighed. *Well, it was worth a try.* Perhaps manipulation of existing shadows wasn't in the arsenal of abilities she'd managed to pick up. It was already fortunate that she had more magical abilities than other mages—if she ignored the part where she had to die in order to get additional powers. Still, the uniqueness was nice and exciting.

She sat down and leaned back against the rock. If she couldn't manipulate shadows, could she create them? Holding her palm up, she tried to envision conjuring up a shadow version of a fireball. When she saw a small wisp of darkness thread thorough her fingers, her heart started to race in excitement and she tried to amplify it, to no avail. She didn't let that deter her. It was midday after all and the sun was strong enough to heat the top of her black hair.

The moving darkness in her palm mesmerized her. What could she do with this? Could she wrap herself in darkness?

Excitement fueling her, Esme thought about her primary magic. Yesterday, Dacio had said she had started to master lightning. Since that had been before her death, she must have only relied on her fire and spirit magic, and between the two areas, lightning seemed to better fit under the fire realm. But how had she done it? From what she could remember, she had never accidentally created lightning before and neither had she seen any other mage do it. Maybe it was like her shadow magic, where she never tried because she hadn't thought of it as a possibility.

This time, she faced her palm toward the cliff, her fingers spread apart stiffly. The heat from the sun made it exponentially easier for her to centralize her magic and generate heat through her body. As she thought of lightning and storms and ozone, warmth traveled from her core up her arms and out her fingertips—as a blast of fire, not lightning. Esme frowned and tried again, creating another spout of flames.

She groaned loudly. "Why can't I remember?" she huffed to herself, growing upset over both her inability to do what she had been able to do before and also over her disconnection to her past.

Everything felt like two halves, separated by a chasm of time and pain. She wished she knew, remembered, so she could feel whole. She wished she *belonged* somewhere, completely, as herself. Back in Atonaco, she was always reminded of how her internalization of the people around her wasn't completely reflected in her image. Close, but not close enough.

Even the intense aura of spirit magic from the island wasn't enough to placate her.

"Control comes from understanding," a deep voice spoke from beside her.

Esme squeaked and threw herself away from the voice. A beautiful figure stood beside the rock, calmly and serenely looking down at her.

"By the stars, you surprised me." She laughed nervously before suddenly processing what they had said. "Pardon me?"

She took a closer look at the stranger who had long, black hair gliding down his back and eyes that were both colorless and somehow every color at once. He wore a loose pearlescent robe, revealing his smooth, pale chest. But the aspect she noticed most was the pure magical power radiating from him, which seemed familiar and calming.

Esme tilted her head and furrowed her eyebrows, trying desperately to recall why the energy seemed so familiar. It was the same peaceful energy she felt when she looked up at the moon in the middle of the night, the same mysterious energy she had felt when she crossed into the spirit realm, and it was stronger than what she had been sensing earlier throughout the island.

Suddenly, she knew who this was. If her guess was right, she was literally in the presence of a deity.

"You're Jing. Aren't you?" she asked. When he—*they*—nodded, she dipped her head in respect and tried to keep her body from trembling.

Internally, she screamed. *Stars above, stars above, stars above.* The deities truly existed! And one stood in front of her! Not that she necessarily doubted their existence, but it was something completely different to meet them in person while still alive. Was she even alive? How was she supposed to act in front of a deity? *How in the nine hells did this happen?*

"At ease, Esme," they said, their voice in a slightly higher and softer pitch. "You should be proud of your astuteness. Now, look at me, little one."

When she looked up again, Jing's form changed back to the one she had seen before in the spirit realm, with softer features and somehow the same outline as their previous presentation. Esme couldn't find the courage to keep looking directly into the deity's eyes. That seemed almost too bold, maybe even disrespectful.

"I'm honored to be in your presence, but if I may ask frankly, why are you here?" she blurted out, wincing after the question left her lips. She was talking to the literal spirit deity, deity of life and death—again.

"It is finally time for us to talk," the deity proclaimed.

CHAPTER 16

Nervous sweat started to prickle at the back of her neck as Esme pressed her lips tightly together and continued panicking on the inside. The spirit deity wanted to talk to *her?* About what?

"Breathe," Jing ordered softly.

The magic-infused air wrapped around her like a blanket and almost felt as if she were using her healing magic. Usually someone telling her to calm down didn't work, but a deity had more power to actually help her. After her heart rate slowed, Esme asked, "What are we discussing?"

"The fate of the mortal realm," the deity said, cocking their head.

Her mind all but rejected Jing's statement, even as she nodded her head. *Of course.* Why would talking with a deity involve trivial matters? Unless they'd found the wrong person?

The corner of Jing's lips lifted up in amusement. "You doubt me."

"No!" she vehemently disagreed, her eyes widening in distress. She cleared her throat to give herself a chance to regain her composure. "I just think a little context would be helpful."

"Come with me," Jing said, holding out their hand to her.

"Where are we going?" she asked, reaching up tentatively and clasping their cool hand.

Immediately, the scenery changed. It took her a few seconds to realize she was back at the Wei imperial palace, immersed in the presence of gaudy gold decorations. However, unlike last time, many people stood in the expansive room, all of them wearing formal outfits and holding fans in their hands. All of them were frozen.

"What in the heavens?" Esme whispered. She almost felt dizzy from the sheer shock of her current location. What would everyone else in the room think with her showing up from nowhere holding a deity's hand once they unfroze?

"This is but a shadow of a memory," Jing said, releasing her hand and untethering her to any potential support in this strange situation. "Yours, on the day of your death."

Startled, Esme whipped her head to look back at the deity by her side. So Raiden's claim *was* true. She really had died. The small flicker of hope that had somehow subsisted within her died out.

The only consolation at this point was that she could finally recover some of her memories. This was the history she had known was there but had never been able to see, touch, or completely connect with. Jing was showing her this memory for a reason, so she looked back at the scene and was unnerved upon spotting herself standing near the edges of the room, beyond the row of tables with teapots and teacups on them.

The other Esme had her dark hair neatly half-tied up in a braided bun with flower pins ornamented throughout, the rest of her hair flowing elegantly behind her shoulders. Her pale purple robes with cloud patterns on the skirt were also formal and looked expensive, along with some of the jewelry she wore. However, in such a grand and formal setting while wearing a decadent outfit, the disdain was clear on her past self's face through her tight expression.

By the stars, are my feelings that transparent?

Shivers crawled down her entire body, a foreboding sense insidiously striking at her heart. She quickly looked around to see if anything poisonous was nearby, as Dacio had insisted that she had been poisoned, but the only viable option was the tea everyone seemed to be served. Even if the tea was poisoned, her past self wasn't holding anything in her hands.

"Go to her, and you will see," Jing instructed softly into her ear, making her shiver.

As if hypnotized, Esme walked over to her past self, weaving through the sea of statues until she arrived in front of herself like a haunted reflection in the mirror. She reached out for her shoulder and was promptly sucked into the vortex of time.

Esme was in a horrible mood. The fight she had with Dacio lingered bitterly at the back of her mind, with her most recent encounter only sparking the memories. Had she really let herself be changed by the imperial palace over the years? Was *she going too far?*

Not wanting to spend more time on personal grievances, Esme scanned the crowd, only stopping when she noticed a familiar man in military robes parading over to her—her younger cousin, Jianli. He wore an insufferable smile on his face, one that always seemed to boil her blood, but never enough for her to act upon it in public. Of course he would be here, *she grumbled to herself. No doubt he would miss discussions over imperial planning.*

"What do you want, Jianli?" she asked in a bored voice when he came within hearing distance.

The prince stood by her, back to the wall and face toward the center of the room, a pleasant and regal smile on his face, even though his imperial standing was shaky. "I just wanted to congratulate you on your... victory from the other day. I wanted to let you experience some success for once, and since I had many opportunities through battle, I worked on my restraint instead," he said without breaking his smile or even looking at her.

"Of course you were," she entertained, although she was certain both of them knew that she had better demonstrated her strength. She had her taste of power, of victory, and they both knew it.

Her indifference must have set him off because he let out a small scowl. "Mingyue," he said, referring to her Wei name, the one she used in the palace and with her mother's family. "You realize that despite your win, you still cannot deprive me of my rightful place. Did you think you could replace my spot with the princess gone? Your command of the language is not remotely close to sufficient and neither is your knowledge of the intricacies that make up the Wei empire. Can you even consider yourself Wei? Why would the people accept a foreign ruler?"

Esme hated how much his words stung. It was already isolating to wonder about that internally, but to be reminded externally felt miserable. Ever since she and her mother arrived in the Wei empire, it had been an uphill hike. She had to catch up on a lot of cultural learning she had failed to appreciate as a child and was still working on years later. More frustratingly, once she came to the palace, she had to learn about the politics, the nobles, the scholars, the history—everything. She still had more to learn, and nothing she did seemed enough. No matter how much she improved, she was still stuck behind a glass wall that everyone else could see but she could only feel.

"This is my home too. I belong here just as much as you," Esme gritted out with a fake smile. At this point, half of her living memories had been spent here in the Wei empire, with the other half from her childhood in Atonaco. She had a home here too. Her family, her friends, her mentor. Her lover. All of them here too, all who called Yin City their homes as well.

"That is up for others to decide," he said.

She wasn't going to quietly take his words.

"Are you really so insecure of your own power and standing that you have to use words to intimidate me?" she asked coolly, sneakily stealing a glance at his expression while trying to act as if he didn't even deserve to be looked at. The prince's left eye twitched, making her feel smug. "Careful, cousin, or they might sniff out your weakness."

How is that for "insufficient command" of the language?

"You demon girl," he hissed and carefully schooled his face back into that of a pleasant celebration host. The light reflected against his purple-red necklace, making it seem like fire was trapped inside. "I would be more concerned about myself, if I were you. You are not the only one capable of making deals."

Esme narrowed her eyes at him. "What are you talking about?" Did he know?

"Please," he scoffed quietly. "Don't feign ignorance. I heard you talking to that creature. Imagine my surprise when I heard my cousin also trying to find the Golden Peaches and dethrone the emperor. You are more ambitious that I thought. In any other situation, I might finally view you like an older sister like everyone tells me I should, but as you are aware, only one of us can be on that throne."

Underneath her sleeves, her fingers tightened and curled into her skirt. Also? Did that mean he was seeking to do something similar? Nevertheless, she was certain their reasons were different. "I think you must have misinterpreted what you heard," she said, deeply aware of the moving people around them, none of whom were close enough to catch their quiet conversation in the large space.

Even if she didn't remember her exact wording, she was certain she had not wished for the emperor to be dethroned, only for better leadership to arise. Furthermore, it had simply been her musing aloud. Neither had she agreed to the deal—this one, at least.

However, if Jianli was talking to the same creature, that could only have ominous and dangerous implications, as he himself was already powerful and destructive enough to conquer the desertlands at a young age. Furthermore, his legion of spies was large and quite influential for a mere prince. What kind of additional power or information was he looking for?

"Regardless, I am here to make you a deal," he said with a small wave of his hand, his wide sleeves swishing along.

"I am not interested," she replied, keeping her chin up.

A quick flash of annoyance manifested in his eyes, but otherwise Jianli didn't look surprised by the rejection. His cold look of determination gave her chills.

"Your loss, Jin Mingyue," the prince remarked. "I offered a way for both of us to have a conversation, but alas, I suppose I must take matters into my own hands."

She froze. From all the stories Dacio had told her, this is what he did best. This was no subtle threat. Jin Jianli never went for his target directly. No, he knew where people's pressure points were, and it was always someone or something other than his target. And she had two major people he could use as collateral damage—her mother and Dacio.

"If you hurt anyone I care about, I will burn you to the ground," she threatened quietly. Lightning would be too quick, too much of a mercy for him if he decided to pursue that indirect path.

Jianli threw his head back and laughed like she had told him a joke. It was loud enough to draw nearby nobles' attention. The edges of his lips curled up, as if he was pleased by the sudden attention before he twisted his expression into one of concern. The prince darted forward, pressing the back of his hand against her forehead, to which Esme stumbled back in surprise.

"Ah, Mingyue, you don't look so well," Jianli said loudly, attracting more eyes.

Esme stepped back and resisted the urge to swat his hand away—or worse. Suddenly, heat drained from her face, the abrupt change in temperature making her dizzy. However, the changes didn't stop there as her chest started to tighten as well. She threw her cousin a half-confused glare.

"Lady Jin, are you okay?" voices asked from around her, echoing in her ears like a bat in an empty chamber.

She blinked quickly, trying to reorient herself.

"Look how concerned Prince Jin is over Lady Jin," someone whispered in the background of the clamor.

"Perhaps Lady Jin is developing the same illness as her mother."

"Lord Jin might be better suited for the throne."

More and more sounds pounded at her head, words from the judges of her life, from the spectators, and she knew she needed to leave.

"Please excuse me," Esme gritted out, storming away from the prince and the rest of the nobles. The room was suffocating her.

Although entering the hallway should have been calming through the lack of crowds and larger space, the cool air failed to ease any of her worries. She quickly walked through the hall, her breaths loud and quick. Was she having a fit of panic? Her chest seemed tighter than usual and her mind was cluttered to a point where it hurt. Just as she turned around the corner, she sagged against the wall for support.

"Mingyue?" a familiar voice called out.

Her eyes looked up at the approaching person. Even before she saw Dacio with their long, flowing black hair and stiff, formal clothing, she recognized them by the sound of their voice alone. Briefly, she wondered if they had been assigned to work during the celebration, but a sudden sharp pain interrupted her.

"I don't feel so well," she said, one hand against the wall and the other reaching out toward Dacio. "Jianli, he…"

Dacio raced over and got there just in time to catch her as she fell forward. She sagged against them as they eased her onto the floor.

"Mingyue?" they cried out, a desperate look on their face. "Esme!"

Her eyes squeezed shut, trying to will the pain away. When she started gasping for air and pawing at her throat, she felt Dacio's hand gently hovering over hers. Soon, soft, calming magic radiated from them and through her, ameliorating her symptoms. Their familiar healing magic should have helped with her fit of panic, and while she did stop flailing, something was still wrong.

"It's okay, love," they said tightly. "Just listen to my voice okay? You're going to be all right."

Liquid traveled down her face from her eyes, her vision blurred red, and that was when she knew this was not from anxiety. What in the nine hells was happening? *Soon, something wet began leaking from her nose, and from the smell of metal, she knew it was blood. Everything looked red, smelled red, tasted red.*

"Da—" she gurgled, trying to open her eyes again. Am I dying? I still have so much to do and say…

She could feel Dacio trembling underneath her. "I'm sorry. I know. Just wait a little longer for me," they pleaded, moving their hand from her throat to her face, caressing it and allowing their magic to flow through her once again.

White pain filled her body instead, striking everywhere at once, so intensely that she almost didn't hurt anymore—a hidden mercy, perhaps given by the deities.

Strength sapped from her body, and when she couldn't hold her head up anymore, she let it roll back into Dacio's arms. Her vision was starting to go dark—no, light? Anything was better than red.

I'm glad Dacio is here. I wish I could have seen my mother again. Maybe father is waiting for me…

"No," Dacio whispered. "No, no, no. No!" Their whispers turned into distant agonizing cries, slowly fading away like an echo in the distance. Just barely, like a sigh in the wind, she could feel something wet land on her face and she could hear choking sounds.

And quietly, painfully, she drifted away, thinking of hummingbirds flying under the sun.

CHAPTER 17

A touch on her shoulder wrenched her out of the memory, the walls of the palace disappearing and transforming into wisps of clouds until all that was left was darkness. Gasping, Esme felt like the floor had fallen from beneath her. She could still feel the blood on her face, dripping from her eyes, and she wasn't sure if she wanted this memory anymore to haunt her every time she closed her eyes. It was hard to breathe.

She wished she could wash that entire experience out of her body.

"Why did you show me this?" Esme croaked to the ethereal deity, clutching at her throbbing chest. "What does this have to do with the fate of the mortal realm?"

The deity cocked their head, thin long hair acting as a midnight curtain blending in the background. Before they answered, she recalled Jianli mentioning the Golden Peaches, the famed peaches of immortality that supposedly grew somewhere deep in the Thunder Forests. They were legend, of course, as no one had ever stumbled upon the Immortal Springs where they grew, but perhaps they weren't so far from reality as she had once thought.

"We must start at the very beginning, eons ago, when the great primordial evil arose, its purpose to destroy all life," Jing started, sounding like a priest or priestess telling a story. "Since its inception, we deities have been battling this beast to keep it in check. However, every thousand years of every world cycle, the primordial evil revitalizes its strength to throw the mortal realm out of balance. If not stopped or corrected, we deities have no choice but to begin another cycle afresh and cut off one of its limbs."

Esme had heard of this story before. Every Atonacan child learned it in school, and it was commonly retold in the temple to remind mortals of what the deities did for them in the cosmos and to honor their continuous sacrifice.

"The destabilization has already begun for this cycle and is near its crest. Unless you can stop Jin Jianli from completing his plan, we will need to step in," Jing said, causing her to shiver.

Gulping, she asked, "How am I supposed to stop this primordial evil in the mortal realm? I'm just a mortal. Why can't the deities do anything about that? You are all more powerful than even the most powerful mortal mage. Are you not?"

They nodded gracefully and closed their eyes, hiding the iridescent colors of their irises. "It is not so simple. Our power is magnified in your realm, and should we make even the slightest misstep, we might destroy your realm. As it stands now, our power can leak through and cause catastrophic natural disasters, and the barriers between our realm are weaker close to your Spirit Festival. Even if we were able to interfere, we would tip the balance too far in another way, like creating a typhoon to water a single plant. Furthermore, my siblings and I are battling the primordial evil in the cosmos; the other realms must also be defended. We must have a mortal champion in the mortal realm."

The hair on the back of her neck stood up, thinking of the deities' fearsome powers inundating the world. Last time that happened, the world was supposedly recreated, with Jing forming the Moonstone Mountains from the wreckage of the destroyed moons, and the combination of Tayanna and Zoraya together using the wreckage of the nine suns and igniting magma from the sea floor to form continents and volcanoes. That had been the start of the current world cycle.

Although she understood why the deities might be hesitant to step in without destroying the realm, she still wasn't sure what role they expected her to have. "What exactly is the emperor's plan? What am I supposed to do?" she asked.

The deity waved their hand and changed the scenery once more, the darkness morphing into a familiar jungle. Esme looked around in the deep greens of the Thunder Forests, droplets of water covering the tops of large, sloping leaves, and a fresh scent of nature inundating the air. This felt too real to be a dream, with the humidity washing over her and even the chittering of animals in the background, but she still didn't think she was actually in the Thunder Forests.

Jing started walking, so she darted after them, walking over the vines on the ground and jumping over a large slithering, molting snake. Soon, they stopped in front of a large spring with crystalline water surrounded by spiky trees with butterflies and peaches on them. Her stomach tightened in anticipation.

"Although his goals are for the mortal realm, they will undoubtedly involve the spirit realm too, attempting to merge everything in one. He craves for immortality in a way we cannot extend to mortals. These peaches are not meant for mortal consumption, and that is why they are in the spirit realm, guarded heavily by the minor deities," they said, walking closer to the tree with thorns in its trunk and reaching up to touch the fruit.

Stars above, Esme thought. Like most other Atonacan and Wei people, she was pious but even this pushed the limits of mortal understanding. Studying and believing was a whole different beast than trying to fix something on a cosmic scale.

"I might have magic, but I'm still only mortal," Esme said, one tone away from sounding like she was protesting. She carefully walked deeper into the gardens.

"That is why you must deal with the mortal aspects before they spiral into a situation where we must step in; the primordial evil has yet to cement its hold here. I would hate to begin a new cycle when the current trajectory has much potential. Do not let Jianli get the Sword of Realms," Jing ordered.

Esme froze. Sword of Realms? Was that the sword Dacio had been threatened to retrieve? The one where if they didn't bring back to Jianli, Raiden would die? *Given all of the clues, likely.*

"What would happen if Jianli were to get this sword?" she asked. "And why didn't you or another deity just take or destroy it while it was out of his possession?"

The deity sighed gently. "The Sword of Realms was a weapon that Zoraya and I created together to battle the primordial evil and try to banish it to one of the nine realms of hell. Last cycle, however, it was corrupted by the evil itself and not only can slice the barriers between all realms, but also is now untouchable to me and the other deities, lest we risk strengthening its power."

Her heart sank. A realm-splitting sword. No wonder it was dangerous for Jianli to get ahold of it, particularly if he wanted to use it to access the Golden Peaches and possibly for another reason. With the memory she just experienced, Jianli seemed power-hungry and glory-seeking, so he could abuse the power of the sword in plenty of ways. After all, within the last two years, the Wei empire had unsuccessfully attempted to invade Atonaco through the mountains, and her own father had perished on the battlefield from the previous emperor's first attempt more than ten years ago.

However, they still had that issue about Raiden. The sword was dangerous in Jianli's possession, but Raiden's life was in the palm of the emperor's hand. Why did she have to make this decision?

"Why me? Why was I chosen for this mission?" she asked, her voice wavering under the burden of the entire realm. Even the peace from the gardens—the Immortal Springs—wasn't enough to appease her nerves.

"Timing, primarily; the emperor's death was the start of the catalyst this cycle. Furthermore, your body was being taken care of while you were considering our agreement to serve a life's debt—return to the mortal realm with a fragment of my power within you in exchange for losing your memories and serving us when the time came. Had you rejected, we would have chosen another," they answered.

"Why wasn't I given instructions when I woke up then?"

"The world does not just tip out of balance suddenly," the deity answered patiently. "It is a slow, painful descent into instability, chipping away small pieces that seem like nothing. You needed to heal first; death is traumatic, as are both birth and rebirth. But you have already activated my gift, which specialized for your greatest need, and the time to wait is over. The opportunity is now here. I have taken a short reprieve to issue you a directive and to allow you one memory for you to understand and learn from."

"What does that even mean?" Esme asked, starting to get warm from frustration. If all deities were this cryptic, no wonder both oracle bones and divinations from priests were so vague.

A butterfly flew toward the spirit deity, to which they lifted their hand and allowed it to land on their palm. Their robes brightened to match the black and white patterns of the butterfly's wings. "I am afraid I must leave. Tayanna and the others await me," they murmured.

Without another word, Jing stepped forward and pressed their cool, free palm against Esme's forehead, sending her back a step and making her blink at the movement.

When her eyes reopened, Esme was back on the bright beach, somehow sitting on the pink sand again with Dacio looking down at her from where she would have expected Jing to be.

"Are you okay?" Dacio asked, extending a hand down for her to take. "I felt strong energy just a few moments ago. I hope you didn't push yourself too hard."

Esme blinked a few more times and then reached for their hand, letting them pull her up to her feet.

Was she okay? Had she been dreaming? Her mind felt like it was racing through quicksand. Deities, death, duties—all a whiplash, something that would be too specific for even her wildest dreams to create.

Now that Dacio was in front of her, she couldn't help but think of when they had shown up in the fragment of memory that she had seen, particularly seeing Dacio with long black hair and more formal clothes and feeling them cradling her body in their arms while trying to heal her. They had called her *love*—something they had not called her within the last two years.

Her face went hot, and not from the return of the intense sun.

"Where is this object again?" Nami's voice called out from behind Dacio, making both of them turn their heads to look at the old woman. Still flustered from everything, Esme had to take a few seconds to process what was happening, remembering that Dacio had left to accompany Nami over to fetch the sword. How long had that dream lasted?

Dacio released her hand and turned toward the village matriarch.

"Of course, I can point out the direction and distance," they said, walking toward the blue waters.

Esme slowly followed along, disoriented. Everything seemed slightly muffled and her mind was still piecing together everything she had just learned. She had to tell someone, but her tongue wasn't working.

Once Dacio had pointed out the general location, Nami shook her hands and then raised her arms, facing her palms toward the sea and planting her bare feet firmly into the sands. Abruptly pushing both of her now faintly glowing hands out and to the side, the village matriarch parted the waters enough to make an alleyway for her to walk through. Some fish and hexapods dropped to the wet sand floor in her path before desperately trying to make their way back through the wall of water on either side.

It was enough of a show to pull her out of her disorientation and bring her back to the present, mortal time. Esme was awed by the way the water mage used her abilities, especially when enacted upon the edge of a large body of water. Still, her thoughts wandered back to the deities, wondering about how much destruction Kai, deity of water, could do with their powers.

Nami looked down at the sword and wrapped it in a bubble of water, which she moved alongside her on her return journey. The sea water slowly started to close back in behind her with every step she took until everything returned to normal and she was back on land. She left the sword resting on the sands of the shallow water.

"Here you go," she said, the sun gleaming against her brown skin and silver-black braids.

"Thank you." Dacio smiled at her before stepping into the gentle swash and picking up the sword to point at the sky. "I could've walked with you to grab it. You know?"

To her surprise, it looked like an Atonacan-styled macuahuitl, with its long flat metal and wooden board with serrated obsidian spikes along the trim. Even if Dacio hadn't talked about its magical aura and even without Jing explaining its function, she would have recognized the strong spirit it radiated. It reminded her of Dacio's magic, and now, of Jing's presence.

The Sword of Realms.

"This is it. We can now return to Yin City and be done with this whole thing," Dacio said, pointing it back down and dragging it along the sand. With its unique shape and lack of sheathe, they would need to be careful transporting it.

The mission loomed over her.

"Not before we get food into your stomachs," Nami sniffed. "No more journeying until you are all full. If you can still move after the meal, you haven't eaten enough. Better yet, rest for the remainder of today so you have energy for the trip back tomorrow."

Dacio laughed, like the sun breaking through a cloudy day. "That sounds like a promise," they said. "I think we have time for that. She of Eternal Hunger would also appreciate trying some of your delicious dishes for the first time."

Although she was happy they had agreed, she still couldn't stop the creeping anxiety lurking in the back of her mind. Still, her tongue felt frozen. Maybe eating would help her break the pressing grip over her, and so she quietly joined the other two in the walk back to the main village, evading the continuous worried glances that Dacio threw her way.

CHAPTER 18

"Did something happen at the beach?" Dacio asked, bringing Esme out of her head and back into reality. She paused mid-bite, still chewing on the spicy, roasted hexapod Dacio had helped Nami make. "You normally would have inhaled your food by now and your eyes are a bit dazed."

She frowned at the grass under the low porch and looked up. Visions from the past swarmed her thoughts, and she realized now that everyone else had already finished their meals and were now participating in weaving activities. "I think I might have met Jing and seen a memory from… *before*."

"Jing, as in the deity of life and death, the spirit deity—*that* Jing?" Dacio exclaimed quietly. "Why didn't you say anything?"

When she turned to face them, she could see an inkling of fear clouding over their eyes. "Because I'm still not sure if I imagined the entire thing or not. Maybe you could verify the memory."

"Anything," they affirmed, still seeming concerned.

Esme hesitated. What part should she even describe? Within the memory, the only part where Dacio had played a role was at the end. She could easily test their perfect visual memory.

"Was I wearing a purple dress the day I was poisoned?" she asked quietly.

Dacio took a sharp breath, like they had been punched in the gut. "Yes," they said in a strangled voice. "You saw *that* day? How much of it did you see?"

With their affirmation, she felt her heart race. More evidence that she didn't imagine the entire thing. Raising her knee up, she rubbed her thumb against the side of her palm and tapped her toes.

"I was at some event and Jianli was being an absolute tyrant to me, and then I felt sick and rushed into the hallway. You were there, and you held me and tried to heal me," Esme said, carefully staring into their pained eyes. They glanced away from her intense gaze, as if the truth hurt them as much as it hurt her.

So it *was* real.

"I also remember being upset with you about something that day, but my memory didn't span far back enough for me to know what," she added.

"We had an argument about how you were drifting away, further into the poison of court politics," Dacio said with their eyes closed. After a steady exhale, they opened their eyes. "There's one more thing I didn't mention before. I know you must be overwhelmed with everything you've learned over the last day, but I don't think I can hide it anymore. There's only so long I can wear this mask around you, and perhaps this might clarify the context of that memory."

Her heart pounded in anticipation, taken aback by how serious and pained they were. Nebulous cosmic problems could wait a few minutes, especially when they were giving her *those* eyes.

"Before your coma, we were... involved with each other. Romantically," Dacio cringed uncharacteristically before rushing through the next part. "Of course, I'm not expecting us to go back to that because first and foremost, we're friends, and second, circumstances are different now than they were before, so obviously feelings are different."

Their cheeks were flushed, but it couldn't have been from the sun as they were both sitting in the shade. Esme stilled and swallowed nervously, slowly.

Oh.

She was the lover?

Heavens.

Everything made more sense. The timing of events, Dacio's hesitant and pained behavior, their discomfort when she had brought up their lover, her fierce protectiveness in her memory. *Oh, oh, oh.* And that drawing in their house back in Atoyatlan—had that emotional drawing been of her? The sadness that hung over them like a shawl—had that always been there or was it because she had forgotten what their relationship had been like?

Even some of Raiden's behavior made sense. When he had thought he had killed her, he also worried about Dacio, perhaps not just because he knew the two of them were friends, but because she and Dacio had been former lovers.

In another universe, she would have been happy or awkward, but in this one, she was infiltrated with a deep, bitter cold sadness, one she couldn't warm up with her fire magic. Reality drowned her, and before she knew it, something wet slid down her cheeks. Stunned, she lifted her hand to wipe at her face and realized that she was crying.

"I'm sorry," Dacio apologized profusely, their eyes widened with panic and guilt. "Um, I—stars—I completely mishandled this."

She started crying harder now, hiccupping quietly and trying to cover her tense and crumpled face. *Lover.* Another thing she had lost, forgotten. Something they had lost. Her heart was tearing itself apart. *It hurts.*

"Oh, I shouldn't have said anything. Or should I have waited longer? Earlier?" they backtracked, and before they could panic anymore, she hiccupped an interruption.

"Wait," she said and shushed them to give her time to reorient herself. Sniffling, she used the back of her hands to wipe the tears off before more of the salt trickled into her mouth. "I wish I remembered—that I knew what we were like before. What might have happened if I hadn't forgotten. I'm devastated because although I can't remember, you do. You never forget anything. And you've stayed by my side this entire time, knowing this."

This, perhaps, was a secret she could forgive because it was so heavy and personal and painful.

Dacio gave her a sad, shaky smile in return. "I know."

Neither of them spoke for a while. Neither of them tried to say it was okay because neither of them *were* okay. Instead, she listened to the sounds of her own sniffling slowly fading away, the consistent crashing of waves against the beach in the distance, the high-pitched cries of birds in the clear skies, and the faint tendrils of casual conversations from the rest of the villagers.

Esme closed her eyes and breathed in through her nose. *In. Out. In. Out.*

When she reopened her eyes, she was conflicted on how to proceed. The two of them should probably address their current and former relationship further, but she still had to tell them about what Jing had said. The problems of deities seemed conceptually easier to understand and tackle than those of mortals and love.

"Jing told me the sword can be used to slice the barrier between realms, and that the fate of the world depends on Jianli not getting ahold of the Sword of Realms," she said expressionlessly.

Dacio, who had been in the process of getting up to their feet, slipped onto their rear, landing on a lower step. "Oh, maybe I should have let you finish speaking." They laughed nervously. The shaky undertones and their frozen smile matched her initial reaction when she had found out. "What exactly did Jing say?"

"You believe me?"

"I've always known the deities are real, and I have always and will always believe you. Your claim also explains the exceptionally strong spiritual energy back at the cove," they explained and then gestured for her to discuss further.

She summarized what the deity had told her and carefully observed their sudden scowl as she mentioned the word immortality in the same sentence as Jianli.

"The last thing any realm needs is for Jianli to live forever. I too might consider restarting the cycle to prevent that from happening," Dacio muttered bitterly, standing up and walking into the sunlight with their hand threading through their black hair.

Esme nodded and followed them. "I think we should also let Raiden know. I don't suppose you've seen him recently?"

They shook their head. "Unfortunately not. We should split up and search for him. The island's small and safe enough where it shouldn't take too long," they said before pausing and dodging eye contact. "You probably need some space to think and process. Just know I'll be here if or when you want to talk."

"Thank you," she said softly, almost reaching out to them before reconsidering. Instead, she looked into their soft eyes, memorizing the way the sun lightened their irises into warm honey and trying to communicate the words she couldn't find.

Swiftly, she turned around and headed deeper into the dense maze of palm trees beyond the buildings. The blunt of the sun's rays struck the tops of the flat, broad tree tops, and she figured if she were a former assassin who wanted to be alone on a small inhabited island, deeper in the forest would be optimal.

Although she kept her eyes out for Raiden and called his name every once in a while, her thoughts kept going back to Dacio. Her former lover. How long had they known each other? How had that relationship started? How long had it lasted before she died? How would she have acted if their roles had been swapped? How much pain would she have been in if her lover forgot her?

Only the wind could answer her now.

"Raiden?" Esme called out again, looking over the tall spry shrubs masking a rocky area. She paused upon seeing a pair of dark boots sticking out from a small boulder. No villager would wear those black curved-toe boots, so she guessed it was Raiden.

She walked around the boulder and confirmed her suspicions. Sitting on the ground, gazing far into the trees, was Raiden. Although he didn't visibly react to her presence, she knew he was aware of her. Slowly, she approached and sat beside him, pulling her knees up and looking into the distance. With everything she had learned recently, she almost forgot that Raiden had had his own shock the previous night.

"How do you do it?" Raiden asked quietly, initiating the conversation to her surprise. She looked over to see the striking mixture of peace and anguish on his face.

"What do you mean?"

"How do you deal with not knowing your past? Of being so close yet so far?" he asked.

Esme looked down at her knees and intertwined her fingers. "Ah, yes, the ever-present question," she murmured. The same question had consistently reared its head since she left Yin City.

"I always wondered about my origins, and I've lived more than two decades of my life not knowing a single clue," Raiden continued. "Now that I know more, I feel more lost. If I had stayed just one day, what would my life have been like these last three years? What did I miss out on?"

His words struck close to home, echoing some of the discordant strings pulling her heart and mind in different directions. Since waking up, she had known she was missing something important. While there was the dull ache of not knowing the basics, knowing she had lost an important relationship had brought her to tears. So she understood, perhaps even too much.

"I still don't have half of my memories so I can't tell you what it's like across the bridge, but I do know that it helps having people who can share pieces of that past with you," Esme said softly. "Like parents or friends."

Raiden winced at her words. "People like me and Dacio, you mean."

"And Nami for you."

"But you at least know Dacio. Nami? She's a stranger to me. This place is unfamiliar. It's like half of me is unfamiliar. Acceptance had never been my goal because it was never an option," he spoke, words spilling from his mouth. Wind rustled the leaves nearby.

Esme had at least known there was an option, albeit one seemingly out of reach. She sometimes couldn't quite feel like she fit, because some parts of her aligned and others did not, because sometimes she wanted to fit and other times she didn't want to be constrained. Neither one thing or another, she floated untethered in the presence of storms. Had her past self ever figured this question out? Surely mastering lightning was harder than understanding oneself.

"Do you know that magic is all about focus and inner harmony? Understanding the flow of yourself and your energy?" she asked. "Self-reflection and self-acceptance are vital to become a great mage. The more aligned with yourself, the more powerful you become. But it's an on-going process."

"And for those of us without magic?"

She thought about the answer, her mind trailing back to all of the recent revelations. "You don't need magic to be powerful, and you don't need to be a mage to go through this process. I don't think we mortals ever resolve all our concerns. There will always be twists and turns, new experiences and information to reflect on and process. Perhaps you'll end up resolving something at the crux of your being and the center of any self-doubts."

The past kept returning to haunt everyone and throw her world off axis, but she had a feeling that when she got through this, she would come out stronger.

They sat there quietly for some time before Raiden said, "Dacio's told me something like this before, that when they finally discovered they were mez, it had been so freeing that they had unlocked their true potential. Something like inner fog transforming to blue, boundless skies. Their magic improved after that."

The mention of Dacio brought a smile to her lips. Although they occasionally experienced some internal conflicts, they truly were confident in the mez part of their personal identity. It was something so admirable and beautiful, both flexible and certain. *Boundless.*

"You know Dacio's worried about you. Right?" Esme asked.

"They're always worried about me. About you too," he said, looking down at his feet. "They hide it so well I sometimes forget. Just another scar from our past because one's weaknesses can be easily exploited." His fingers drifted up to his face, where the visible scars showed.

Although she knew where his statement was coming from, she hated the message it sent about having people to love and care about. "We shouldn't be reduced to being one another's weakness when we are also a source of strength," she affirmed.

However, she couldn't help but think of the tension among the three of them, given the secrets coming to light. Until all the important ones came out, the three of them weren't going to fully be able to support one another.

"Well, we were thinking of heading back to Yin City tomorrow. If you haven't eaten already, you should. I have important news to share with you, and you should have the energy to prepare yourself," Esme said, getting back up to her feet. "Come on. Let's go."

Raiden sighed and rose from the ground. "That doesn't sound ominous at all."

Taking the same path back, Esme led him into the burning brightness. She had to let her eyes adjust before continuing over to the common area. Among the villagers was Nami, who was smiling and chatting with another person before she spotted the two of them approaching. She immediately wrapped up her conversation and walked over to them. Given his height, Raiden could make anyone look small, but Nami looked especially small next to him.

"I've been looking for you," Nami said gently with a hesitant smile. "Please come and eat. There's still plenty of food left."

Esme looked at Raiden to watch his reaction. Foreign hope and yearning colored his face as he looked down at his grandmother. "I would love to."

CHAPTER 19

Nami couldn't stop fretting over the three of them. Esme's bag was filled to the brim with fruits and dried snacks for the trip back to Yin City, and the matriarch had spent the last half hour praying under the morning sun in the four cardinal directions and to all the major deities for their safe journey and good health. There was no doubt how much she cared about them, and Esme was glad she got to meet the woman who helped take care of her during her coma.

"Thank you for everything," Esme said, holding Nami's soft and warm hands in hers.

The old woman's face brightened even as she shook her head, releasing her hands and stepping back. "No need to be so polite, child. Kunhai will always welcome you with open arms. You are all a part of our community." The last sentence she spoke while facing Raiden, who stood stiffly as if he wasn't used to that kind of statement and warm attention.

Surprisingly, he stepped closer and looked down at his grandmother, saying, "I promise to come back and learn after everything in Yin City is settled."

His words had a visibly positive effect on Nami with some underlying tension easing, but there was still hesitation from both parties. Esme imagined the old woman would have liked to hug her grandson before sending them off, but the two of them were still unfamiliar with each other, and Raiden was also carrying the clunky Sword of Realms with one hand. Nevertheless, this was the brightest she had seen either of them since they found out about their relationship.

"I would love that," Nami said softly, this time looking at all three of them. "Don't keep me waiting too long."

Dacio ducked their head, and the three simultaneously thanked her once more before finally leaving the village of Kunhai. Since Esme was already wearing her warmer Wei robes, she could only feel the heat of the sun on her face as they made their way toward the portal. She was already missing the peaceful, sunny atmosphere of the isles and they hadn't even left. The mission ahead of them was too daunting, and after briefly recapping everything to Raiden, everyone seemed to feel the trepidation in the air.

At the center of it all was the obsidian-rimmed sword. In the center of the board were intricate drawings of the sun and moon, with patterns of wind and water made of metal etched throughout. Although Jing said they had made the sword with Zoraya, the metal deity, it was clear that all five major deities were represented somehow in the weapon.

As the master of weapons, Raiden was in charge of the supernatural sword. Every time Esme looked over at him, he was eyeing it like he was expecting it to bite him.

"You know, if I could stop him from getting his grubby hands on the weapon, it would be a noble way to die," he said nonchalantly, to which both Esme and Dacio glared with the heat of ten suns at him.

"*Or*, maybe instead of sacrificing Raiden to spite the emperor, we can try to find another metallomage to extract the pin," she suggested, raising an eyebrow.

"That's a much better plan than running away and letting Rai die," Dacio said, before sending him a sneaky, smarmy grin. "Besides, the last thing we want is bringing Rai to the palace and allowing him to accidentally commit regicide and destabilize the entire Wei empire."

"Hey," Raiden protested automatically in mock outrage with his free hand over his heart. "It wouldn't be an accident. Not with him, at least."

Dacio snorted while Esme felt the corner of her lips tilt upward. Unfortunately, the playful atmosphere disappeared in a blink when Raiden coughed and staggered in his step, his brows and lips pulled tightly. The smile dropped off Dacio's face.

"Is it the pin?" they asked, stepping closer to him with spirit magic already called to their fingertips. Although they seemed prepared to alleviate Raiden's pain, Esme felt a soothing rush of energy flow through her body, ready to respond as well. Raiden held his free hand up to keep them both away as he let out another cough, but he quickly straightened his back and inhaled deeply.

"I'm okay," he said, rubbing his chest and averting his gaze.

Esme wasn't satisfied with his answer and his gentle refusal to let either of them help, but he continued walking in the direction of the portal as if nothing had happened. She looked back at Dacio, seeing her worry mirrored in their face. When she caught up to Raiden, his face was firm with resolution.

Even if she hadn't recognized the cove from two evenings ago, she knew they had reached the portal from the magnified aura alone. The other two stepped through the portal, and she gave the island one last view-over before following them in, eyes closed as the magic washed over her.

"Stars, not again," Esme murmured to herself when she opened her eyes to a gray setting instead of an iridescent white-blue one. A quick perusal of the environment made her realize that neither Raiden nor Dacio stumbled into the spirit realm along with her. She couldn't tell if it was simply her luck or her pull to the spirit realm through her profession and past.

At least she knew how to get back. However, as she started to light up her fingers, a familiar voice stopped her.

"Mingyue," a chiming voice called out.

She froze. *Is that...*

Esme turned to face the image of her mother. Her fingers started shaking and her heart pounded faster. There, suddenly in front of her, looking exactly like in her childhood memories stood a finely dressed Wei woman with the same eyes and smile as her. Elation and horror battled within her. *Why is she here?*

Her mother stepped closer. "I could feel you yearning. For your childhood. For peace and safety, so I came," she said sweetly. Although she wore an elegant Atonacan dress with a bright red shawl and blue skirt, her hair was styled in Wei fashion with ornaments and pins woven throughout it. She certainly looked like a noblewoman, now that Esme knew the context that had flown over her head during childhood.

Yet, something seemed very wrong. The air around her felt heavy and suffocating, and her skin prickled with anticipation. Every muscle in her body seemed to tighten, as if expecting to flee or fight. When she took a closer look, she realized her mother's eyes were actually glowing slightly. The aura was the exact opposite of what she felt in Jing's presence.

"Who are you?" Esme whispered, taking a step back. "And don't say my mother."

"What gave it away?" her "mother" asked, delight flashing in her eyes.

"Everything," she replied with a frown. "Now, who are you and why do you look like my mother?"

"Should I wear another form?"

Then, like a shimmering mirage, her mother's features morphed into those of the high priest of the Great Temple of Atoyatlan, with his high, sharp cheekbones and turquoise-adorned nose and earlobes. However, he wasn't wearing his ceremonial outfit or paint and was dressed simply in a colorful cape and loincloth.

Anger ignited within her, countering the hesitation and fear. "Stop it," she demanded. "This form stealing is not only disrespectful but also insulting. Show me your true form."

He morphed again with a brazen grin, his features softening until it was the face she saw staring into still water or into her obsidian mirror. Narrow eyes, tumultuous black hair, golden brown skin, and painted full lips. "And if I said this were my true form?"

Esme glared at her false double. "I think I will just leave then," she threatened and re-ignited her fire.

Her threat managed to work because the mirror dropped. Finally, the being presented inhuman characteristics. Flesh decayed into sharp bone, like that of a humanoid Dreadful, acting as a mask over half of its face with horns of an ox sprouting from the top. An ominous orange light glowed in the darkness of its eye socket. *It's a demon*, she realized, chills washing over her. However, it wasn't like any Dreadful she had seen, not that she had encountered very many. The rest of its shape was that of a human, and this creature was too sentient with morphing abilities to be like the others.

"Fine, if you insist. I only aimed to give you a familiar face," it said, yawning.

Inwardly, she panicked. Why in the nine hells did supernatural beings continue talking to her? What did this one want? *More importantly, why am I still here?* The sluggish heaviness in the air seemed to lure and trap her.

"Why would a Dreadful want to show me a familiar face?" she asked.

It cocked its head to the side, asking, "Why do you assume that I am a Dreadful?"

Esme shifted uncomfortably on her feet. "Why wouldn't I? The bone mask and demonic air... but you don't seem completely demon..."

"Fair observations, alas, I am more than a simple demon; I am an Evolved, the final stage of any powerful Dreadful, and I can offer you something you want," it crooned sweetly and slowly approached her. Holding up its palm, visible sparks zipped between its bony fingers. The fire in its eyes burned brighter. "I can feel it in the air. You just want to return home, to your family, but you feel powerless against the tides of reality, just like you did years ago when you accepted my bargain for more power." Although its skull failed to demonstrate any facial expressions, its tone turned almost jovial.

The demon's words made her still. "What do you mean?" she asked, narrowing her eyes. What was the Evolved implying? The memory of the day she died crept to the front of her mind. Jianli had accused her of making deals with *that creature*. Is this the creature he had been referring to?

"Last time you only had a taste of lightning," it said, freezing her blood. Her mastery of lightning had come from a *bargain?* "Alas, that was always meant to be temporary as once we absorb something from you mortals, we can only lend it out for so long. Regardless, I believe you anticipate needing help soon."

Her face felt tight with stress. "I don't imagine any of this comes for free."

It laughed, the discordant sound echoing off the jagged rocks of the mountain cliffs surrounding them. "Of course not. You have a delicious deity-given gift that I have yet to encounter if you were interested in a more long-term power-sharing agreement."

More and more, the implications made the hair on the back of her neck rise. Although this so-called Evolved was clearly different than a Dreadful, it still seemed similar in that it wanted to absorb something from mortals. The simpler demons wanted to replace the mortal memories and emotions it had lost and while she wasn't sure what the Evolved's ultimate purpose was, it wanted more magical abilities. No matter how she cut it, this whole situation seemed nefarious. What were the consequences of agreeing?

Esme decided she didn't want to know. She remembered her past self's doubt from whatever agreement she had made last time. "Interesting offer, but I'm going to have to refuse," she said, taking a step back.

"Hmm, perhaps I mistimed my offer," it mused. "Disappointing, but not irredeemable. I'll let you continue on your journey." It waved its open, fleshy palm to the side.

Warily, she let her fire come roaring back in her hand. As she replicated what she had done last time and hoped that it was indeed the process to return to the mortal realm, the

Evolved changed its appearance once more into a stranger dressed in Wei minister robes and eerily assured, "See you soon."

Firelight flooded her view, and when she dropped it, she was back in the mortal realm, the Evolved's words echoing in her head. *What did that mean?*

"Esme!" Dacio's voice exclaimed right before she felt a body slam into her side. She would've tumbled over if Dacio hadn't held her in a tight hug. "I thought I lost you again," they murmured, their distressed tone and words punching her in the gut. How had she missed all the signs of their affection before? Regardless, she clung onto their familiarity and reoriented herself.

"Don't worry. I'm here," she said, rubbing their back and making eye contact with Raiden, who visibly relaxed under her gaze. They both must have been concerned and she didn't know how much time had passed while she was in the spirit realm again. Telling them would only worry them more even if nothing really happened. Still, she wondered if she had made the right decision.

"Maybe next time I should hold on to you to make sure you don't take another accidental detour," Dacio suggested, pulling back but keeping their hands on her shoulders.

"I wouldn't want to further delay our return to Yin City." She smiled back awkwardly and reached up to nervously push a strand of hair behind her ear.

Raiden looked up at the cloudy skies. "At this rate, we'll arrive back at the Wei capital well after darkfall. We better hope we don't run into any demons in the Emerald Forest this time."

Esme shivered at the idea. She was done with demons, but she had a feeling they weren't done with her just yet.

CHAPTER 20

When Raiden used his plum blossom charm-key to get into the base under Yin City, the three of them found Reina practicing on her knife-throwing in the weapons room to the side of the foyer. However, since Daiyu had been collecting information from the palace, they needed to find her before exchanging new information. The four of them weaved through the dimly lit passageway until they reached a different entrance than before, exiting into a storage room in what seemed to be the back of a teahouse, based on the cans of tea leaves and pots that filled the shelves.

"Wow, the tunnels are quite extensive," Esme noted while looking at the labels on the metal cans and recognizing types of tea from the northern deserts. With the easy access to multiple buildings, there must be a significant level of trust between Reina and anyone who was connected to the tunnels. "If you don't mind me asking, Reina, how did you end up joining The Six?"

The Lady of Shadows sighed and then took off the ribbon on her wrist to tie her black, yellow-orange decorated braids into a coiled bun, hiding away the bright colors and showing the silver studs in her ear. Instead of continuing her trajectory out of the storage room, she pivoted to face her.

"My oldest sibling often sold convincing replicas of various works of art. The Six noticed his work and convinced him to join the forgery arm, so he disappeared for a few months. I decided to join so I could find him and bring him back, which I eventually did, and I happened to pick up useful skills along the way," she said, vaguely reminding Esme of her own journey to rescue Dacio.

"Wow, so even before joining, you were committed to helping people escape," Esme said, stepping away from Raiden and around Dacio, who was also browsing the types of tea. Sometimes she wondered if she ever did enough. What would it be like to do what Reina did?

Suddenly, a tall, dark-brown man with short, curly hair curiously popped his head into the storage room. Esme froze instinctively.

"Ah, Reina, it's you… and company," the man said, passing a glance over the four of them. "Are you looking for Daiyu? We were just talking about you."

"Only good things, I hope," Reina responded with a charming smile. "And, yes. Do you mind bringing her back here?"

He nodded with an equally warm smile. "Of course. Make sure to stop by later for a chat over a cup of tea," he said before disappearing back through the cloth doorway curtains and into the store.

"Best to take this conversation back into a location less prone to interruptions," Raiden said before he turned around and headed back into the tunnels, black hair and cloak flashing behind him.

Reina made a motion for them to leave first, so Esme nudged Dacio with her elbow and then followed Raiden into the darkness. They walked further in until they stood in a better-lit intersection. The stale, cool air almost made her sneeze, only impeded by the faint, fragrant smell of tea drifting into the tunnels. After a minute, Reina returned with Daiyu in tow.

Initially, Daiyu's posture was tense, with her sharp jaw tight and her shoulder bunched together under her cloak. However, she relaxed after giving the three of them a thorough glance, particularly Raiden. "Good, you didn't give the sword to the emperor."

Raiden shook his head, shifting the Sword of Realms further into sight. The fire light reflected off the obsidian shards. "No, not yet."

"Good," Daiyu affirmed again before dropping, "because the emperor intends to use that sword to bring more demons into our world and conquer Atonaco."

"Sorry, what?" Esme asked, flabbergasted. Her voice echoed weakly in the tunnels.

The emperor *wanted* more demons in the mortal realm? Conquering the north made sense given his track record, but how was Jianli supposed to control the demons, and why would he ever need them? Additionally, she thought he only wanted the sword because he was going after the peaches, which were in the spirit realm so he needed it to access them. She wished Jing had been more detailed when discussing Jianli's plans.

"Do you have a timeline for his plan? Or more details? He isn't doing anything right away. Is he?" Dacio asked, their nerves clear through their pinched eyebrows. Raiden placed his gloved hand on their shoulder, but that only eased them slightly.

"When I overheard him talking to his advisors, he only mentioned the sword with respect to the Spirit Festival, which still doesn't happen for a few days," Daiyu answered, rubbing her thumb over her bottom lip.

The Spirit Festival again. Jing had mentioned that the barrier between realms was weak, and while she had known that before, it gave more credence to his supposed plans to bring more demons into the mortal realm from the spirit realm. She *had* wondered why Jianli had insisted on that day specifically as a deadline.

"Emperor Jin is looking for the Immortal Peaches, which apparently exist and are located in the part of the spirit realm overlaying the northern part of the Thunder Forests," Daiyu said, essentially confirming what Jing had said and that the strange event on the island indeed happened.

Reina scoffed and leaned against one of the stone walls. "And that's why he wants to invade Atonaco again? Did he not learn from his own failure years ago and from history? The mountains are hard to penetrate and Atonacans are known for their military skill and knowledge, as well as having the advantage of knowing the land well."

Esme knew that too intimately, with her father having been part of the military.

"If he's looking for the Golden Peaches, and if he were to have access to a realm-splitting sword to gain access to the spirit realm, why is there any need for invasions or demons?" Esme asked.

"Hah. The invasion part is easy. He's a greedy glory-seeker. When he helped the empire annex my family's ancestral lands years ago, he couldn't stop boasting about bringing more prosperity to the Wei empire while ignoring the destruction he left behind. Atonaco is just another Rainbow Desert to him. And if he has failed in his plans before with his deity-blessed magic, I'm guessing the demons are supposed to help turn the tide of the invasion," Reina said, looking like she was two seconds away from rolling her eyes.

"That sure sounds like him," Raiden agreed. "What else did you find out, Daiyu?"

"As we knew from earlier, only Atonacan dignitaries and Wei commoners were invited to the celebration in the palace, and none of the nobles or civil officials that both Jin Jianli and the previous emperor had put in place while consolidating power. It turns out that the demons are very, very hungry and demand sustenance in exchange for helping him take over the north," Daiyu said. Her voice seemed winded near the end from explaining everything.

Esme felt sick at the implications. Were the commoners there just to *feed* the demons? Those were the emperor's own people! Although, given his track record of going as far as killing his own cousin as well as employing assassins like Raiden, she wasn't sure why she would overestimate his propensity for feeling guilt. So much for trying to bring prosperity and glory to the Wei empire. Conquest for glory was the mask of a rotting, hollow beast.

Employing assassins... Esme wondered if all of Raiden's assignments had been for political purpose or if Jianli had been secretly feeding a demon all this time. *Or both.*

With her arms crossed and fingers tapping her biceps, Reina let out another scoff. "That's probably why the Atonacan dignitaries, including the great speaker himself, were invited. Not only would the demons be fed, but Jianli could also destabilize the political system of Atonaco before he swoops in and takes over to cement control in a chaotic political environment. Two birds, one stone," she said, earning a nod from Daiyu.

As horrifying as the plan sounded, Esme was still confused about one important aspect. "So we know he wants to use the sword to bring in more demons, but I wouldn't call them trained beasts by any metric," she said.

"That's the final piece I learned right before I left," Daiyu said, frowning. "When his advisors seemed bored from the conversation, Jianli reminded them he could control the demons whenever he wanted through 'the bloodstone.'"

Eerie.

If the bloodstone truly controlled demons, it probably wasn't from the mortal realm, and it certainly was dangerous in Jianli's hands. Esme reached up to rub her temples and alleviate the headache she could feel forming. The pressure was mounting. However, all of this information was advantageous to counteract any of Jianli's actions.

Before, committing to defy the emperor had been an abstract decision, commanded by the deities and with the threat of the mortal realm's fate over her head. Now that she could see enough of the pieces to realize the truth, she had to do something about it. Merely keeping the sword away from her cousin wasn't a long-term solution.

Even without the threat of realm-splitting and demons, the Wei empire—particularly Yin City—seemed to have its fair share of structural problems that wouldn't disappear by just keeping the sword away. The consolidation of power, the invasion of the desertlands many years ago, parts of the city crumbling in on itself, the fact that the nobility used members of The Six on one another and on the citizens of the city. Most of the problems seemed to start with the emperor, with his blend of poison spreading throughout the city like the roots of a decaying tree.

Suppose they ran away with the sword or got rid of it somehow, like throwing it into a volcano. How long would they last before Jianli came after them? Or found a different way to accomplish his goals? He had already waited three years and still seemed dedicated to the cause. The rest of the problems would also remain. No, limiting the possession of the sword only delayed the emperor's plans and failed to address the root of the problems. Even without any additional powers, he could still make others suffer.

"We have to stop him," Esme declared firmly. "Not just keep the sword away, but stop him. With all of the heinous crimes the emperor has committed, why can't we just overthrow him right there?"

She couldn't help but remember how unsatisfied she was with the previous emperor in her memory, even though she didn't remember why. Maybe part of her personality was wanting to overthrow emperors.

But was it her place to suggest that? She didn't live here—anymore, at least.

"That's what I've been thinking since he ascended to the throne after those mysterious circumstances surrounding the previous emperor. I know many who reside in Yin City would agree with that sentiment," Reina agreed, making her feel less like she overstepped a boundary.

Dacio opened their mouth and then closed it before opening it once more. "As much as I agree, this would be extremely dangerous. He not only has his metal magic but also supposedly has demons under his control. With Raiden under his threat, if we do have to give the sword back, there's not much we can do. His speed gives him an advantage for both offense and defense," they said carefully. As they talked, their pendant flashed in the available light.

With what she knew of metal, it took significantly more energy and focus to create it, so moving and manipulating was a faster method, much faster than manifesting other elements. *What was quicker than metal then?* Just as quickly as she had asked herself that question, she knew the answer. Lightning—a power she still hadn't been able to bring back and one she had refused from the Evolved.

Flashing Esme a concerned glance, they added, "I also don't want to lose you again."

Their words stole her breath. The fear was palpable, and she completely understood. Her cousin was dangerous and had succeeded with stealing her life before while making both Dacio and Raiden's life a misery.

I don't want to lose you either—or anyone else I care about. No more. No more loss. No more suffering, either hidden and visible, she thought. Instead, she asked, "How do you know we'll be safe if we don't deal with this? If we don't, who will? Who else knows what we know? We can't run from this, not anymore, not with the stakes for both Atonaco and the Wei empire itself, as well as the entire mortal realm."

"I know," they replied softly, casting their gaze to the side, past her and onto Raiden. "Rai, what do you think?"

Raiden quietly contemplated the question and sighed, closing his eyes. "As much as I've avoided… everything these last three years, Jianli is unfortunately a magnet that draws me back. I'd appreciate not having his specter haunting me for the rest of my life. However, I agree we need to tread carefully."

"Of course. Our advantage is the information Daiyu gathered. We know what he needs. If we can take that away, well, it certainly makes the fight easier," Reina said. "Let's take this one step at a time. We have the sword right now, so we should consider what to do with it."

Although Esme didn't want the sword to get to Jianli, they still had Raiden's problem. Dacio clearly had the same thoughts because they said, "My spirit magic couldn't remove the metal pin from Raiden's body, but perhaps a metallomage might be able to do something. If we can resolve the ultimatum without handing over the sword, we can take out one of the three legs to Jianli's plan."

"And if the mage can't do anything?" Daiyu asked.

Dacio stayed silent for a few seconds and then exhaled before giving them all a slow, heart-warming grin.

"I suppose no one ever said anything about promising to not steal the sword back after I returned it," Dacio said cheekily, drawing a smile out of Esme. "It *would* give me great joy to steal from Jianli in particular."

"True," Reina remarked. "You three try to see if we can figure out the sword problem tomorrow morning, and Daiyu and I will see if we can address the bloodstone problem. Whether successful or not, we will regroup afterward to discuss next steps. Sounds good?"

Everyone nodded.

"Fantastic!" the Lady of Shadows exclaimed with a glint in her eye. "Now, rest up and prepare to make Jin Jianli regret his plans."

CHAPTER 21

Although they still had time before the official deadline and there were certainly metallomages in the Academy of Magic back in Atonaco, the trip would take too long even with the help of portals. Therefore, they had to search near the city. As agreed, Esme, Raiden, and Dacio split off to hunt down a mage, and after haggling with a Wei jeweler and buying some new trinkets, Esme managed to track down the location of someone who might be able to help.

Since Dacio knew the location well, they led the way to the Yin City cemetery, near where an old mage lived.

The scenario reminded her of her first day in Yin City, when Raiden had taken her on a brief walk throughout town before they had gone to the palace. She recognized a few streets and buildings this time and was ready for the transition between the well-kept and dilapidated areas. With more context of Wei history and the emperor, she eyed the cracks in the walls and glass in the streets. Walking through the city made it seem like all that gold that Jianli had supposedly found when he conquered the desert was simply a legend. Raiden himself had said something about there being even more cracks than before, a clear manifestation of the persistent grip of the past suffocating the present.

"Hey, Rai, isn't this near the bakery where we first met?" Dacio remarked as they approached the cemetery. Rows of small grassy mounds and stone burial markers stretched out in the distance. Even the closest buildings to the graveyard left generous space to clearly separate the land of the living from the land of the dead.

"I'm not the one with perfect visual memory, but it seems about right," Raiden replied with a small smile at the corners of his lips.

"How times have changed… and not," Dacio murmured. A light breeze ruffled the large sleeves of the pale green robes they had borrowed from the Chens, which matched the color of their jade earrings.

Sometimes Esme forgot how deep Dacio and Raiden's friendship ran. She tried to imagine them as teenagers, walking through Yin City and trying to forget their roles together. With the timeline she pieced together, she figured that they had been friends even before she came into the picture. Did the three of them have many memories together? Perhaps she could ask for more stories later.

"Found it," Dacio said, nodding their head in the direction of a building that matched the description of what the jeweler had told her.

Metal flowers framed the doorway surrounding a small stone-walled complex. A small hook acted as a pulley to a system of bells attached to the trim of the doorway. A red sign with a large, auspicious Wei word on it hung upside down on the door.

Dacio moved forward and pulled on the pulley. Then they waited for someone to answer. The sound of people squabbling in the background ensnared Esme's attention, making her wonder what was happening behind the walls. Catching a snippet of dialogue, she realized the people inside were arguing over who to send to answer.

Eventually, a short teenager came to answer with a slight pout. "Hello?"

"Hello, sorry to interrupt, but we were directed here to find a metallomage. Would we happen to be at the correct address?" Dacio asked politely, responding back in Wei.

"That would be granddad," the teenager said, their gaze darting in Esme and Raiden's direction. "What do you want?"

"We wanted to ask for your grandfather's expertise," Esme answered vaguely in Wei, glad she could still speak decently. She suddenly understood why everyone who had been in The Six was so evasive. It was hard to know how much to reveal and how much to keep safe.

She looked though the open doorway and saw many people of a wide range of ages walking around in the background. Although the exterior of the house seemed small, it still held many generations of a family within. Perhaps some members lived in the unit next door.

"Please follow me," the teen said, turning on their heel and allowing their loose black hair to swish around.

They did not have to go far before reaching a porch, where an old man sat at an outdoor table and played a game of tiles with three other people spanning three separate generations. Although the exterior of the house looked chipped, the space inside the walls was as warm and lively as the sunny, almost spring-like day.

"Granddad, we have some guests who would like to speak about magic with you," the teen said.

The old man didn't react to his grandchild's statement

and continued playing the game, drawing the next tile and letting out a whoop of victory. Quickly, he showed all his tiles and made the other three players groan.

"Just in time," he said gleefully, finally giving the newcomers his entire attention. "So, how may I help you youngsters?"

Dacio dipped their head in respect. "We were recommended to you as a master of metal magic who could potentially help us with a... delicate problem."

"I'm no master but I can take a look," the metallomage said, stroking his silver-threaded beard. He slowly rose to his feet, excused himself from the game, and started walking away from the table. The teen giddily took his spot and started another game.

As the mage led them past a small shrine dedicated to Zoraya and some minor deities and into a cramped craft room full of tools, he asked, "So, are all of you visiting the city?"

"We're here for the festival," Esme partially lied, feeling uncomfortable with just how easily the half-truth came out.

"Of course. Festivals always bring an influx of visitors, and with the empire ever-expanding, many people come to the capital. I couldn't quite place your accents because yours"—he tilted his head at Dacio—"seems more standard and very fluent, and I can hear a bit of Atonacan in your voice." He looked at Esme.

Her lips flattened and she forced an appeasing smile on her face. Although it was true she came from Atonaco and the question probably came from a place of curiosity, it only went to "other" her. When she had exchanged currency in Port Kai, the innkeeper had assumed she was Wei from her appearance, and here, she was assumed to be Atonacan from her accent.

Things never seemed to align. If she had been on a different continent and mistaken for either half, it wouldn't have bothered her, but within the two empires, there always seemed to be a decent chance of failing to pass.

"As much as we are looking forward to the festival, we do have a little magic problem we would like to resolve first," Dacio said, stepping forward and taking the attention off her.

Inwardly, she stewed, upset for getting upset. She was not concerned with the opinion of someone who didn't know her and she wasn't looking for his approval—just his services. Esme briefly wondered if Dacio felt similar, as they looked Atonacan but grew up in the Wei empire. The old man's words weren't necessarily the compliment he thought they were in their case.

Dacio continued explaining the situation and gestured toward Raiden, who had been silent since he entered. "Our friend here stumbled upon a trap in the forest and I've had no luck in trying to remove it from his chest because of the lasting nature of enchanted metal and its resistance to my spirit magic."

"Interesting. Let me take a look then," the metallomage said, walking toward Raiden and lifting his hand up. Even before the mage did anything, she noticed the corner of Raiden's nose crinkling up, as if preparing for something.

Sturdy, cool magic prickled Esme's skin as she watched Raiden's face twitch deeper in wary discomfort. Even the mage's face scrunched up in irritation as he moved his hovering hand around. She rose to her toes to get a better view. Raiden let out a sharp gasp, prompting the immediate dissipation of magic in the air.

The metallomage reached up to tap his chin. "The signature of this magic is very potent indeed. It is many leagues above my own, surely done by someone who was classically trained, and it also repels my magic." He frowned. "I'm afraid you will either need to discover the enchanter or perhaps find a better trained scholar to reverse this."

Raiden's face darkened, his lips flattening. Esme imagined her expression matched his. This meant they would probably have to seek Jianli himself.

"Are you certain?" Dacio asked hesitantly, their hands wringing together.

"Unfortunately so. Whoever laid that trap deserves some punishment from the deities. It's too dangerous to simply let it be out there like that, even if the intent was to hunt animals," the old man tsked.

Dacio thanked the mage and excused all of them from the premises. As soon as they closed the metal door behind them and stepped back into the streets, they sighed. "It was smart to grab the sword first. Let's head back to discuss our backup plan."

Biting her lip, Esme looked over at Raiden, who clearly had a dark cloud hanging over his head, and she reached over to touch his upper arm. "We'll get you out of this."

Disappointment diffused into the air around them on the walk back to the tunnels. She barely paid any attention to her surroundings this time, trying not to let this setback overwhelm her. As long as they kept going, they had a chance. However, the look on Reina's face when they reached the base warned her of yet another hurdle.

"I see you three didn't fare much better," Daiyu remarked from the side, near the shelf of scrolls. Reina was next to her, filtering through a stack of scrolls and pausing her search to greet them.

"I take it you two figured out what the bloodstone was," Raiden replied. He waited until both Esme and Dacio stepped into the room before closing the door behind them.

"Not only did we find out what it was, we know where it is, and that's the problem. It's around his neck in the form of a necklace," Reina said flatly. "I don't think we'll have much luck trying to get something that close to him unless we want to directly take him on, which I want to avoid for as long as possible."

Esme's stomach sank, as did her shoulders. Not only was the stone going to be hard to take away, they were going to have to return the sword. Even with their information, they were still not in an ideal position.

"We also hit a snag. It looks like we will have to steal back the sword after we give it up, but unlike a necklace, it may be easier to take. At some point, the sword has to leave his possession," Dacio said.

Theoretically, that was true, but with her limited knowledge of the emperor, she would guess Jianli to be more hypervigilant over potential threats.

"Given that you stole it the first time, Daci, don't you think he might be more protective of it this time around?" Esme asked, chewing on her bottom lip. Her fingers played with the edges of her long sleeves.

"Among the five of us, we have me, two spies, a thief, and someone who can blend into shadows," Raiden said. "We can simply steal the sword while Jianli goes to sleep. Even emperors need to rest at some point."

Dacio walked over to the wall and sat down by the low table, one knee raised for their elbow to casually rest on. "Let's think this through. Rai and I go directly to the palace with the sword. Jianli removes his pin in exchange. We pretend to leave but sneak back for the sword using our knowledge of service passageways."

Before anyone could add or opine, Esme jumped in, hands now clenching her sleeves. "You two aren't going alone. You'll need backup, or at least someone to sneak around while the attention is on making sure you leave the palace complex," she said firmly.

"I agree with her assessment," Reina said smoothly. "Esme and I can trail while Daiyu manages the external affairs should things go completely awry. We will stick to the shadows and watch, only intervening as a last resort."

Now Dacio was nervously biting their bottom lip, and Esme knew they were probably worried about her, so she reached over to grab their trembling hands. Words got stuck in her throat, but she managed to send a tendril of healing magic to them as a replacement for her understanding. Their trembling ceased.

"We go tonight," Reina ordered with a sharp nod. "Let's go make Raiden a free man again."

Esme couldn't help but feel her stomach jump with worry. Too many things could go wrong, and she prayed to the deities—if they weren't too busy fighting off the primordial evil in the cosmos—for their aid. Night, although still a few hours away, waited for them patiently, like a jungle cat stalking its prey.

CHAPTER 22

Esme's pulse fluttered underneath her skin, still spiked from when Dacio announced their and Raiden's presence to the royal guards at the entrance of the imperial palace complex. As she and Reina found an alternative entrance, she was struck with yet another sense of déjà vu, one more sobering than last time now that she knew what had happened to her three years ago in the palace.

Instead of heading to the throne room, the royal guards led Dacio and Raiden to a small rotunda near the gardens in the middle tier. Although the lanterns and the gently falling snow made the night slightly lighter than normal, Reina directed her behind the shadowy shrubs surrounding the rotunda. The structure was not completely walled, so if anyone took a peek over the ledge and looked down, they could be spotted. Her heart pounded fervently as she crouched and waited, trying not to disturb even a single leaf or twig.

Although she was no trained spy, she still had magic and an expert at her side. Luckily, the peaceful, walled nature of the garden and circular structure made it easy to hear sounds in the isolating quietness. She was also grateful for Daiyu's spare black uniform so she could both better move around and not get her nice clothes dirty.

The sound of metallic marching dragged her attention toward the archway leading into the garden. More palace guards arrived, with the emperor himself walking amongst them. His robes flowed elegantly behind him, creating the image of an imposing stone guardian walking the mortal realm, but Esme knew what festered under the image.

"Always an overachiever, Dacio," Jianli mused while walking into the rotunda and disappearing from her hidden viewpoint. "If my eyes do not deceive me, it looks as if you accomplished the little mission early."

Even without seeing him speak, she could hear his smirk.

"Yes, I got your sword. Now fulfill your end of the bargain. I assume you still keep your promises," Dacio said firmly.

"Of course, I must be a man of my word. For everyone's sake, I will take the sword first. No need for our dear Raiden to be holding it while my gift is still waiting near his heart," the emperor said.

A few seconds passed before Dacio said, "Just do it, Raiden."

If she hadn't been listening so intently, she might have missed Raiden's quiet footsteps and the swish of his cloak as he walked. A brief thought invaded her mind as she tried to imagine what was happening inside the structure. What would happen if Raiden were to just permanently take care of the emperor right there? After all, he had a realm-splitting sword in his hand.

No, she reminded herself. They still needed the emperor to retract his threat first.

"Beautiful. Was that not easy?" the emperor asked, informing her that Raiden must have given over the sword. Esme clenched her hands into tight fists, her nails biting into her palms. Would Jianli follow through with his promise? Her eyes darted to her periphery, observing Reina's calm manner.

A sharp grunt echoed in the air. She recognized Raiden's staggered gasp and had to physically restrain herself from leaping up to see what was happening. It sounded like Emperor Jin was following through on his end.

"Fetch someone to clean this mess," Jianli commanded, barking at one of the servants in the sideline.

What mess? Did he not extract the metal in the same fashion as he inserted it?

Footsteps descended from above down the steps of the rotunda until finally Jianli reappeared in Esme's view with the Sword of Realms in his hand.

Was that really it? Perhaps he really did keep his promises.

No sooner had she thought that when the emperor stopped in his tracks and turned back with focused, narrowed eyes. Chills ran down the back of her neck. The look reminded her of the one he wore the night she died immediately before he had lunged forward and feigned concern, coincidentally around the same time she began to feel ill.

"I am afraid I must delay my side of the bargain until after the celebration. Leaving things to chance is too risky given your history of slipping through my fingers and stealing objects right before I can execute my plans," Jianli said slowly. "You still know a little too much from your days of service for my comfort, so while I will still honor my promises, I must keep my enemies closer."

His words sent off warning signals.

"Guards, take them to the dungeons. Do not let them out of your sight," he ordered before turning around, whipping the edges of his black and red robes with wide sleeves around as if slicing through mist and wind. The beads in his crown jingled quietly, swaying side to side.

As he walked away and the guards started to converge on the rotunda, Raiden lurched into view toward the emperor. Esme internally screamed and wanted to leap up to her feet to prevent him from continuing in his tracks. Reina pulled on her arm hard, dragging her ear over so that she could whisper into it.

"Remember, last resort. We lose the element of surprise if we reveal ourselves here and now," Reina warned quietly.

Esme couldn't look away from the scene, not even when Jianli pivoted around to see Raiden going after him.

"Your word is worthless," Raiden hissed, venom in his words and his even composure cracked. Dacio ran to his side and tugged at his arm, creating a strange mirror of her and Reina's situation.

"Not worthless, simply delayed for a few days. This was meant to be one last mercy, as I spare your lives, but if you want to make this more difficult than it needs to be, so be it," Jianli said coldly.

The rush of magic in the air was the only warning she had before she saw metal fly off one guard's armor and zip at Raiden. *No!*

However, Dacio threw themselves in front of Raiden and took the blow with a stab in the stomach. Esme threw her hand up to cover her mouth and prevent any whimpers from coming out. *Daci.* They staggered to the ground while Raiden caught their weight. She couldn't breathe. *Were they okay?*

"You!" he hissed at the emperor.

"They suffered from the consequences of your actions, so save your glare. Let this be a gentle warning, if you may. We both know that wound is something they can handle as a spirit mage," Jianli responded. With a wave of his hand, he used his magic to rip out the metal shard, stretch it out into a ribbon, and coil it around both Dacio and Raiden, binding them together with blood and steel. "Nevertheless, I tire of this. It is late enough already and I am ready for sleep."

Emperor Jin walked away, leaving the guards to their duties. Although she could see Raiden fuming from her spot, he provoked no more.

Stars above, this is a nightmare. Their plan was already falling apart and it was only just supposed to get difficult. Her fears ignited, her mind wandering down the path of imagining everything getting exacerbated. At least Dacio hadn't provoked the emperor too through their ice magic, albeit they might not have been able to react or counter quickly enough. *Oh, Dacio.*

Instead of jumping in to help, Esme forced herself to wait until the guards left along with Dacio and Raiden without further aggression and quiet settled back into the dark gardens.

"That… was not ideal," Reina said after a few minutes, once there were no other sounds aside from the faint rise and fall of their breathing and the sound of snowflakes gently hitting the ground.

"That's an understatement," Esme croaked, still worrying about Dacio. If Jianli had been just a bit more merciless, would she have seen them die in front of her? She prayed to the deities for Dacio's safety.

Reina placed a palm over her shoulder to calm her. "They will be fine, and the plan is still salvageable. The attention is still on the two of them, and while one of us needs to free them, the other can still go after the sword while Jianli sleeps."

Esme slowly breathed in through her nose, trying to gather focus. Panic would only inhibit everything. Dacio and Raiden needed their help.

"Daiyu's waiting position is closer to the dungeons than where we are, so she can help break them out. One of us needs to go with her and the other needs to follow Jianli, who is probably heading toward his bedchambers with the sword," Reina pondered aloud. "My skills are suited for either. Do you have any preference?"

As much as she wanted to help rescue Dacio and Raiden, her ability to blend into the shadows would better suit a stealth mission. "I can go after the sword. If the deities are on my side tonight, I may even be quick enough to help out in the dungeons afterward," she decided.

"Then here's what you need to know," Reina responded before telling her about all the necessary details for how to get into the emperor's chambers without being seen and where to head afterward. She quickly erased the map she drew in the snow as to not give their plans away to any straggler. "If you don't show up within an hour, we will go in after you. Got it?"

"Got it," Esme affirmed with a nod, one that Reina mirrored before they both took off into the dead of night, heading in separate directions.

She chanted Reina's instructions in her head, repeating them over and over while letting them guide her through the palace. Though she had once resided here, she had forgotten everything and was now re-discovering. She was to sneak into the emperor's chambers and steal a realm-splitting sword—something that could only send her pulse to the stars.

Her heart was all but ready to leap out of her chest, and ascending to the third tier of the palace complex didn't help. Even her hands were shaking as she tied her thick hair back.

As she waited in the dark to let time pass, she wondered how anyone could do this job without passing out from stress. She tried channeling everyone else's cool and calm personas and pretended she knew what she was doing. As long as she could control her own magic, it would still be okay.

She crept into the emperor's dark bedroom from the secret escape tunnels and made sure to open the door as quietly as possible. The only light available was the one coming from the dim lanterns in the corner of the room. Briefly, she wondered if she should risk summoning a small flicker of fire or simply let her eyes adjust to the dark. Perhaps the available light would reflect against the macuahuitl's obsidian shards or its metallic, celestial designs from a certain angle and she just needed to find the spot.

For extra precautions, Esme drew the abundant darkness and wrapped it around her. She looked over at the bed, where the emperor slept, and listened to his even breathing. Reina had warned her of the purposely creaky floorboards as anti-spy measures, so she cautiously tiptoed around the room.

As expected, the emperor's bedroom was large, but it was surprisingly sparsely furnished, with only a short table on one side, a changing curtain near the back, and small ornamental statues and vases placed throughout. Many oddly shaped metal structures were also scattered throughout. At least that meant she had fewer areas to search.

Her next hesitant step sank deeper than prior ones, warning her with a small creak and making her heart stop. Luckily, she had felt it first and hadn't put enough weight to make a large sound. She looked forward at the changing curtain, wondering if the sword was behind it. Perhaps warping over would be safer—as long as she didn't land on a creaky board when she re-materialized.

Esme warped over and poked her head around the divider, failing to find the sword. Was it even in the room? What if it was being kept elsewhere? Drawing back, she realized how close she was to the bed canopy and the vulnerably sleeping emperor. How had he survived this long if someone could simply sneak into his room while he slept without the guards outside knowing, especially when he was hated by many?

She remembered how Jianli used people's weaknesses and secrets against them: the thinly veiled threat from her past, Raiden's metal pin, and coercion aplenty.

Here slept her murderer, her own cousin, his throat bare and unaware. If he died right here, where did that power go?

But acting upon any of the creeping, dark desires frightened her. She saw the effects of killing on one's mind and conscience in Raiden, who still suffered under his guilt now. Unclear were the implications for the afterworld. And what if she enjoyed her revenge? Would Jianli's hold over her ever break after that?

Jianli turned to the other side, facing away from her, and then she saw it. Above his head, mounted to the wall was the sword. *Of course it's right next to him.* But *why* would anyone want to sleep with a literal sword over their head? What if it fell down in the middle of the night?

The location didn't make her mission easy either. The sword was not the lightest object out there, and if she had to reach out and keep it up high, that was going to require a lot out of her... although perhaps it wouldn't be a complete shame if she dropped it.

Esme gently shook her head, evicting those thoughts. Maybe she could warp, grab it, and then warp back? *No, too risky.* If only she had metal magic to float the sword over.

She decided to test out her physical strength and stealth, approaching the bed from the side where the emperor's back was turned, tiptoeing up the flat steps. She was so nervous she could pass out. *Stars above, why in the nine hells did I decide to do this again?* Carefully, she pressed her knee into the headrest to establish her balance and was surprised to feel the texture of metal instead of wood. Eye on the prize, she reached out for the sword, hoping she would be able to hold it steady.

"Bold," a low, raspy voice chilled the blood in her veins.

Suddenly, she was thrown back to the wall with a sharp yelp, cold metal wrapping around her body and pinning her to the side. Magic that was not her own filled the air.

"Guards," the same voice barked. The doors opened and allowed light to flood into the room, letting her see that Emperor Jin was actually awake. "I knew it was a matter of time before you—"

He froze once he saw her face, his snarl disappearing. If she hadn't been so surprised, she would have reveled in his stunned expression.

"No…" he whispered, blinking. "You, you *died*."

CHAPTER 23

Jianli immediately turned around and blasted the metal doors closed behind the incoming guards, preventing more people from entering or seeing into the room. "More light!" he ordered. "You will not speak of this to anyone. Understand?"

His guards complying with his orders, Jianli turned around and faced her again. Unlike the previous times she had seen him, his hair was not pulled up into a bun and hidden under a crown. His appearance reminded her of how young he was—younger than her given what he said the day she died, although she wasn't sure by how much.

The cold, unforgiving metal pinned Esme against the wall like she was a mere decoration, and the curious, unbelieving look Jianli gave her made her feel like an exhibit of a mythical animal. With the metal right against her, the emperor could have stabbed her already but was simply choosing not to. If the situation deteriorated, she was ready to call upon her shadow magic. *Or perhaps I should leave now?*

"Are you here to take my throne in revenge, Mingyue?" Jianli asked, interrupting her mental calculations on how to escape. He held out his hand and used his magic to levitate the sword over to his side.

Her eyebrows raised in surprise. *Of all the questions he could ask, he chooses this one?* The silent question must have screamed itself through her expression because he laughed.

"Still transparent, I see. You must be wondering why I am not asking why you are alive. Never did I expect to see you again in this lifetime, even though there had always been a possibility when no one could ever find your body," he mused at the end, as if trying to rationalize the situation to himself. "However, the timing is obvious, given our mutual friend Dacio returning to Yin City. Why would death ever separate the two of you anyway? Perhaps I underestimated their power. Perhaps they are not as disposable as I thought."

"Of course they aren't disposable." She glared at him, before flatly adding, "And Jing revived me."

His eyes widened with a brief flash of fear, making her feel smug, but then it morphed into a disbelieving scoff. "So even the deities side with you over me? What is it about you?"

She squinted at him, but before she could even respond, he grew frustrated. "Even back then, when my claim shouldn't even have wavered, they all talked about you. *I* was the one who annexed the desert and added the gold stores. *I* was the one who had a plan to expand the empire, in line with the previous emperor. *I* was the one who grew up in the empire, who was taught everything from birth, but you come in and disrupt the natural order," he said bitterly. "I toiled away to get to where I am, yet they all overestimate your abilities and ambition and underestimate mine."

What exactly had she done in those missing years? Dacio said she hadn't been too involved in court affairs but apparently, court affairs had involved her anyway.

"Have you ever considered that people don't like you?" Esme asked dryly, silently judging his entitlement. "Also, you weren't and still aren't the only one who works hard. What is about *you* that makes you think you deserve anything at all?"

He laughed harshly in response and walked closer to her. His dark hair framed his fervent dark eyes. "Because it is my birthright. I will push further than any other mortal because I know I can. Deityhood is within my reach. With no land to rule, a prince is useless, powerless; an emperor is not. Since death marks a transition in power, a mortal is vulnerable, fragile; an immortal is not."

Esme wondered how Jianli got this way. Had the primordial evil infected him somehow? Or had he always been told gilded promises and internalized them? Mortals did not become deities within their life in the mortal realm; the only route was through death in the spirit realm, and limited to being a minor deity.

"If you choose to get in my way again, I will make sure to finish the job I started three years ago," he said, stopping and painting his face with regal composure once more.

The cool metal retracted from her body, releasing her, but the long strands morphed into a thinner, sharper shape. His threat was clear despite her release. Esme couldn't help but remember what had just happened in the gardens. Metal was too quick as both a defensive and offensive strategy. She wasn't sure if shadow was faster than metal.

"I suppose one good thing about you here is that I can draw the rest of the rats out in one go. I take it the extra presences in the palace are related to you, and if they are not, well," Jianli said before turning back to one of the two silent guards in the room. "Summon the Serpent."

Serpent?

"My current assassin will keep you company and wait for any rats that come for you," he said.

Her eyes widened. Now was a good time to try and escape. The previous curiosity to talk with Jianli in her current life was now washed away by the reminder of the situation. However, as she started to draw in her shadow magic, the unmistakable energy seemed to have caught his attention because before she could dissipate, a sharp pain stabbed through her feet.

Esme shrieked at the fierce, raging blaze stemming from her feet, and she saw that the hovering metal spikes were now piercing through both of her feet, staking her to the ground. *Pain.* Tears sprang to her eyes, and she lost her sense of space and time. *Is this what it feels like to burn?*

"You are not going anywhere until I decide what to do with you," Jianli hissed, his fist clenched in front of him.

As something hit the side of her head, the white-hot pain turned into darkness.

"Mingyue, can you hear me?"

Her mind was groggy. She felt like she was drifting, but land was in sight, right in front of her. Just a little bit further...

"Can you open your eyes?"

The sweet voice hypnotized her to follow. She gathered the strength to open her eyes and had to blink away the blurriness in her vision. A person with sun-kissed, brown skin and short black hair blinked at her, their beautiful dark eyes filled with hope and fear. The room she was in was unfamiliar and empty of any decorations.

"Where am I?" she rasped.

The stranger gave her a gentle, shaky smile, tension slowly easing from their posture and their features softening. "You're currently in the healing center of the Great Temple of Atoyatlan."

Blinking, she tried to remember what happened that would have caused such a major headache, but she only drew a blank, and the harder she attempted to recall her most recent memories, the more discomfort she felt in her head. "Did I hit my head? I can't remember what happened."

They threw her a worried glance and reached over to brush their cooler fingers against her ever-warm forehead. The sudden movement surprised her, but the pressure in her head was slowly siphoned away through their calming touch. The air around her prickled her skin. Spirit magic.

"Better now, Mingyue?" they asked.

"Yes, thank you," she said, curious that they knew her Wei name that her mother would occasionally use with her as affection. Did her mother tell this healer? "And what's your name? Who should I thank for healing?"

The healer froze. Devastation and panic invaded their face. "My name? Do you not remember me?" they asked, growing more alarmed.

Confused, she took a closer look at their face, from their long eyelashes down their high cheekbones and round nose. There would be no way she could forget someone who looked like them. "Should I know you?"

They withdrew their hand and scooted back, staying silent for a few seconds. A tense smile crawled onto their face and she couldn't figure out why their eyes were suddenly glistening. Why did her heart ache?

"Esme?" a frantic voice whispered, jolting her from her dream. The accompanying shake to her shoulders made her eyes fly wide open to see Dacio leaning over her. Clear, heavy relief washed across their face with determination quickly replacing it.

"What's happening?" she asked groggily, leaning against the wall, before finally noticing the action in the background of the emperor's chambers. Her eyes widened at the sight of Raiden dispatching the guards in the room like they were immobile metal poles. The red feathers on the soldiers' falling spears make it look like sparks jumping toward the ground.

A throbbing pain in her feet made her wince as she made the movement to get up.

"Shh, stay still. He'll be okay. Let's get these spikes out first," Dacio said, prying her attention back. Their face was hard and tense as they glared at the metal stabbing through her foot. "I am a healer at heart, but I might kill him if I see him again. He is lucky that Reina and Daiyu are leading the attention away from here."

They took a deep breath, as if to calm down, before looking back into her eyes and saying, "This'll hurt, but it'll be quick."

Kneeling on the ground, Dacio yanked the metal out, causing her to yelp and them to wince, and they quickly hovered their hands over her feet, summoning their familiar spirit magic. As much as the throbbing pain hurt, she knew that she was in good hands. There was no better healer or spirit mage in the world.

Comforting warmth spread through her toes, and they both watched the holes in her feet patch themselves back together into smooth skin and muscle. If she had been using her own healing magic, there would have been a scar. It was too bad that her boots now had holes in them.

"You don't have to do this," Raiden's low voice said, drawing both her and Dacio's attention back to the other side of the room, where they saw him fighting a black-clad, bone-masked person. Unlike the rest of the guards, this opponent wielded a sword.

Esme's eyes widened at the sight of someone somehow managing to expertly evade Raiden's attacks and come close to striking him. They seemed to dance around each other in a lethal circle, and the mirror of their steps made her realize who this must be—the assassin Jianli had sent over.

"I wore that mask once upon a time. What does he have over you?" Raiden tried again lowly, dodging the slash of his opponent's sharp, curved weapon. Both of them were moving too fast for her or Dacio to directly intervene.

"Nothing but my calling as the Silent Serpent," the assassin replied coldly, lunging for Raiden's throat, as if aiming to kill instead of incapacitate.

It didn't seem as if talking him out of this would work, and Raiden seemed to understand that when his face hardened into serious focus.

This was the Hand of Death. The Assassin of the Night.

"I'll give you one last chance to stop this," Raiden warned, staying on the defensive.

Instead, the Silent Serpent pulled out small throwing knives and faced Esme and Dacio's direction, revealing the full-face mask. It reminded her of a demon. Dread spiked in her veins as his intended actions became clear. Dacio breathed sharply and quickly called upon their magic, the air around them turning bone-chillingly cold.

Raiden leapt in front of the way, extending his sword to block the knives before Dacio could even construct a barrier of ice. As the clear ice wall rose from the ground, high enough to block their heads, Esme saw the assassin using the opportunity to strike again, knocking the sword out of Raiden's hand.

He jumped back, weaponless.

But the Hand of Death didn't need a weapon to fight.

When the Silent Serpent didn't stop his advance, Raiden jumped back again and quickly yanked off his left glove with his teeth. Instead of dodging the next attack, Raiden actually stepped closer and grabbed the assassin's sword hand.

"Got you now," Raiden said, using his unoccupied gloved hand to shove him back to the wall with a loud thud.

Esme rose to her knees to get a better view over the top of the ice wall.

Shocked, the assassin struggled back, but he quickly started gasping for breath, and then something strange began to happen. Blood dripped from under his mask, staining the bone-white design red like he had been bleeding from his eyes and nose.

As he began to sag in Raiden's grip, Esme suddenly couldn't breathe from the hauntingly familiar visuals. *Wait, this can't be...* The Silent Serpent stopped moving, silent forever.

By the stars.

Esme fell back from astonishment and landed in Dacio's arms, barely registering Raiden wearing his glove again and then walking over to them with a troubled look on his face. Blinking, she looked up at Raiden, noticing the regret in his eyes, perhaps from just killing the Silent Serpent, but it had the same soul-crushing weight that he always wielded around her.

"I died the same way," she spoke hollowly, trembling and trying to make sense of the unconnected dots of information.

Raiden stilled, paling.

Dacio tensed from behind her. "I know how similar it looks, but the memories from the Eastern Isles should tell you it wasn't Raiden. He was with me for hours leading up to the celebration that night. I don't know how Jianli replicated the symptoms though," they assured.

Her eyebrows tightened together in confusion. Hadn't Jianli touched her forehead right before her past self started suffering from similar symptoms?

"No," Raiden said, his breath ragged and broken. "I'm the reason you died, Esme."

CHAPTER 24

"What in the heavens are you talking about?" Dacio demanded, their arms tightening around her. "You weren't even there, and she didn't die either."

"Dacio!" Raiden snapped. "When will you accept what happened? You *know* she died. I saw the look on your face when you couldn't sense her spirit anymore. It was the same devastation you had every time someone died and you couldn't heal them."

Instead of being exasperated by the same argument the two always seemed to have, Esme emotionally prepared herself. She wanted to hear his explanation for why he thought he was the reason she had died.

"No, no," Dacio said, squeezing their eyes shut. "You need to stop trying to paint yourself as villainous and cruel. That's not you. You don't have to blame yourself for everything bad."

"But it's the truth. The soul-ripping truth. I transferred my power to Jianli that night," Raiden confessed. His entire posture was tense, his face pained in such a way she could *feel* the truth emanating from him even before she could understand it.

Esme let out a sharp disbelieving huff. "How?" she asked, her throat dry and unable to get any more words out. *The only method of transferring power between them was... oh no.*

He looked back at her, his eyes glistening. "I made a deal with an Evolved. I desperately wanted to stop killing and to leave Yin City, but I couldn't while Dacio was still within striking distance of Jianli, so I made a deal to lend my power for a few hours in exchange for the Evolved to help release us. I didn't realize the effects of my deal until after you died," he said, his head drooping in shame.

The words fell heavy among the three of them, seeping into the air.

"We could've left together so that Jianli couldn't use us against each other anymore," Dacio offered weakly, drawing Raiden's gaze again. Prince Jin must have coerced them both into staying in service by threatening the other.

"Would you have left your father here? What about Esme? Could you have left her? Or would you have asked her to leave her family and ailing mother?" he demanded swiftly in Wei.

Dacio pushed her up into a sitting position and rose to their feet, partially blocking her view of Raiden. "You asked whether I would've been willing to leave, but you never even gave me, gave *us*, the choice to make a decision. Why didn't you say any of this before? To me?" they asked back in Wei, their voice cracking. Their face was full of anguish and confusion, the clear display of betrayal matching the storm inside her. "We went through so much together and you couldn't tell me this? *Why?*"

"Because I felt guilty and was ashamed!" Raiden exclaimed sharply. "With one *stupid* deal, I got Esme killed and I helped our blackmailer steal the throne. How was I supposed to face you and tell you what I did when I knew this would finally be a horror you couldn't look past, a mistake you couldn't justify?"

Esme curled into herself. This explained all of Raiden's behavior around her. His abilities hadn't been the only thing that had created that air of distance and hesitation between the two of them, but the fact that he had inadvertently contributed to her untimely demise. From the way he had almost fled back in Atoyatlan at first sight to the guilty glances he gave her and his offer to safely guide her to Yin City and rescue Dacio. All of it was because he had felt ashamed of his involvement and wanted to avoid making the same mistake again. All of it was because of a stupid, yet understandable, deal.

A storm of conflicting emotions crashed within her. They had all suffered from secrets, whether they held them or drowned in them. She was so *tired*. So many lost opportunities. Lost memories. Fractured relationships.

The scent of blood and death drifted over.

"So your solution had been to run away? Was that why you didn't stay in the Eastern Isles after I asked you to help bring Esme there? Why you barely spoke to me in the last three years?" Dacio demanded. Their hands were clenched into fists at their side. "This—all of this *hurts*. I thought you had just been enjoying your freedom all this time, but you just abandoned me."

Their words seemed to hit Raiden like a slap to the face. He visibly cringed.

"Daci," Esme interrupted quietly. Too many intense emotions hung in the air, and she was nervous that something would ignite and irreparably burn everyone. None of them seemed to do well with absorbing secrets without having had time to process them alone, and as a pyromage, she could only address one fire at a time.

Dacio didn't seem pleased and looked like they were about to add fuel to the fire, so Esme reached up to put her hand over their arm, drawing their attention. They looked down at her and then away before inhaling and exhaling deeply. She knew those actions well, as she also did the same to center or calm herself.

Calmly, hollowly, she said, "We have bigger things to worry about now."

"We do," Dacio said coldly, reaching down to lift Esme to her now-healed feet. "We still need to retrieve the sword. Do not doubt me when I say that we are going to have a long discussion about communication and honesty after this is all over. Frankly, and I know how ironic this is coming from a former spy, but no more lies, either direct or via omission, from now on. We need to trust each other if we want to take the emperor down. Now, do you have anything else you would like to share while we have the opportunity?"

Raiden swallowed hard, suddenly looking awkward from where the conversation ended. "Nothing else that's important." He coughed, looking away.

"Good," Dacio clipped.

However, before anyone could even move to leave the room, they heard the door open from behind them. Esme froze for a second and then quickly looked back to see who opened the door.

Now in formal robes with the realm-splitting sword at his side and beaded crown partially masking his eyes, the emperor stood at the door, looking at the three of them with an equal mix of disdain and disbelief woven through his lips. A squad of guards and servants hovered behind him, waiting in the hallway.

"I leave for an emergency and this is what happens... although I suppose I can now solve two problems at the same time," he murmured, taking in the dead and unconscious bodies on his chamber floors. When his eyes landed on the Silver Serpent, he added, "By the stars, what a waste of a perfectly good assassin. Pity."

Not wanting to be there any longer, Esme dashed toward the secret entrance on shaky legs, dragging Dacio alongside her.

"I did not dismiss you," Jianli thundered from behind as the strange metal structures in the room flew and blocked their path.

Esme glared at the morphing metal and gripped Dacio's poor hand harder. *Well, I suppose the three of us can just take him down now.*

"Looks like your handiwork, Raiden," the emperor said, nudging the Silent Serpent's body with the tip of his boot. "I wonder why you took your gloves off only for him since no one else is bleeding on my floor."

Raiden glared at him. "I'd take off my gloves for you too," he growled. "I've been told that you learn from your pain and suffering, and I would be delighted to make you a very wise man."

Jianli tsked at him, unfazed. Instead, he replied with more show of power as he raised his hand into a fist, sending Raiden's sword flying away from him and into his unoccupied grasp. "You don't need this then," he said.

Drawing energy from her calm rage, Esme summoned flames to her hands, heat rushing through her entire body until sparks started falling from her hair. She was done with him.

"You three are nothing but mere flies buzzing at a dragon and it is time for you to go," Jianli snarled, brandishing the jagged obsidian sword.

She threw her fireball at him, making it expand and morph into the shape of a tiger charging toward him. However, he blocked the blast with the metal divider in the room, the flames spreading out like waves crashing against a cliff. Esme tried to prevent the heat from blasting back at the three of them.

"No lightning this time? Or did you lose that when you died?" the emperor asked with a sneer once the flames subsisted.

Esme felt the air around her cool with Dacio's magic. Jianli must have noticed too because he moved the metal structures behind them, hitting the three of them like a moving wall and jolting them forward. With them now closer, Jianli swung the spirit-infused sword—but not at them. Instead, a giant slash appeared in the air in front of them opening up into a portal. Spirit magic inundated the air, making it clear what was on the other side.

"I bring gifts!" he yelled, and tossed them into the fissure. All of them grunted as they hit the gray-scale floor. "Eat them as you please," he commanded coldly before slashing the sword once more and closing up the portal behind them to leave the three of them in the spirit realm.

Hells.

Quickly, Esme looked around to see if the emperor had indeed summoned demons. Aside from Raiden and Dacio, no other living persons were in the empty chambers. They were all clearly in the spirit realm given the gray hues of their environment and because a skeletal figure stood where the Silent Serpent's body was previously. It was hard to tell what the spirit's expression was given the lack of facial features shown through its bare skull. However, she imagined he might still be processing his death given the way he silently stared at the floor.

She wondered if spirits also perceived the spirit realm as a gray, hollow mirror of the mortal realm or if they saw something else before heading off to their next destination.

Dacio nudged her with their elbow before whispering, "How did you get out of here last time?"

"I used the light from my fire," she replied. "However, we should leave the room, or even the palace, so we won't end up right back where we came from." With this being her third time in the spirit realm—since her coma at least—the initial novelty was wearing off slightly, but not enough to keep fear from running through her veins.

"Good idea," Raiden said, already stalking toward the doorway while avoiding the Silent Serpent on the way over. "We should leave before we—"

Just before he got to the door, a few large figures suddenly blocked the way, stopping him in his tracks. Esme's pulse jumped when a legion of tall, clawed creatures stalked in, taking up expansive space and sucking any hint of joy out of the room. Heaviness suffocated her. Even the Silent Serpent noticed their presence and stumbled back.

"Hungry..." one of the creatures rasped, sniffing the air around the dead assassin. This particular Dreadful had the skull of a monkey with the teeth of a tiger. Six more uniquely different demons looked over at them with hollow eyes.

It was *definitely* time to leave.

CHAPTER 25

No one even had to say anything before the three of them took off in the other direction toward the side entrance. Trying to fight off seven demons at once in a closed room was suboptimal, and the unfamiliar scream behind them suggested the Silent Serpent thought similarly.

"One of you two should lead the way. I don't know these passages and hallways very well!" Esme huffed loudly as she sprinted into the dark. Even though Dacio had healed her feet earlier, they still felt sore and uncomfortable, and she didn't know how much longer she would have to run.

"Why don't you use your powers to let us escape?" Raiden shouted as he dashed by her and led them back into the lighter main halls, which were filled with only normal spirits.

"And lead the demons back into our realm? Absolutely not. We need to evade them first," she said, looking back to see the legion squeezing through the narrow service tunnel and into the hall behind the Silent Serpent, who was also running away. Strangely, the first demon that came out ignored the other wandering spirits, maybe because they weren't the targets.

Raiden made a sharp turn in the middle of the long corridor, and Esme barely adjusted quickly enough to make the turn as well. The air around her cooled, and she realized Dacio was drawing their magic. They used their motion to gracefully pivot around and waved their hand diagonally upward to build an ice wall across the entire hallway.

"Daci!" Esme hissed, urging them to hurry.

On the other side of the ice wall was the Silent Serpent, whose bare skull looked like it was in a state of perpetual surprise. However, he must have actually been surprised because his trajectory slowed up to the ice wall. That deceleration was enough for the Dreadful to catch up to him. Esme watched in horror as it picked him up, squirming and screaming, and devoured him whole, with its jaw elongating to consume his entire spirit.

Chills racked her entire body, but she forced herself to turn around and continue running, lest she wanted to be the next demon snack. A raucous crash behind them told her the demons had shattered through the ice wall, but Dacio's magic had given them more of a buffer.

What would happen if she used her fire magic to attack in the spirit realm? Would she end up inadvertently sending the demons to the mortal realm? She decided to not risk it unless absolutely necessary.

Raiden led them down the hallway, where at the end a pair of doors led outside the building. Unfortunately, since they were not spirit-walking, a few precious seconds were spent on physically opening the door—a phenomenon that would need to be processed at another time. A massive central courtyard greeted them outside, which was almost completely lined with imperial buildings save the outdoor steps down to the second tier.

They dashed down the stairs, the stomping noises behind them telling her the three of them were indeed targets and needed to do more than simply running. However, given the incident back inside the hallways, the Dreadful still interacted with physical magic, and that could possibly delay them enough for her to open up an escape.

Once they reached the bottom of the steps, Esme looked across the open space on the second tier, where a gate lined the entrance to the next set of steps.

"Dacio, block their path again at the gate, and I'll get us out," Esme ordered. Everything felt so fast: her breath, her heart, her plan.

"Understood."

Heat flooded her veins, partially negating any cooling effects from Dacio's magic as they built wall after wall behind them to block the incoming demon swarm. As soon as they crossed the threshold and the last shard of ice left Dacio's fingertips, she pulled both of them to her and released the fire building up within her, surrounding them all with light.

Please work.

A large crashing sound was replaced by the whoosh of the fire dropping. Her relief of seeing the warm colors of a nascent sunrise was promptly destroyed when she looked back to see the Dreadful tagging along behind them. Esme's eyes widened as she was immediately pulled down the other set of stairs by Dacio. They were back in the mortal realm and the shrill scream from afar indicated that not only had the demons re-entered their realm in front of living people but also that said people could see them too.

"*Hunger!*" a smaller, almost humanoid Dreadful chittered loudly.

With servants frozen in fear and so many people to choose from in the lowest courtyard, the attention on Esme, Dacio, and Raiden suddenly became less concentrated. One servant dropped her tray of food and ran screaming into the building. The lack of anyone in regal outfits made her guess that they were closer to the servants' quarter.

What have I done?

Raiden cursed beside her. "If only I had my sword," he growled, visibly frustrated.

Her breath was completely ragged and her heart pounded furiously from having run all the way from the top level and from the horror of releasing demons into the mortal realm.

"You want to try to use your death touch on it?" Esme asked breathlessly, already drawing up more flames to her hands.

"You're *joking*," he hissed. "Too close, too slow, bad idea."

Another scream interrupted their quips, bringing her attention to the descending legion of Dreadful, one of which used its claws to slash at an innocent bystander.

"No!" Dacio shouted, throwing their hands out and shooting ice spikes at it. Although the shards hit their target, the bear-faced demon was single-minded in its pursuit of its prey and bent down to rip out their heart for consumption. Another demon knocked into the first, fighting over the corpse.

Esme felt sick to her stomach, but she managed to keep enough focus to use her fire and place a painful barrier between a few of the demons and some of the fleeing people. Servants and officials alike ran past her without even sparing a glance although one was picked up by another bird-like Dreadful. The flight of an ice pole kicked her back into action as Dacio tried to bring down the flying demon.

As she was about to make prisons of fire for land-constrained Dreadful, a loud metallic commotion from behind preceded a small brigade of alarmed guards with spears and swords. Although a few guards also ran away, the rest followed their commands and faced the Dreadful.

"The emperor himself might come now," Raiden warned from the side. He looked out of his element, surrounded by ice and fire and demons without a weapon in his hand.

"Why would he come out for this when the guards are here?" she asked, moving her hands to the side and throwing fire over another demon. It shrieked when it shriveled up.

Having used a fair amount of magic, she was beginning to feel weary. They would have to deal with this situation soon, or else she might faint. At least they were down two demons, one from her and one from Dacio.

"I don't think you understand how powerful he is, both magically and politically. He's the one who single-handedly led the campaign to conquer the desert. You might have mastered fire back then, but he was the master of metal," Raiden spoke quickly.

Another Dreadful burst into ash when enough guards focused their attention on it. However, one was caught off guard by a sneaking demon from behind as it swiped them in her direction and knocked them down. Their sword dropped from their hand, clattering and skidding across the stone ground. Raiden darted over to grab the now-free sword to rearm himself.

At this point, only guards, demons, the dead, and the three of them were in the courtyard. Raiden joined Dacio in their fight. To avoid blasting fire and ice at one target, Esme turned to the one the guards were facing, letting streams of fire turn into a flaming serpent to strike from above. She slowly walked backward until her back was to the wall for both defensive and long-range offensive purposes.

As she moved the fire, she had to keep her knees from buckling under the sheer exhaustion, and it didn't seem as if she was the only one. Further in the distance, Dacio was also beginning to sway side to side, making sloppier, slower movements. Esme's shoulders tensed. Since they had arrived at the palace, Dacio had been stabbed, healed both themself and her, built walls of ice in the spirit realm, and skewered demons back in the mortal realm. Even they had their limits and she was sure they were approaching them.

"Raiden!" Esme called out. "Daci's about to fall. Get them to the side."

He nodded sharply, beheading the demon and then tugging Dacio away through a cloud of dust. Esme's gaze flickered over them to act as their eyes, but she noticed a familiar regal figure walking down the steps from above. Inwardly, she cursed. Three demons were still left, and while the chaos could give her, Dacio, and Raiden cover, they needed to escape *now*.

Dacio slumped against Raiden, who immediately bent down to carry them on his back. To give them more cover, Esme extended the fires upward to block the view while she slid back into the darker edges. The movement was weak, and given the metallic-smelling liquid dripping from her nose, she didn't have much energy left.

If the emperor didn't want the Dreadful wreaking havoc within his own palace walls, he could deal with the consequences of sending her to the spirit realm. Esme urgently waved for Raiden to come over. Dacio was completely passed out, blood on their face.

"I command you to stop!" a loud voice boomed just as Raiden arrived at her side. Facing the three demons with a stern, unwavering expression was the emperor. Next to him stood a thin minister, who would have held more of her attention had she not seen the flash of purple radiating from the emperor's chest. The bloodstone.

Like tamed beasts, all three creatures paused their motions and faced the emperor, bewildering her. It was that simple?

"I want all witnesses gathered and someone to clear the mess away. None of this gets out. *Do you understand?*" Jianli barked at one of the guards, perhaps a captain based on their more decorated armor. As he descended the stairs, his voice carried enough for her to hear, "I have a feeling I know who set this fire and where these demons came from, so you and I will take care of that troublesome obstacle."

Esme winced at the comment. The fire did give it away. However, the more urgent worry was escaping before Jianli caught them again, so she pushed Raiden in the other direction. When she took one last look back at the center of the courtyard, she stumbled after making eye contact with the emperor's mysterious companion, who gave her the eeriest of smiles.

Only when she was halfway back to the tunnels did she realize why the emperor's advisor looked so familiar. He had the same face as the one the Evolved had worn right before she had left.

CHAPTER 26

Esme had been so exhausted when they returned to the tunnels that she had passed out across the plush chair. The last thing she remembered was Raiden placing Dacio on the bench next to her. Now, hours after waking up, she was paying the price of sleeping in such an uncomfortable position with a crick in her neck. Her entire body felt sore, as did her morale.

Although everyone made it back in one piece, they had all failed. Jianli had both the Sword of Realms and the bloodstone, as well as his magic and the power of the emperor's seat. The only consolation was that Raiden now didn't have a metal pin inside him.

"What do we do now?" Esme asked to the group. The uphill battle now seemed like trying to climb the Moonstone Mountains, and even Daiyu must have thought the idea seemed exhausting because she was lying on the floor with an arm under her head and a knee propped up like she was taking a nap.

Silence filled the air, making ample space for spiraling thoughts. Nothing she had learned in her life, that she remembered, would have prepared her for a situation like this. Her face was starting to hurt from how tense her jaw was.

Raiden, who was the only one standing, said, "Jianli certainly knows we're back in the mortal realm, so I imagine security will be tighter around the palace during the festival. Even the escape tunnels and service passageways will be guarded now."

"The more concerning part is all of the innocent people at risk, the commoners and Atonacan dignitaries who were invited into the palace for the celebration," Reina said quietly, her gaze unfocused and her arms crossed.

"Do we have enough time to prevent people from attending?" Dacio asked. "While we figure out how to disrupt his usage of the sword, we can minimize the damage." Esme looked over at them, noticing the dark shadows under their eyes.

"What about your network, Reina? Or do you think you can use your connections to nobility from your spy days, Daci?" Esme asked, looking between the two.

Reina ended up answering both questions. "We can certainly involve my overall network, spies and non-spies, to prevent invitees from entering the palace, but Daiyu and I will have to spend a whole day recruiting them. As for the nobles, not only are their armies too far to mobilize, but also Dacio and I did our parts of tightly securing their alliance to Jianli through their secrets."

Dacio winced at the second comment. *Oh.* Esme forgot to make the connection between information-gathering and political control because of how they phrased their job as performing.

"Perhaps I can still convince them to lead the Atonacan dignitaries away from the palace at least. I know which nobles may be most likely to help," they suggested, although their idea still failed to address infiltrating the palace again. Daiyu made a hum of approval from the floor.

"The easiest battle to win is one that never starts at all," Raiden remarked. "We certainly can take preventative measures, but we need to think of the most important player—Emperor Jin."

The first step would have to be getting to him. But with the usual paths probably blocked off, she wondered if there was a way to blend in with the other guests somehow. Or could they find a way to be invisible?

Suddenly, Esme perked up. "I could use my shadow magic to bring us in. Or maybe if we can figure out how to get into the spirit realm, we can just stroll right through."

"Let's test the shadow magic first," Dacio said, shivering. "The spirit realm isn't without its issues—demons, mainly."

"I second that. Stick to the enemy we know and delay facing demons for as long as we can," Raiden agreed. "Time would be better spent on honing in your current abilities rather than trying to figure out how to access the spirit realm."

Reina pursed her lips and tapped her chin with her fingers. "Esme, can you move through the shadows with someone? Would it be possible to cover all of us with magic?"

Thinking of her experiment on the island, Esme admitted, "I haven't tested that out yet. I can, however, summon some wisps of darkness. I can train to see how far I can get with my magic."

"I can act as your test," Raiden volunteered, garnering her attention. "I don't have the same connections everyone else does and don't have a specific task yet."

"And what happens if her magic doesn't work?" Daiyu asked. Although she was still lying down, she was now tossing a knife up and down absentmindedly.

Everyone went silent, and Esme could feel the pressure mounting on her shoulders. If she couldn't figure it out, would they have to leave things to chance?

She felt lightheaded.

"I believe in you," Dacio soothed her, gently patting her shoulder and making her smile nervously. *No pressure.*

As much as she had mused about how wanting to overthrow emperors was a part of her personality, there were profound consequences to the actions they were going to take—ones that made her nails bite into her palm. Whether they won or failed, the mortal realm would be shaken to its barest bones. Such destabilization was rife for change, either good or bad. If Jin Jianli was to be removed, a power vacuum would be left in the Wei empire, and she wasn't sure if that would mean someone else would take the throne or if the three underlying kingdoms and the desertlands would separate off again.

She wished Jing had given her a hint about what was supposed to happen.

"Maybe I'm thinking too far ahead, but what's the plan for after? What do you think the ministers and other officials will do?" Esme asked.

"Why don't we wait until we get that tyrant off the throne first?" Daiyu suggested dryly toward the ceiling. Her long hair sprawled around her head like dark rays. "If we can take him down, we can take on anyone."

Reina gracefully rose to her feet. "Let's begin preparations. The sooner we execute our preparations, the better standing we will have in two days. While you two work on Esme's magic, the three of us will try to gather as much support as possible."

Everyone mumbled their agreements before the stress of deadlines got them all on their way to start their respective tasks.

Wanting more fresh air and to avoid potentially damaging anything within the base, Esme suggested practicing in the forest outside the city walls. Indifferent, Raiden simply walked beside her on the way out before directing her to a more secluded area of trees where no random straggler—or enemy—could accidentally stumble upon them.

First, Esme tested out her shadow-warping, which now felt as simple as summoning a fireball. Hopping from one place to another with relative ease, she moved on to transporting objects, which she had done once when they had fought demons on the way to the Eastern Isles.

After being satisfied with the basics, she stared at her arms and hands, drawing dark energy from within herself and her surroundings to let it flow to her fingertips. Unlike when she had tried to create wisps of darkness in Kunhai, the weather and location here made forming dark fog easier. Entranced, she moved the opaque haze around until she wore it like a cloak.

"What do you think?" she asked Raiden, twirling around in his direction.

He stood leaning against the tree, his arms and legs crossed in a half-casual, half-closed off manner although his dark eyes seemed engaged. "Although it might seem disorienting to see a floating black mass during the day, that could be very useful if or when you want to distort someone's sight," he noted, stepping away from the trunk and heading closer to her. "Why don't you try it on me?"

Her eyebrows shot up. "Try it on you?"

"Yes, I want to see how the shadows affect one's senses," he said.

"You really trust me that much?"

"I trust your abilities, regardless if this particular skill is new. You're a trained mage and I've watched you take down multiple demons now without hurting any bystanders," he said, waving his hand before opening up his posture.

Esme scrunched up her nose but was curious herself of shadow creation's utility. Moving her hand like she was actually taking off her cloak, she made the shadowy mass float over to Raiden, tightening the edges and hovering it around his eyes. At the first signal of distress, she would be ready to pull it back.

However, Raiden only said, "Good start. Hard to see. Why don't you move it closer? If you're worried, you can drop it after a few seconds."

"What if I send your head to the spirit realm or something?" she asked nervously, suddenly thinking more carefully about all the ways this experiment could end badly.

His lips curved up, followed by a snort. "Then we found another way into the imperial palace through the spirit realm," he said smugly.

By the stars, how's he this nonchalant? she fumed. However, since he did give permission, she proceeded testing and covered everything above his mouth. He turned his head back and forth, and after counting for five seconds, she let the darkness drop.

"Hells, that really could be useful," Raiden said, his eyes widened. "My hearing was muffled too. You can truly mess with someone's senses that way—which could be a good offensive or defensive move."

"Could you still breathe? Or do I run the risk of killing someone through this?" she asked. "Actually, no, I don't want to test this out on you. This brief experiment gave me enough initial information and stress. I should focus on the shadow warping part."

A flash of disappointment crossed his face before disappearing. Without any protest on his part, she moved on to warping with another person. Was physical contact required to take something with her? Or simply physical proximity? Esme stepped toward him until he was close enough to elbow. She closed her eyes, focusing on the center of her energy and trying to expand it out to envelop him before stepping through the shadows to a distant tree.

When she reopened her eyes, she was immediately disappointed that Raiden wasn't next to her. That just meant she needed to try another method. She warped back to his side and held out her hand.

"Maybe holding hands will work better," she suggested, already thinking about an infiltration strategy should this method work.

However, Raiden made no motion to comply. The air filled with confusion and awkwardness.

"What's wrong?" she asked.

"Even though I'm wearing gloves and although nothing happened last time, I can't just forget about my abilities and what I did to you three years ago," he admitted, averting his gaze. "I'm sorry."

Esme's heart sank, reminded of the revelations from before Jianli threw them into the spirit realm. *Oh yes, Raiden had played a role in my death.* Despite the awkwardness, the atmosphere wasn't as emotionally charged as when she had found out, and although she still felt betrayed, she didn't think he would have agreed to whatever deal he made had he known she would be one of the victims. Since meeting him in Atoyatlan, she had only seen him try to protect her and Dacio.

Remembering the scene Jing had shown her, she searched for words in her head. "You might have agreed to an ill-conceived deal, but you didn't kill me. Jianli did. He used your magic to poison me, and even if you hadn't made that deal, he would have found another way to get rid of me," she said slowly.

Upon thinking aloud, she realized she hadn't *lost* her memories, her history, her life. No, it had been *stolen* from her, washed away to the sands of time. Something Dacio said what seemed like a long time ago echoed in her head. Emperor Jin stole from *her*. The more she let Jianli's actions torture her, the more his actions agonized others, the more power he had over them all; that was unacceptable.

With his brows furrowed and lips flat, Raiden clearly remained unconvinced. Before he could argue, however, she added, "The only things you were guilty of were keeping all of this a secret and being fiercely loyal. You stayed as an assassin to protect Dacio, and you made that bargain to protect them and yourself."

He gulped quietly. "My actions have consequences. I still have blood on my hands that will never wash off," he murmured.

"Acknowledge your wrongdoings, but don't let that stop you from doing better. Forgiving yourself doesn't mean you have to forget or cover up your mistakes. This is the perfect opportunity to make due to Yin City, to its people, so perhaps no one in the future will have to make the same difficult decisions you did," Esme replied, still thinking about her own past. "I don't think anyone leaves the mortal realm without breaking any glass."

Even her past self had kept secrets and had apparently made some shady deals of her own, and while she still didn't know much from when she had lived in the Wei empire, she knew circumstances were not the same as her life in Atoyatlan the last two years. The set of choices she had in each place differed. An eagle could thrive in the sky, but clip its wings or put it in a cage and it would have to fight to survive, its potential cut short.

More and more, she was learning of the lights and shadows everyone had, some more literally than others. Every action had some sort of sign: positive, negative, or neutral. Yet, these actions had context that colored them differently, pushing them one way or another, judged only by the universe itself. The most significant context was that they were mortal. Imperfect. Complex. Light wasn't always good, as it could blind as easily as reveal, and darkness wasn't always evil, as some of the greatest acts of courage and love happened in the dark.

Light and darkness weren't so separate at first thought.

Raiden nodded. "That's the least I could do—helping out."

She held her hand out toward him again, silently offering another opportunity. He hesitated one last time before finally reaching over and grasping her hand.

Giving him a small smile, she attempted shadow warping again, closing her eyes and pretending he was an extension of her. This time, the darkness weaved out of her and successfully coiled around Raiden, allowing him to warp alongside her. When they rematerialized together, he inhaled sharply, as if in disbelief.

Flashing him a sturdy grin, she mused, "I think we've got our way into the palace."

CHAPTER 27

Evil butterflies fluttered in Esme's stomach, her nerves lit by an insidious sense of doom. Despite having gone through the plan many times over, she could still imagine a million ways everything could go wrong, and the anticipation only exacerbated her apprehension. The worst part of the plan was waiting for nightfall. Once loud noises began setting off throughout the city as distraction, they would head toward the palace. Until then, they were sitting in the tea house, huddled around a table, drinking tea together.

She only got a few sips in before she couldn't stomach anything. The anxious, fidgeting energy from her restless half-sleep last night failed to leave her body. The only thing she was looking forward to was the end of the night, post-endeavor, whether it included fighting or not.

Thinking about battle, Esme leaned over to quietly ask Raiden a question. "So, infamous assassin-turned-demon-hunter, any advice for fighting if it so happens to come to that?"

He cocked his head in confusion, stopping mid-sip before moving the cup away from his lips. "Are you worried about your magic?"

Esme shook her head and gripped the now-lukewarm cup. "I meant general advice. Fighting the Dreadful is my only experience and they're rather mindless creatures, unlike people like Jianli or even his guards."

"Well, don't die, for starters," he replied with a straight face, earning a snort from Daiyu, who continued sipping tea with an amused expression on her face.

"That's... not helpful at all," Esme said after blinking a few times in exasperated silence. It seemed like a fairly obvious rule of battle, perhaps even the only real rule, but his delivery was underwhelming.

"Fine," he sighed before finally divulging less vague pieces of advice. "Don't hesitate. Hesitation can cost you your life, or someone else's. You must also focus your mind and keep control of yourself. Be aware of your surroundings."

Aside from the first part, the rest of his suggestions were familiar because they were key ingredients to using magic—awareness and focus. When he framed it like that, the daunting idea seemed easier to digest. Still feeling inexperienced, she turned toward Dacio, who had their eyes closed peacefully, as if trying to enjoy the last moments of quiet before everything ramped up.

"Daci?" she called for their attention. When they opened their eyes, she asked, "Were you also trained to fight?" Was she the only one of the five who didn't know physical combat?

"Mmm, I was although I was never very diligent about it because I'm too reliant on my ice magic, so don't worry about being alone if that's what you're concerned about," they answered, one corner of their lips lifting.

Their words eased her tension more than the tea ever could. A smile slipped onto her own face. "Of course I'm not alone. I have you—you all," she said, looking at the rest of the group. Daiyu and Reina smiled back at her.

A loud boom shattered the peace, making her jump from her seat and her heart stutter.

"That's the signal," Reina said, gracefully rising to her feet and smoothing her outfit. "Let's go."

Esme hopped up with the other three. "What was that noise?" she asked.

"Only the fire powder meeting the royal armory. That will surely get His Imperial Majesty's attention," Daiyu said, briskly walking toward the entrance.

"Deities be with you, Reina, as we surely are," the owner of the teahouse called out as they left the establishment and moved into the lantern-lit streets.

Smoke rose in the distance where the armory must have been. The display caught enough attention because she heard people postulating that the large booms were simply fireworks as they weaved through the cover of the crowd, avoiding the gaze of the royal guards who seemed to be running to investigate the explosion. This first distraction would delay invitees from showing up at the palace and would divert attention from the main gates.

When they dashed up the hill of the imperial palace, she began to prepare herself and tapped into the abundance of darkness around her.

Night was the territory of spies, assassins, and shadow mages.

They slipped into the crowd waiting at the front gates. As expected, guards were checking every person before allowing them in. Although she was dismayed by the number of people who followed through with their invitation, it only took a few seconds to realize some of the members of the crowd were dissuading others from entering—Reina and Daiyu's efforts at work. She even saw some Wei nobles intercepting the few early arriving Atonacan dignitaries; it appeared Dacio managed to get a few nobles on board.

"Are you ready to go now?" Reina asked quietly. Esme looked back at the gates and the shrinking crowd before them. As long as she could see where she wanted to warp, she was ready.

"Yes, hold hands, everyone," she ordered. Raiden took her left hand, Dacio took her right, and Daiyu and Reina tagged onto Dacio's side. Esme just had to repeat what she had practiced yesterday, extending her sense of self to incorporate everyone. They were all connected as one unit, and as a unit, they would dissipate into true shadows.

Esme carefully guided her magic as it washed over her and spread down her body before she let it flow outward through her hands. As soon as she was satisfied that they were all connected, she seamlessly warped past the crowd, past the guards, and across the threshold deep into the first level of the palace grounds. Like breathing pulsing mist, they flew through, undetected against the natural dark. She released the magic when they reached the dark corner beneath the steps, and everyone materialized again.

Last time they had been here, people had died. The stone floor, however, looked impeccable. Untouched. Erased.

Daiyu seemed the most enthusiastic about the trip through the shadows if her thin raised eyebrows indicated anything. "That was so cool," she whispered. "I felt like air itself."

"Where to next?" Esme asked, still holding onto Dacio and Raiden. As long as guards were roaming around, they needed to be ready to evade roaming eyes.

"If this were a private event for nobles and government officials, I would've guessed the Hall of Wonders, but given the size of the crowd he invited and the fact that he intends to feed them to demons, he'll probably ask them to congregate in the Courtyard of Heavens—the highest tier," Dacio murmured over the lively chatter from the approaching crowd.

"Jianli himself will probably be on the highest tier while the commoners will be asked to stay on the central tier to emphasize his status as emperor," Raiden opined.

Reina poked her head out and looked into the better-lit areas. "With everyone taking the steps up to the second level, same as the rotunda, we should go through the interior to—wait, is that Mrs. Chen?"

Esme looked in the same direction Reina was facing, her eyes widening with fear when she saw the amicable, old woman who offered her home to them. Why was she here? The palace was dangerous.

"Did you two not warn her?" Esme asked quietly, fear rising at the back of her throat.

"We did," Daiyu insisted with a frown. "She volunteered to help persuade and draw people away from the celebration. Only those who know how to fight were given the option to infiltrate palace grounds, so she shouldn't be here."

"More incentive to hurry. Find Jianli and take the sword," Raiden said in a hushed tone. "Let's go through that entrance."

With a quick nod, Esme called upon the smooth, inky darkness and let it flow through her body to prepare for the second jump. Each time she warped, it got easier, and with the night high above them, the trip was smooth from the corner of the first set of stairs past one of the open entrances of the long, connected building. When they materialized again on the interior, past the guards, Esme immediately transported them to the end of the interior hallway in the direction of the upper levels.

However, this time, a pair of patrolling guards stepped foot off the staircase and jumped back in surprise from their sudden appearance. The Lady of Shadows reacted quicker than Esme could warp again. Reina flew out of the lineup and dove at them. Her precise and quick motions flowed like water, her arm striking out like a viper at their exposed temples. The two guards dropped to the ground, one right after another.

Wow, she thought, gaping. *I need to spend more time with Reina after this is over.*

Raiden released Esme's hand and walked over to snatch an equipped sheath from one of the guards. When he turned around and saw her giving him a judgmental look, he paused mid-step. "What? I'm still missing mine and this sword needs a new family anyway."

Daiyu snickered quietly but quickly recovered. "Let's go before anyone realizes these two are missing."

Esme looked over and realized that with Reina and Raiden separated from the chain, only she and Dacio were still holding hands. Her face heated up and she reluctantly released their hands, letting her fingers brush past theirs before resting her arms at her side.

"I think we should use stealth for now so Esme can reserve some energy for later if necessary," Dacio said, eyeing her from the corner of their eye.

Since he was closest to the stairs and was now armed, Raiden led the way up to the second level. A quick peek through some of open doors on the left revealed the gardens and rotunda where Raiden and Dacio had given back the sword and had been captured. All of the rooms, which she figured were offices based on the furniture, were either empty or had closed doors. On the right were doors toward the outdoor corridor and the grand central courtyard, where a large group of people was gathered.

Raiden slowed before they reached an exit and gestured at Reina to come over. Esme watched them sneakily approach the stationed guards outside before they struck like twin vipers. With little flair, they both dispatched the guards and caught them with their arms, preventing the loud clash of metal catching anyone's attention and dragging them out of sight. Once the coast was clear, they all slipped into the outer corridor, darting behind the pillars for cover.

Esme looked around for Jianli. However, her eyes couldn't help but be drawn to the center courtyard. To her dismay, throngs of people walked up the grand stairs, more than she was comfortable seeing. The abundance of metal in their surroundings made her even more apprehensive.

"Found him," Raiden said in a cold voice, forcing her attention back to him. He jerked his chin in the direction of the third level, and Esme looked over to see the emperor standing at the top of the next set of steps, just as Raiden had predicted earlier. From what she could see, Jianli was standing next to that eerie companion of his—the one that was probably an Evolved—and his entourage of personal guards and advisors.

Vibrantly dressed figures started walking up the second set of steps toward the emperor, and she recognized the colorful cape patterns and formal staffs. Those had to be the Atonacan dignitaries, including the great speaker Itzcoatl himself, invited to talk with Emperor Jin, unaware of his plans to use them to destabilize the north. A group of Atonacan warriors trailed behind.

"He's too out in the open," Reina murmured from beside her. "Perhaps we can stretch his attention if we sneak and simultaneously attack from different directions."

Raiden glided toward the next post, guiding them closer to the highest tier and presenting a plan. "I can attack from behind. Reina and Daiyu, you can strike from the library side. Dacio and Esme can warp from the other side of the stairs from the records building."

Daiyu pulled out a small flute and flashed it at them mid-step. "I can try to use this and slow Jianli down or incapacitate him so our coordinated attack won't be as easily deterred. It's not a guarantee that it will be fast enough against his defenses but it could give a large enough window of opportunity for Esme to warp to the emperor's side, take the sword, and warp away while the rest of us focus on facing the emperor and escorting the Atonacans to safety."

A headache started forming behind Esme's eyes. As much as she didn't want the group to split up, it was probably better to have multiple fronts of attack.

They weaved back into the indoor halls at the end of the second-level corridor, hyperaware of any movements in their surroundings. This time, Daiyu and Reina took care of the guards in front of the next set of indoor staircases.

"We will give you a signal before Daiyu blows her dart. Now, hurry to positions," Reina whispered fiercely after they reached the highest level. "Go and good luck."

With one last nod, Raiden took off along the long corridor. Esme looked over at Dacio and held out her hand, ready to warp over to wherever they needed to be. They slid their hand into hers and tugged her back out into the cooler air.

"Do you see the corner mirroring us?" Dacio whispered into her hair. When she nodded, they said, "That's the records hall. We need to get there, and although I did say we should save your energy, time is of the essence."

"I understand," she whispered back and gave their hand a squeeze before turning them both into moving shadows and flying undetected across the open courtyard.

As soon as they materialized again, Dacio swiftly pulled her back indoors to avoid the guards just walking into the outdoor corridors. Her breath caught in her throat. This entire stealth trip was reminding her of their previous trip, which had failed spectacularly.

Suddenly, the air felt heavy, and not because of her worries corrupting her sense of reality but because of other, familiar reasons. Dacio must have sensed it too because she felt a flash of cold energy manifest at her side. When she actually scanned the interior of the dark wooden hallways, she found the unsettling source.

There, leaning against the wall next to a doorway to what looked like the records room, stood another Esme.

The Evolved.

The false Esme turned toward her, a wide smile unnaturally splitting her face. "I told you we would meet again."

CHAPTER 28

Dacio immediately crouched down and put their hands against the floor. Ice crystals spread from their fingers, slowly at first before shooting like arrows down the hallway. When they rose back up, a thick ice barrier shot up with them until it closed off the hallway.

"What was that?" they asked shakily, still looking in the direction where the other Esme was. "How did… You don't have a twin, do you?"

She shook her head. "No, but I do know who—what—that is," she said, staring straight ahead and waiting for the Evolved to act.

However, the false Esme merely came in through the far door of the records room in front of the ice wall. Her hands were raised in the air, her eyes glinting. "Why the hostility?"

"Please stop wearing my face." Esme glared.

The Evolved complied, morphing its appearance to that of the emperor's advisor. "I am here to extend my offer once more."

"And once more, I will decline it," she immediately replied. With what Raiden had told her, bargaining with an Evolved didn't ever go as intended, and she was even more glad she had rejected the offer the first time. Dacio stiffened beside her, probably piecing together the clues of its identity.

It pouted. "Shame. I would have loved to see Jin Jianli get electrocuted."

Esme's eyes widened at that statement. *What in the nine hells?* "Are you two not allies?"

"If one holds your leash would you consider them an ally?" it asked, reminding her of the bloodstone.

Did that bloodstone also control the Evolved? With that information, she couldn't decide how to feel. How much of its actions were its own?

"But that doesn't necessarily make him an enemy either. Does it?" Dacio asked quietly.

"Correct, after all, hunger has been a long-lost friend these last few years and he is proficient at addressing it," it admitted ominously, walking closer. She didn't want to imagine what satisfied its hunger. "I was directed to deal with whatever magical mischief shows up. Unfortunate for the emperor, his word choice was weaker than normal, so here I am, dealing with you two. He never specified for how long or what exactly to do. This is what he gets for breaking his side of the oath."

"Oath?" Esme asked curiously.

"Two lives taken for two lives saved," it said vaguely, flashing them a toothy grin of sharper than normal teeth and waving them off. The dark aura intensified. "Fortune is on your side. I will stay out of your way. That is all I can and will offer."

She and Dacio hesitated. However, with no additional motions or comments from the Evolved, and because her last conversation with it had been civil, she nodded and walked toward the end of the hallway near the center of the complex, hoping with every step she took that she could at least trust its word for now. The suffocating aura disappeared from behind them, lightening the feeling of the hall.

Although nothing happened, she hoped this would be the last time she came face to face with an Evolved.

Esme peeked out the door before tugging Dacio back out to the exterior corridor. She darted behind a pillar and then warped them both to the last pillar at the end. It was dark enough where they arrived so she didn't even need to create shadows to cover them, and it was close enough to catch fragments of the conversation the dignitaries and the emperor were having.

"We thought with inviting us after many shortfalls, you would have given up on this fruitless endeavor, but it seems like we forgot how persistent and underdeveloped children were," one of the Atonacan dignitaries said in formal Wei, the accent similar to her own when she talked in Wei.

Ouch, she thought, her gaze darting over in time to catch Jianli's chilly reception. The aggressive and direct statement would have been strong to anyone, but he was the emperor, and to imply he was a child when he wasn't was a clear power move. Given that she was near his age, she knew she would feel insulted too.

"Fear not, I have learned that I must pursue an alternative strategy. However, I must implore the speaker to better monitor how dignitaries are trained these days. If it were not for the festival and for my mercy, it would be within my rights as emperor to carve out the tongue of someone who dares sully the seat of heaven and earth," Jianli said smoothly, staring intensely at the dignitary who had just spoken.

The great speaker of Atonaco, the leader of religious, diplomatic, and military purposes for all the city-states that comprised the Atonacan empire, cast an elegant warning glance at his subordinate. Esme remembered seeing him in her childhood memories from the ranking ceremonies her father had participated in, but since her coma, she hadn't seen the great speaker. She wondered why he had come to the Wei Spirit Festival. Was he looking for war or for peace?

"Apologies," the dignitary bowed toward Jianli. "Regardless, we remain unwavering in restricting access to our sacred forests."

It was even more of a slight that the dignitary had the last words instead of the great speaker, with the implication being that Emperor Jin wasn't worth speaking to, leader to leader.

Again, she looked over to watch Jianli's reaction, which reminded her of the one he wore immediately before he had poisoned her. He was being denied access to the Golden Peaches, his path to immortality in the mortal realm. Surely, retaliation was spelled in the books, and she had a feeling Jianli would act on his plan soon.

"So be it. I knew what your answer would be even before I asked," he said, before dismissing them with a graceful gesture of his arm toward the second level. "Please enjoy the rest of the festivities."

The Atonacan dignitaries bowed to Jianli whereas the speaker blinked at him with a tight expression before they turned around to walk back down the steps. The dismissal and power pull and push were apparent to everyone.

With Jianli now isolated, Esme looked for a signal from Reina or Daiyu on the other side. As Jianli started moving toward the steps, an insidious sense of panic crawled up her body and gripped her throat. Were they being held up? She clenched her hands into fists, her nails biting into her palms.

The emperor stopped at the edge and raised his hand, prompting a cascade of chimes to fill the air and snatch attention from the crowd. The people below looked around to see what was happening, and the noise of the audience died down. *Oh, stars above,* Esme lamented.

"Welcome, Yin City!" Jianli exclaimed loudly and unexpectedly. She would have thought the emperor would have told another official to make the announcements instead. "You should all be honored to witness the birth of splendor. Rest assured, your sacrifices will bring us forth to a new age and make the empire one that is finally united. On this day celebrating the dearly departed, the best way we can honor them is by making their legacy eternal."

She couldn't quite see people's faces below, but some of them must have been confused by his words given the cheers. However, any jubilance was quickly cut off by the loud screech of metal tearing itself from edges of the palace and moving over to block the exits of the central courtyard.

"Where's the signal?" Esme whispered to Dacio, whose expression displayed the same tension she held inside her. Each second of waiting was a risk, but which decision was worth it? Risking charging in too early or too late?

When Jianli pulled out the Sword of Realms, she heard a piercing whistle from below, instead of from across the courtyard. Regardless of whether Reina or Daiyu whistled, the emperor's attention was distracted.

With hope and anxiety flooding her body, Esme leapt.

She turned into shadows, warping over toward Emperor Jin and reappearing to launch herself, shouldering him from behind. Both of them flew over the steps, since Jianli had been standing near the edge just moments before, and in mid-tumble, she warped again to the side so she was pressed against one of the walls bordering the steps. In any other situation, Esme would have enjoyed seeing the emperor tumbling down the steps of his own palace. Instead, she was more focused on the sword that had dropped out of his hands and was toppling down.

Esme darted after the sword, stopping it from its fall. Her heart was racing, ready to escape from bone and flesh. Barely a second after she had a firm grip on the hilt, she felt the sword being tugged—Jianli's magic. The pull of his powers was stronger than her two arms, so she flew along with the sword until she was face to face with a furious, slightly battered emperor. Jianli glared at her with the force of a dozen depraved demons behind his dark eyes.

"You," he hissed, lip bloody and eye bruised from where his face must have hit the step. Given his lucid state, Daiyu must have missed her dart or he must have evaded it when she had warped.

If she hadn't already been trying to hang on for dear life, she would've freed a hand to blast a fireball at his face to add injury to insult. Instead, something crashed into her back, mimicking what she had done to him not even moments earlier. Esme tumbled forward and her hands flew out, releasing the sword. Before she could hit the stone steps, she slipped into the shadows and redirected herself to a different position.

However, that was enough time for Jianli to grab ahold of the sword once more.

"No!" Esme yelled out. She let her blade-sharp focus drive the vehement fire within her and conjured up a ball of flames to blast at him.

Jianli reacted quickly, moving his free hand in front of him, the motion followed by a flash of metal—an armor-clad guard—to block the fire. Given how quickly he blocked her attack, the guard must have been the object that had hit her from behind.

From above, shards of ice spiked down, bringing both of their attention up to the top of the steps where Dacio stood. Esme could barely see Raiden in the background targeting the remaining guards. The emperor dodged the next few ice spikes and continued to use his own personal guard as a shield.

Just as she was about to launch another fire blast from her fingertips, the emperor raised the sword and slashed it in the air, cutting through the mortal realm and causing the fireballs to enter the spirit realm. *Hells*, she mentally swore.

Bile rose to her throat. The portal was now open, and the only way to close it was through the sword. *Unless there's another way?* Quickly, she wondered if shadows could close portals, given that light and fire could open the path back into the mortal realm.

"I summon you to my side," Jianli yelled into the portal. A purple glow emitted from his chest, reminding her of the bloodstone. If she took that away, he would lose control over the demons.

A lone sword sailed through the air from above. Once again, her attention trailed up the steps until she saw Raiden. Behind him stood Daiyu and Dacio. Reina wasn't in sight, but with the whistle that had come from below, perhaps she was in the central courtyard.

Jianli easily batted the sword away with his magic and completely reversed its trajectory so that it soared right back at Raiden, who dodged it. Raiden sprinted down the stairs, and with the emperor's attention on him, she warped toward Jianli. However, with the number of times she had revealed her shadow magic, Jianli must have predicted her plan because as soon as she rematerialized, she was immediately greeted with the sharp end of a sword. It was a miracle she was able to avoid skewering herself on it as she threw herself to the side.

The emperor stepped away from both her and the portal. Esme's eyes widened when she realized why. A legion of demons charged from the spirit realm in her direction. She scrambled up to her feet and slipped back into the darkness, warping to Raiden's side just in time to avoid the invasion of creatures.

"Hells," Raiden muttered from beside her.

Hells indeed, she thought as she saw the demons start trickling in and sniffing around for prey. People ran to the sides, pounding at the metal blocking their way. While the great speaker and his warriors remained fearlessly to fight, other people fled screaming into the buildings, barging into the palace. Perhaps some of them would find their way out through the interior hallways.

A few demons looked above and started heading in Esme's direction.

"Fuel yourself for battle, my army," Jianli ordered, his voice booming over the shrieks in the background.

He raised his arms and clenched his hands into fists, causing spikes to form at the metal barriers he had shoved into place. Some of the metal that had once been decorations suddenly became an instrument of death, catching people in its path. The Dreadful lunged forth at the people who were in the process of running away.

"This has to be the worst time to be a close-range fighter," Raiden groaned. "If I survive this, I need to learn long-range methods."

"Less complaining, more action," Esme gritted out. "I'll hold off the demons for now. You go after Jianli. Get his stone. Without it, he can't control them. I'll help out when I can."

He nodded and charged forward. Following distantly behind him, she turned her focus on the demon that was lunging at Raiden, and intervened with her fire magic. Sweat started lining the back of her neck as the toll of all the power she had been using began straining her. She continued and repeated her strategy of boxing the Dreadful in a prism of fire.

A figure darted into the courtyard below, and it took her a few seconds to recognize Reina's braid of braids, shining orange tips flying like streaks of ember in the darkness. From above, she could hear Reina barking orders to guide people out of the palace.

"I've got you," Dacio's warm and familiar voice came from behind, sending relief to her core. They were okay, albeit justifiably worried. "There are so many of them." As if emphasizing their point, more Dreadful streamed out of the portal.

"Raiden is trying to get the stone away from him. You handle the demons for now," she panted out, whipping her hand to the side to incinerate one last demon before she took off. Ice shards rained down in her peripheral vision as she sprinted down the steps. She could hear Dacio following in her wake.

The emperor and his former assassin were circling each other, although Raiden was now without a sword. Esme reacted immediately and conjured up cool wisps of darkness into her hand, shooting them at the emperor to surround his face and blind his view, just as she had practiced. Using the distraction, Raiden lunged for Jianli's neck. She couldn't tell if he was simply going for the stone or if he was going to kill Jianli right there. Her question was answered when Raiden yanked his hand back, revealing a glowing purple stone. Esme's heart leapt to her throat.

However, before Raiden could issue a command, Jianli wildly swung his sword around and slashed at his side.

"Rai!" Dacio yelled and ran down.

As Raiden slumped over, Dacio threw a blast of ice at Jianli and forced him back. Esme noticed the bloodstone necklace on the floor. With Dacio at Raiden's side, she trusted they were the best person to help him, so she rushed after the stone.

Upon grabbing it, she could feel its otherworldly power radiating into her body. The curious stone was surprisingly more than just purple, but rather a blend of pink, blue, and violet, and it looked like it contained liquid fire inside of it.

So much power lay in her hand, in this one little stone—pure destructive power, power to change the fate of the world.

She fought the lure of its enchanting song, and yelled, "Stop!"

"No!" Jianli screamed, swatting at the wisps of darkness. None of the Dreadful paid any attention to his shriek and stopped their rampage to stand in streams of blood.

Esme couldn't even be relieved by the halt of demonic activity because Jianli turned his ire on her. Even though she could have predicted his move, she still didn't react quickly enough to dodge the smaller dagger he threw at her hand in his attempt to knock the stone from it. She let out a short, pained scream when the blade pierced through her hand, burning her, and forcing the stone out near the portal. As Jianli staggered up the stairs for the stone, she ignored the pain.

Neither shadow nor fire alone could stop him. But perhaps a combination of the two would work. Like the positivity and negativity essential for lightning, she internalized harmony and disharmony, light and darkness, sun and moon and shot a stream of dark fire at Jianli. Faster and deadlier than warping, her magic struck him and forced him to drop the Sword of Realms before he could even pick up the bloodstone.

Black fire blanketed his body, and it must have been scorching because he screamed in agony. Shadows drifted from her fingertips and flames flickered at the edges of the strands of her hair.

She did not need any compromise to break boundaries; she was boundless.

Quickly, she returned her focus back to the mission. The chasm between realms was still open, and as long as Jianli was here, he was a threat to everyone he had planned to sacrifice—both the people of Atonaco and the Wei empire. His pained scream made her wince and she dropped the shadow fire. Although she wanted him stopped, she had no intention to burn him alive. *Trapping him in the spirit realm, on the other hand…*

With that idea, Esme warped over to Jianli, hoping she still had enough energy. She took advantage of his pain and surprise, using her momentum to tackle him through the schism and into the other side. The scent of burnt hair and clothes trickled past.

Both of them let out a wheeze as they crashed into the ground, but only Esme had been prepared for it, so she recovered quickly and staggered up to her feet. She still needed the sword to close the portal, but before she could get far, Jianli used his foot and kicked at the back of her knees, making her jolt forward and fall to her hands and knees.

Esme looked back through the portal and made eye contact with Dacio, who looked stunned when they realized where she was.

"Find the sword!" she shouted, throwing a glance back to at Jianli, who was hobbling to his feet with a glare lining his charred face. From the burns on his body, it seemed as if the shadow fire was more damaging than normal fire. How he was still standing was a mystery.

"What are you doing?" Dacio shouted back, drawing her attention back to the mortal realm. They were now closer, their eyebrows pinched with fear and bewilderment, and they seemed caught between continuing healing Raiden and helping her out. Their eyes suddenly widened before they yelled, "Stay down."

An ice shard sailed into the spirit realm, over her head, and crashed into the emperor's shoulder. Since there was no metal on this side, Jianli was unable to deflect with his magic.

Somehow, he managed to stumble past her, storming toward the portal. Her face tightened in determination and she crawled onto her knees and lunged at his legs to prevent him from returning to the mortal realm.

Over the emperor's grunt and attempts to shake her off, Esme held on, ignoring the pain from her injured hand. She gritted her teeth and gave a new order. "Daci, use the sword." Jianli could not return.

Even from the other side, she could see the edge of Dacio's jaw tightening. They staggered away from Raiden's side, reached down for the sword, and lifted it up with uncertain arms. "Promise you'll come back."

"I will," she called out before Jianli thrashed his legs and clocked her in the side of the head, forcing her off. Dazed, she rolled to the side and reached up to touch the tender side of her head.

"Dacio! Don't you dare!" Jianli screamed in the background. When Esme looked back over, she realized that the only sources of color left in the realm were from her and her cousin.

The gateway was now sealed.

CHAPTER 29

"Not so powerful now." Esme laughed, pushing herself off the floor into a seemingly casual sitting position. However, her muscles were coiled and ready to react. Being in the spirit realm with her murderer was bound to be unpredictable.

Jianli went as rigid as a threatened jungle cat. "You," he spat out, gritting his teeth when he broke off the shard of ice in his burnt shoulder and shattered it on the ground. "This time, I will make sure you never return, even if it means I personally have to separate your head from your body."

"How are you going to do that here?" she asked, gesturing to the gray realm around them.

Briefly, she wondered if it was wise agitating him when she wasn't so sure if she could use her fire magic without accidentally creating a way back too early. Would shadow fire work instead? Or would she have to rely on purely shadow magic, albeit that would only be useful in illusory and evasive maneuvers? However, if her dizziness was any indicator, she was reaching the limits of her energy sources.

He glared at her, helpless for the first time. No sword, slow creative magic with the absence of metal in the spirit realm, not even a way to control demons. No power, it seemed. He had sacrificed his own family, his people, his morals. Power had meant so much to him, but without it, he was nothing. Jin Jianli had tried to play with a realm that he had no business manipulating, and now his ambition had exposed a weak and rotten foundation. The only thing he had left now was his own physical strength.

This man stole her life. Stole her history. Stole from others. He would steal no more, hurt no more, if she had anything to do with it.

Suddenly, human-sized skeletal figures appeared in the expansive courtyard, slowly materializing into view. That moment of distraction was all Jianli needed to attack her.

"I can still kill you the old fashion way," he growled, grabbing her shoulder and raising his hand for a strike.

Esme instinctively raised her left arm to block his direct punch but wasn't stable or prepared enough to prevent her forearm from smacking the side of her face and jostling her to the right. Although the strike disoriented her, she managed to call her magic to set herself on fire, imitating the way she had turned her body in shadows, and prevent Jianli from grabbing her again.

Jianli stumbled back from her flaming arm, far enough for her to put distance between them and stumble to her feet. Fearing she would open a path back, she extinguished the fire. A small part of her was thrilled that her clothes remained unburnt, but dissecting how everything worked would have to wait.

Something dripped from her nose, and even without wiping or sniffing, she knew it was blood. Jianli might not have much power now, but neither did she. What other resources could she use to fight? Or would she have to continue evading?

She hadn't completely thought her plan through for the spirit realm. Her eyes darted in the environment, reminding herself of the spirits wandering in the background. Given the concentration of ghosts, she guessed that most, if not all, of them were the victims of the emperor's plan.

Resentment infused the air, acting like a beacon for spirits to gather around.

"Do you think I *enjoy* harming my own cousin?" Jianli demanded, baring his teeth at her. "This is larger than all of us."

"You're right. It is larger than all of us, certainly more than you can handle," she responded, to which he gaped. "While I don't care about your motivation, *they* might." She gestured to the dozens of eavesdroppers.

The serious tone of her voice must have made him second-guess any initial doubt because he looked around. Behind him were the figures of the people who had died earlier that evening, the same trampled people who were now converging on the reason behind their untimely demises. She wondered if any other previous victims of Jianli stood in the crowd too.

Rage lit a fire in their eyes, directed at the emperor.

"Who are you?" he demanded, stumbling back in Esme's direction. "Get away from me."

"Don't you see, Jianli?" Esme asked quietly. "You are standing in front of the consequences of your greed and arrogance, and now we shall both see how much power truly matters."

Although she wasn't sure what the spirits could do to him, they could certainly scare him and absorb his attention enough for her to escape and leave him in the spirit realm to face his punishment.

He threw her a hateful glare, and she couldn't help but feel smug satisfaction from his finally broken composure.

Smoke lifted from his body where he had been burned, his hair a disheveled mess. A cruel, disdained sneer etched in his face. "Spirits? They are dead and powerless; they cannot do anything to me."

"Are you sure?" the spirits asked in unison, the clicking of chattering bones sending chills sprinting down Esme's entire body. "You are in our realm now."

Esme surreptitiously stole a few paces in the direction of the steps between the middle and high tiers of the palace grounds.

"I command you to stop. I am the son of heaven and earth, and I am your emperor. You listen to my orders," Jianli tried again, although the slight tremble in his voice undercut his message.

"You are no emperor," the spirits said simply before swarming him.

To Esme's surprise, the spirits seemed to have some physical presence in this realm because as soon as they surrounded Jianli, he flinched back and scrambled away.

"Do not touch me!" he screamed, whipping his gaze around like a cornered animal. A low hum filled the air, and he clutched his head as if in torment.

She watched in horror but was unable to figure out what he was experiencing physically or mentally. He jerked away, eyes wild and unfocused, like he was seeing things in his head. His breathing was choppy, almost raspy.

"Jin Mingyue! Help me!"

She didn't budge.

Why should I? He had to face the consequences of his own actions, and she wasn't obligated to help him, not with what he had done to her, to those she loved, and to other people, who loved and were loved. Even at the end, he wasn't remorseful.

She had a feeling that if she left now, she would never see him again.

"Long live the son of heaven and earth," Esme murmured and limped up to the middle of the stairs. From above, she took one last glance back at the huddle of skeletal ghosts, unable to see Jin Jianli under the squirming dome of justice.

"Now, let's head back," she muttered to herself as she ascended to the top of the steps, entering the Courtyard of Heaven. With the adrenaline wearing off, she started to ache all over and feel sore. Her fingers ghosted over her shoulder and the left side of her face, from where Jianli had grabbed and hit her. She wondered if she had enough magic to heal the forming bruises in addition to her injured hands and scuffed knees after she returned to the mortal realm.

As she gathered herself again and attempted to head back, she could only feel the cold from the realm of death instead of the usual warmth of magic flooding through her body. Her heart stuttered a beat. Esme tried again, attempting to keep the shaking panic at bay, but only the barest of flickers kissed her fingertips. The ground beneath her felt shaky—or perhaps that was simply the strength in her legs sapping away.

She was stuck here in the spirit realm.

Her magic was depleted.

Esme let gravity pull her to the ground and she leaned against the stone walls of the upper palace complex. How long would it take for her to replenish part of her magic? How was the situation on the other side? Was Raiden alright? Dacio? How many people had died?

The stress of the past week overwhelmed her. Tears sprung to her eyes. Her breath was ragged and shaky, death on her mind.

But she was still here, still flickering against all odds.

Eventually, her breathing evened out. She looked up in front of her and tried to recenter herself. Focusing on the intersection of light and darkness in the spirit realm, she took comfort in both. No matter where she seemed to go, light and dark were inseparable. They were part of a whole, yet whole individually. They were more than what people constrained them to. It was that peace in understanding that gave her the strength to continue.

Slowly, she rose to her feet, pressing her palm against the wall for support. Here in the realm of ghosts, she stood alone.

Or perhaps she wasn't as alone as she thought.

"Jing?" Esme asked, chancing on the deity hearing her call for help. During her first visit to the spirit realm, Jing had found her somehow, so perhaps they could do it again.

"Esmeralda," an unfamiliar sonorous voice answered back, the sudden sound frightening her into a jump.

She turned around and saw a stunning dark-skinned figure in a bright red and orange feathered gown, gleaming like the sun. The abundance of colors blinded her and the sheer power radiating from the stranger indicated this was no mere spirit but something more. Unlike Jing's calm and serene aura or the Evolved's heavy and ominous one, this stranger's was intense and vitalizing, so it wasn't either of them in another physical form. If anything, she recognized the same feeling as the one she had whenever she let fire run through her veins.

This could only be Tayanna, the deity of fire. Her patron deity and the source of her magic.

As Tayanna approached, Esme could better see her face, with her high and wide cheekbones and maroon-gemmed eyes. Bright oranges and reds blended seamlessly into her dark hair.

Esme dipped her head in respect and was taken by surprise when she felt a warm hand grab her chin and lift it up. Eyes wide and body stiff, she looked up into the curious maroon eyes of the fire deity. Tayanna didn't have the same smooth, soothing aura as Jing, but she still had a comforting bright energy that made Esme feel slightly more at ease.

"You've exerted yourself," Tayanna noted, tilting her head. "Be sure to rest before completing the next leg of the journey."

"Next... leg?" Esme asked. Any semblance of joy within her deflated. Was bringing Jianli here not enough?

The fire deity released her chin and gave her a coy smile. "There is always work to be done in the battle against the primordial evil and its influences. Fret not, Esmeralda, for you have accomplished the first major step and the next should be simpler. Years ago, we lost two items that Jin Jianli found. Retrieve and return them to us," she started, making Esme guess that she was referring to the Sword of Realms and the bloodstone. "The rest we shall take care of either through calling upon another champion or after we have weakened the primordial evil in the cosmos."

Hesitantly, Esme asked, "Is that it?"

Tayanna let out a chime-like laugh, her eyes twinkling like crackling embers. "Would you like more?"

"I think I'll just start with finding those two items first," she replied, her face heating up. The mission seemed easy enough given that both the sword and stone were back in the central courtyard. "Speaking of those steps, I would need to go back to the mortal realm to complete them and am currently a little stuck here..." she trailed off.

"Of course, child, I can help you open the door this time," Tayanna said, stepping back. "You have our blessings and gratitude."

Without warning or explanation, the fire deity simply waved her hand and threw a dome of fire over Esme, who raised her hand to block the sudden and sharp light. When the fire dropped, she found herself back in the Courtyard of the Heavens on the top of the steps. Immediately, someone bumped into her—a stranger carrying an injured person on their back.

"Where'd you come from? Eh, never mind, get out of the way. I need to get to the medical wing," they said gruffly.

With wide eyes, Esme stepped out of their path, disoriented with the situation. Exhausted physically, mentally, and magically, she looked around and tried to figure out what had happened while she was in the spirit realm. The remaining demons were all frozen, and dead bodies were strewn across the courtyard. The metal barriers were still mounted and blocking the main gates, and injured people were being helped by those who managed to escape the deadly events. Already, she could tell the energy in the air had dampened.

"Esme!" a familiar voice called out. She looked in the direction and saw Dacio near the bottom of the steps waving at her while helping a person to their feet.

It took a few seconds to realize she was moving, skipping steps on the way down to greet Dacio, weakly throwing her arms around their shoulders and embracing them. She closed her eyes and listened to their steady heartbeat, comforted by their arms curling around her.

"You came back again," Dacio murmured against her hair, which must have looked like a mess after everything.

"You can't get rid of me that easily," she said, smiling and earning a snort. After pulling back, she felt the heat of their eyes catch every bruise and cut on her face. Before they could worry further, she asked, "How's everyone? Raiden? Daiyu? Reina?"

They sighed wearily and stepped out of the path of an incoming group. "After I sealed the rift, I finished healing Raiden, and we've all been escorting people out or giving medical attention. I don't have much magic left, if any, so we're now directing people to the medical building on the third level where more healers are waiting."

She couldn't tell if the shadows under their eyes was from the lighting or from their exhaustion. "Do you still have the stone? Where's the sword?" she asked, suddenly remembering Tayanna's request.

Dacio reached into the pocket created by the cross collar over the sash of their outfit and pulled out the broken chain that held the pretty stone. "I have the bloodstone. Raiden should still have the sword."

Esme released a sigh of relief. "Keep that safe with you. We still need it, and we'll need the sword too," she said, watching Dacio pocket the stone.

When she quickly glanced at the rest of the courtyard, she found a familiar tall, dark-cloaked figure in the thinning crowd. Raiden must have spotted the two of them because he started walking in their direction, clear relief on his sweat-and-ash-lined face.

"You look better than before," Esme greeted with a small smile.

"Generally people look better when they're not stabbed or impaled by something," he responded dryly, cracking a smile. "I'm glad you're back. Jianli?"

"Let's just say his victims are currently in charge of his punishment. I'm not sure if he's dead but I don't see an easy path back for him," she said. Without fire magic or the sword, the only way back would probably be through a deity's help, and she didn't think any of them were too eager to help him out anytime soon.

"I can think of an easy solution to make sure he stays there," Raiden said, glancing over at Dacio. "Stone?"

When Dacio lobbed it over at him, he easily caught it with his left hand and used his right to take out the sword and slice at the air, creating a fissure. Esme and Dacio automatically took a step back from the rift and watched as he lifted the stone up into the air.

"Return to the spirit realm," he commanded, shouting in the direction of the statue-like demons. "If Jin Jianli is still alive over there, make sure he doesn't come back."

The creatures lumbered in accordance with his command, walking past them back to their home. Their collective action almost made her reconsider her opinion on the Dreadful. They were all still terrifying, but most of them had been controlled and out of their natural habitat. After the last one crossed over, Raiden raised the sword and sealed the gap again.

Only then did Esme finally feel relieved, the stiff tension easing from her neck and shoulders like shrugging off a heavy hand after years of being pushed down. Although they had made many missteps, they had narrowly avoided a disaster with no return.

However, just because most of them escaped this disaster didn't mean others remained unscathed, and Esme was reminded of that fact when she heard a soft wail from behind her. She whirled around and saw Reina kneeling next to a body, hands covering her face. Her heart dropped, fearing that it was Daiyu on the ground. A few steps closer revealed that it was Mrs. Chen. Heaviness flooded her body.

They all sprinted over to Reina's side. Esme instinctively bent down and tried to see if she could scrounge up some spirit magic to heal the old woman's fatal wounds, but like before, she was still depleted and couldn't do anything. Dacio looked down with tears in their eyes, and it didn't seem as if they had any magic left either. Tears streamed down her cheeks as she recalled Mrs. Chen's warmth and willingness to help those in need. Her throat felt thick with remorse.

"She was one of the first people I ever helped," Reina whispered hoarsely.

Esme leaned over and hugged her, feeling her clutch back at her like a lifeline.

The night had been a victory, but it didn't completely feel like one.

CHAPTER 30

Even days after defeating the emperor, the road ahead of them seemed long. Dealing with the fallout of the massacre, the disappearance of the emperor and a sudden power vacuum, and the diplomatic tension between the Wei and Atonacan empires placed everyone on shaky grounds, not to mention the problems that existed before Jianli almost shattered the mortal realm.

At the center of the fragile infrastructure was Reina, who was sprawled across the bench in a quaint, public garden, arm over her eyes. "The logistics of reorganizing the city are even more challenging than trying to stop a murderous tyrant from destroying the realm." She sighed. "If only Jianli and the previous emperor hadn't phenomenally distorted all of the government structures, perhaps we would have an apt leader to deal with this."

The curved roofs of the central pavilion blocked the sudden rays of sun. The light drew Esme's attention to the bright plum blossoms against the remaining snow on the trees in the eastern side of the gardens. They reminded her of the symbols associated with Reina and the tunnels.

How did one just find a replacement leader? Did they try to find the previous empress? Did they trust any of Jianli's subordinates or allies? Prior to her death, Esme herself had been seen as a potential, valid replacement in the eyes of the court, even disregarding her blood connection to Jianli. However, she was woefully unfit. Even though she must have learned a lot while she lived in the imperial palace before her death, all of that knowledge was gone, including any information about who was who.

Not that it completely bothered her. She didn't *have* to remember or know. Esme decided she was going to stop letting other people and the past torment her. She would learn on her own terms.

With other things out there, like jewelry-making, spirit-guiding, and magic innovations, leading a nation wasn't for her.

Her eyes darted toward Dacio, who was chatting privately with Raiden across the pond. As Jianli's former imperial spy, they would have the knowledge and connections, but she figured they weren't completely interested in revisiting their old occupation. Raiden also didn't seem to be the type who wanted to be involved in bureaucracy either, as he had a lot to work through with himself first.

Reina, on the other hand...

"I know a good candidate," Esme offered after processing her thoughts. She looked over at the Lady of Shadows.

Reina opened one of her eyes and looked at her expectantly. "And?"

She took a deep breath. "I'm looking at her right now."

Abruptly sitting up, Reina's mouth gaped open, a choking sound coming out before slowly morphing into astounded and incredulous laughter. "*Heavens,* you're serious," she half-stated, half-asked. "Me? A former spy and current head of a shadow league?"

The more Esme thought about her idea, the more certain she was in Reina's qualifications. "You are already a leader of the people. Maybe not in name, but in spirit. You know the people living in and out of Yin City. You know their stories. You listen and address their concerns. You fight for them," she started, gesturing to Dacio and Raiden, who were still engaged in what seemed like a serious conversation.

Reina's face fell again, but Esme continued. "You have the experience of leading. You, a former spy, know the ins and outs of the court. You know the games they play, who they are, how to interact with ambassadors of other nations. You've forged your own path before, and I believe you could help address the wrongs because you're passionate and most importantly, *you care*," she said.

Only a fool wouldn't be able to see Reina's potential.

"I think you overestimate my capabilities," Reina whispered back, her dark eyes shiny with unshed tears and her chest barely moving with her breathing.

"Sounds like you're underestimating yourself," Daiyu's voice sounded from behind Esme, making her jump and turn around to face the newcomer, who sported a simple ponytail and a black outfit that matched Reina's.

One of these days, she was going to add bells to everyone's belt sashes or make them get a taste of their own medicine through her shadow magic.

"I simply think it's something to consider, and I'm not saying you would have to go through it alone because many complex issues remain to be resolved," Esme clarified after turning back to face Reina, who seemed like she was pondering about the idea.

Daiyu glided past Esme and slid onto the stone bench next to Reina, draping an arm over her shoulder. "Think about it. We could raid the imperial coffers and finally get some nice outfits," she sang mischievously. Reina rolled her eyes with a smile on her face.

"We shall see—about the leadership part, not the raiding," Reina said. Her dark, fine brows arched at her second-in-command, who pouted and glowered.

Esme grinned at them both and slowly backed away, leaving them to banter between themselves and joining Raiden and Dacio. When she noticed the tense atmosphere, her smile faded and her steps slowed. Gaze darting between the two, she hesitated and wondered if she should go back to conversing with Daiyu and Reina.

"Everything okay here?" she asked cautiously. The other two looked away from each other. That was not promising.

After a few seconds of silence, Dacio answered, "We were talking about Rai's ability and the past... your death."

Her eyes widened. *Oh.* No wonder they both looked tense although neither of them seemed ready to go for the other's throat. It also seemed like Dacio was finally accepting the fact that she had indeed died three years ago.

"Have you reached any conclusion on either topic?" she asked.

"Just my apologies for my past actions, like not telling them about what I had done and then not supporting them afterward while they dealt with you," Raiden said, cringing and scratching the back of his neck. Still, the temperature seemed to be at a reasonable level between them.

"I was bringing up the suggestion again that fear was and still is the underlying cause of the two topics," Dacio said, their eyes darting to their side as if gauging his reaction. Yet another repeated conversation, this time, the one that had sparked the argument between them at Kunhai.

Raiden nodded hesitantly and then calmly. "I'm done letting fear isolate me, and I will try to do better."

Invisible strings pulled at Esme's heart. Tears started to prickle at the corners of her eyes. They still had many—*many*—issues to work through, but they were working through them together, one step at a time, one conversation at a time. Healing together.

"This means we're going to see if you can control your death touch. Right?" Dacio asked in a higher pitch, as if trying to soften their message with a more lighthearted tone.

He winced. "I don't entirely... trust myself."

Esme gave him a gentle smile, understanding that overcoming fear wasn't something that could be done so quickly or simply. However, she trusted he would learn from his mistakes because they had tormented him for so long. He would work on his fears because he knew the benefits he could reap if he did so. Many people would be there to support him this time.

"I trust you," she said, looking over to Dacio to back her up.

"As do I," they quietly chimed in. "Even when you keep secrets, even when you think you've gone too far, I believe in you because I know your bones—what makes you *you*. So when you're ready or you need me, I'll be here for you."

"Hells," Raiden whispered, voice wavering slightly. "You really have your way with words."

Esme cracked a smile, as did Dacio. *What an understatement.*

"Are they enough to make you stay longer, by any chance?" Dacio asked.

Stay longer? She threw him a quick look. Where was he going?

He sighed. "I made a promise to Nami, and honestly, I want to rest for a bit," he admitted.

"Wait, are you leaving for the Eastern Isles today?" she asked, her eyebrows pinched together tightly. When he nodded, she followed up with, "Why didn't you say anything earlier?"

"Because I just decided before we came to the gardens," he answered. "Don't worry. I'll be back before you know it."

She glared at him, partially upset by being blindsided by his timing but completely understanding the desire to rest and reflect. "You weren't just going to leave without telling any of us, right?"

He blinked. "You mean, leave quietly like Reina and Daiyu did?"

Esme whirled around, noticing the other two were gone. *Stars above.*

"Well, when you come back, Dacio and I can try to guide you through your magic," she said when she turned back.

"At your own pace, of course," Dacio added.

Raiden flashed them a wry grin. "I think once I've figured myself out a little more, I'll be ready to go. I've been waiting for years already." Maybe it was because he had his gloves on, but he surprisingly stepped forward and embraced them both as a temporary farewell.

Although Esme was happy for him and she was sure they would meet again soon, she couldn't quite keep the heartache away as he embarked on his own personal journey. New beginnings also signified an ending, and endings weren't always easy.

"So, what should we do with the sword and stone?" Dacio asked, gently kicking at the ground, reminding her of the aforementioned items stored safely in the base. "Throw it back into the sea?"

Esme shook her head. "No, the deities want them back in the spirit realm," she said. "But if you really wanted to dispose of them in the mortal realm, I would suggest throwing them into the volcano by Atoyatlan. They would be much more difficult to retrieve, assuming they remain intact."

Dacio let out a hearty laugh. "That could do the trick," they mused. "I suppose they *are* safer in the spirit realm, and I hope they stay there this time."

She smiled and suggested, "You should come with me and meet a deity yourself."

Their eyes widened comically before they gave her a sweeping smile. "Let's go now. I want to use the sword," they chattered excitedly. The shadows that once lived under their eyes were gone, emphasizing their unmistakable freedom from secrets and enemies.

"Wait, I want to use the sword too," Esme said.

They stared at each other, narrowed eyes glinting at the silent challenge.

"How about this. You can use it first *if* you tell me a story," she offered first, sitting down on the stone bench and patting the space beside her.

Dacio raised an eyebrow and slid over to her side. "What kind of story?"

Looking off into the distance, with both the gardens and the tiled roofs of the city, she smiled. Yin City was a city reborn, one with a dark past but a brighter future, one with more hope and compassion coming to light. "Anything about me, about you, about us. Something worth remembering."

She was never going to regain her memories from her first time in Yin City, outside of those from the day of her death.

Those pieces were simply lost to time. However, she still had people who could tell her stories. For now, that was all she could really ask for. The past was important, but the future even more so. As long as she could continue making new memories while learning about the old, she would be content because she was still whole—standing strong against the tides of time and life, adjusting to whatever it threw her way.

"Of course," they said softly. "Hmm, why don't I tell you about the time we went to visit a temple and ended up making bets on a ball game next door featuring the reigning champion from Atonaco?"

"Hmm, did we win?" Esme mused, remembering watching those games in childhood with her parents.

Dacio laughed. "Of course not, but we left the tournament unsure of whether you just started a diplomatic issue between Atonaco and the Wei empire or whether you were going to get a marriage proposal from the star champion."

"*How?* Those seem like drastically different outcomes," she asked, flushing.

"Well, you see, it started..."

She nodded, resting her head against their shoulder to get comfortable and settle in for the story. There, she listened and imagined and watched the gentle clouds pass through the bright blue skies before they eventually darkened into the moonlit midnight cover, laughing at the stories Dacio was mirthfully acting out. Sometime in the middle of the story, she used her fire magic to light the stone lanterns throughout the gardens, amplifying the atmosphere.

When her eyes grew sleepy, she sighed. "I would've loved to remember everyone's reactions, especially my mother's."

Dacio hummed and then grew quiet, as if lost in thoughts—or just resting their voice. After a while, they asked, “Shall we go find her?”

Esme froze against their shoulder, eyes wide awake. She pulled back and looked at them, asking, “Do you know where she is?”

“I don’t right now, but I have the skills and connections to figure that out. We could probably also find my family in the meantime. I haven’t seen them in a while,” they rambled, seemingly ready to continue their thoughts before she interrupted them with a fierce hug.

“I would love to do both,” she murmured, embracing them tightly and then releasing them so she could stare into their eyes. “Thank you.”

Above them, the brilliant moon seemed to wink at her.

EPILOGUE

A small child with eyes that seemed to glow and teeth a little too sharp sat on the ledge of a short bridge in the imperial gardens, swinging his legs back and forth as he listened to the conversation behind him.

"Mingyue? Is that you?"

He looked across the stone-rimmed pond to see Esmeralda standing across from a pale-skinned woman with black and silver hair pulled up in a bun. Both had the same glistening eyes as they stared at each other. The spirit mage healer hovered in the background, keeping their distance as Esmeralda's mother reached forward to touch her daughter's cheek, as if she were trying to figure out if she was truly there.

"Yes, it's me," Esmeralda choked out. The light from the stone lanterns highlighted the shimmer in her eyes.

"You're okay," her mother said, her tone tilting upward like a half-question. "I'm sorry. I'm sorry I couldn't go with you." Her gaze drifted back toward the healer. "Thank you for keeping her safe, Dacio."

They chuckled nervously. "I wouldn't say *safe* is the most accurate description of the most recent events, but we're all here now and the main threat shouldn't haunt us anymore."

Snorting quietly to himself, the child looked back over at the melting snow. He could smell spring around the corner. The currents of time formed a familiar cycle, one that would be extended longer in accordance to the will of the deities. However, threats were never truly gone—only waiting in the shadows for the right time to arise.

"How were the last few years?" Esmeralda asked her mother after embracing her.

"That is a loaded question. Is it not? To say it simply, it was much easier once I found out you survived. My dear, sweet Mingyue, my little emerald moon and sun, my Esme. I am glad the universe and the deities have allowed us to reunite," she responded.

The child tensed at the mention of the deities. He looked up at the star-strewn skies, where the moon hung radiantly. With his luck, Jing would probably be the one to find him if he stayed here any longer, so he quietly hopped off the ledge, scampering off into the darkness. The imperial palace was no longer a viable hunting ground—for now.

The rocky beaches of Yin City summoned him from the imperial palace. He weaved through the city visible, but undetected, until he arrived at the beachfront. Glowering, he crouched on a large, jagged rock and prepared himself for company. The stars, the ancestral dead, traversed across the skies, and he continued waiting until the barest hint of orange settled on the horizon to the east. Soon, the sun would emerge from its bath.

"You missed out on a fascinating conversation," a smooth voice said, verifying his suspicions. When he turned around, he saw Jing's eyes glowing as if two of the original moons had been treasured by the deity of life and death and captured on their face. "You also caused quite a commotion this time."

"What can I say? I am an agent of chaos," the child smirked, but he wondered what the deity's plans were for him. He could sense that the primordial evil had been dealt a major blow in this realm, and given Jing's visit, the deities seemed to be winding down the battle in the cosmos just enough to have time to chase him down.

"Even chaos needs to rest," Jing said, all but floating to his side. They used their obsidian blade and cut open a gap between realms. "The others await you."

He rose to his feet and looked through the portal, considering the deity's offer. *Rest.* Did peace and satisfaction come with it too? Regardless, his time here was at an end, although perhaps for another, it was only just beginning. Silently, he didn't bother replying, and approached the schism. As he stepped through realms, he turned one last time and watched the sun rise brilliantly.

The people of Yin City would wake up to the dawn of a new day.

ACKNOWLEDGMENTS

Going on a new journey can be terrifying. Writing and publishing a book certainly felt this way for me, with obstacles along the way (*coughs* imposter syndrome) and an uncertain outcome. That's why support was so vital for the creation of this book. Like with Esme, Dacio, Raiden, Reina, and Daiyu, I saw how making it to "the end" and accomplishing goals would not be possible without champions and teamwork. *Fulfilling this dream* would not have been possible without you.

Thank you first and foremost to my family for supporting my journey—from being my inspiration to listening to me talk about the whole process. Thank you to my friends who hyped me up and had my back as I embarked on this exciting and absolutely nerve-racking adventure. You are the magic in life.

Massive thanks to my editors and publishing support: Stephen Howard, whose enthusiasm helped me keep going (and for making that wicked cool map from my excel sheet map idea); Jessica Drake-Thomas, who encouraged me and listened to and addressed my many concerns; Eric Koester, who helped set up this program in the first place; and finally Brian Bies and the rest of the team at NDP, for believing in me and my book.

Special thanks to my beta readers: Marina Zhang and Grace Smith for being my #1 cheerleaders (I appreciate you guys so much); and Shay Fibbernacci and Catalina Aguirre. Your thoughts and input helped me tremendously, both from an emotional standpoint and in writing.

For their support and encouragement, great thanks to: Aba Kpeglo, Adunoluwa Obisesan, Amy Kay Kerber, Andrew Schad, Anezka Kovarik, Angela Cao, Angela Murray, Angelica and Kimi Jackson, Anny Lin, Abenah Peasah, Bob and Ilona Rouda, Bryant Wong, Caleb J. Nixon, Carmen Swanson, Catherine Huang, Cheyanne Simpson, Chiung Wang , Cindy Gu, Colette Moder, Daniel Gonzalez Diaz, Danielle Bragale, Doris Schirmacher, Douglas Diggs, Elaine Zhang, Elly Kim, Emily Lentz-Hoops, Faith Esperanza Jones, Gina Ciganik, LuAnne Pederson, Grace Chuan, Heather Knutson, Iris Abrahantes, Jaime Nat Osuna, Jane Schneider, Jennifer Barshack, Jessica Yen, Jisoo Cheong, Juan Aleman, Julie Lentz, Karen Satterlie, Karen Schaffhausen, Kathryn Tso, Kevin Qian, Leah Yost, Linda Yu, Marco Nocito, Marie Capra, Matt and Karen Sundeen, Matthew Perry, Megan Teske, Melody Phu, Mimi Wahid, Minwoo Kim, Miranda Fernandez, Monica Bolinger, Nabihah Khalid, Neil Gonzales, Nicole Goridkov and Jose Guajardo, Noah Risley, Nory Klop-Packel, Oby Nwodoh, Patty Chiang, Rachel Wu, Roger Shinmoto, Rona Wang, Sarah Vu, Shelby Laitipaya, Sujay Kazi, Theresa Las-Peters, Victor Chau, Victoria Juan, Wen-Hong Wang, the Wang family, the Weng family, and Yi Shan Chiu.

You guys rock!

PRONUNCIATION GUIDE

CHARACTERS

Esme: EHZ-may
Raiden: RYE-den
Dacio: DAH-see-oh
Reina: RAY-nah
Daiyu: DYE-you
Jianli: JIAN-LEE
Mingyue: ming-YUE
Nami: NAH-mee

PLACES

Atonaco: ah-dho-NAH-co (soft "t" and "c" sounds)
Atoyatlan: ah-dho-YAH-tlan (soft "t" sound)
Yin City: "een" City
Wei: WAY

DEITIES

Alejo, Deity of Wind: ah-LE-ho
Jing, Deity of Spirit: JING
Kai, Deity of Water: KY (rhymes with sky)
Tayanna, Deity of Fire: tah-YAH-nah
Zoraya, Deity of Metal: zoh-RAH-yah

Made in the USA
Monee, IL
11 May 2021